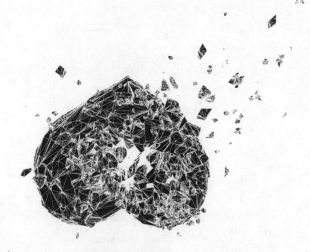

THE
WINNOWING

VIKKI VANSICKLE

Scholastic Canada Ltd.
Toronto New York London Auckland Sydney
Mexico City New Delhi Hong Kong Buenos Aires

Scholastic Canada Ltd.
604 King Street West, Toronto, Ontario M5V 1E1, Canada

Scholastic Inc.
557 Broadway, New York, NY 10012, USA

Scholastic Australia Pty Limited
PO Box 579, Gosford, NSW 2250, Australia

Scholastic New Zealand Limited
Private Bag 94407, Botany, Manukau 2163, New Zealand

Scholastic Children's Books
Euston House, 24 Eversholt Street, London NW1 1DB, UK

www.scholastic.ca

Library and Archives Canada Cataloguing in Publication

VanSickle, Vikki, 1982-, author
The winnowing / Vikki VanSickle.

Issued in print and electronic formats.
ISBN 978-1-4431-4886-3 (softcover).—ISBN 978-1-4431-4887-0 (HTML)

I. Title.

PS8643.A59W56 2017   jC813'.6   C2017-901514-1
                                               C2017-901515-X

Photos ©: iStockphoto: cover background: mythja;
cover heart and throughout: Jolygon.

Text copyright © 2017 by Vikki VanSickle.
6 5 4 3 2 1   Printed in Canada 139   17 18 19 20 21

DARBY, NEW MEXICO, 1989

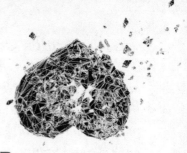

CHAPTER
ONE

I'm flying.

At least that's what it feels like. What I'm really doing is running. But it's the smoothest, easiest action in the world, like I was born to do nothing but run. I barely feel the ground below me. I could burst into song and keep on running without breaking my stride.

But then things change.

First it gets hot. Stinging sweat drips into my eyes. I rub at them with the back of my knuckles, which only makes them sting more. When I blink the tears away I find myself lost in smoke so thick I can't see my own hands in front of me. Then I lose my footing. I fall on my knee, hard. I look down and it isn't grass and dirt below me but thick, black gunk, glowing red like embers in the belly of a campfire. It swirls around my feet and hands, lapping at my wrists and ankles.

I push myself up, palms stinging, and I keep running.

I run and run but I can't get ahead of the lava. It roils and burps, splashing my calves with burning drops. I hear

3

screaming and the stampeding of feet behind me but I don't dare slow down to see what's happening. I try to run faster but the lava swirls higher around my ankles. Something is burning and I know it must be my own flesh that's making that horrible smell, but I don't want to believe it. I can't. I'm screaming for help and then—

Ceiling, walls, a bed below me. The familiar shapes and shadows of my room came into focus as I sucked air into my lungs in hungry gasps. The air was fresh and cool against my skin but I could still feel the grit in my eyes. My legs ached. My calf muscles were tight and the soles of my feet burned as if I really had been running.

I unknotted the damp bedsheet from around my knees and was shocked to find my feet scratched and covered in open sores, dirt and grit ground into the broken skin. The pain was real. The running had been real. Only, the lava couldn't have been real, could it?

That's when I knew. It had started. I was going ACES. I sat back against my pillow, letting the moment wash over me. For years I had waited and wondered when it would finally happen. The Adolescent Chronosomniatic Episodes were all tied up with puberty. The same part of the brain that triggered boys' voices to change and girls' periods to start also triggered the vivid night terrors scientists called the ACES.

Yesterday, Saren went off to the Barton Center for Adolescent Health to be winnowed, putting an end to the ACES and the dangers of adolescence. Now it was my turn.

I heard the thin, reedy whistle of the kettle protesting in the kitchen. Gumps was awake. I pulled my softest pair of socks over my throbbing feet and hobbled to the kitchen.

I cleared my throat and said the words I'd been dying to say since I knew what they meant: "I've started. I'm going ACES."

Gumps kept his back to me as he prepared the tea. "Is that so."

"Yes. Was I screaming?"

"I thought maybe you were dreaming about a bad date."

I took my usual seat at the table, rolling my eyes even though I knew he couldn't see me. I wished he would turn around. "Gumps, don't be funny, this is serious."

"There's nothing funny about a bad date, believe me. But you don't have to worry about that for another fifteen years."

"GUMPS!"

"Okay, ten."

Gumps was the funniest person I knew, but it made me crazy when I wanted him to be serious. "You should probably call Barton."

Gumps stopped joking. He turned, sat down at the table and blew the steam from his tea, somehow managing to fit his long fingers through the slender loop of the handle.

I wondered about that tea. Gumps preferred coffee. It was my grandmother who had been the tea drinker in our family. She was serious about her tea, warming the cup first and only drinking out of real teacups. If you served her tea in a mug, she would say, "Mugs are for coffee," dump it out and start again. She had a full bone china tea set from some other era, painted in delicate pink and orange roses and rimmed in gold. When I was little and something was bothering me, she used to brew a pot and we'd sit at the kitchen table and figure out a plan. The tea, the teacups — who was Gumps trying to cheer up: me or himself?

"The Barton Guide says to call right away. The longer you wait the more dangerous it becomes," I reminded him.

"I know what the guide says." Gumps looked so sad I lost the will to continue badgering him. Gumps didn't like to talk about going ACES. It made him uncomfortable. But it had to be more than the ACES that was making him sad. My grandmother had been dead for a year; it was just the two of us now. Maybe the idea of being alone in the house was bringing him down. A splash of guilt curdled my excitement.

"When I heard the screen door slam I thought maybe you were stargazing. You were obsessed with comet-spotting, you and Saren, a few years ago."

"I remember," I said, trying to keep my impatience to myself. Now was not the time for a trip down memory lane. I didn't see what this had to do with me getting to Barton. Plus Saren was already there. I could be there by lunchtime if only Gumps would cooperate. "We used to bring the couch cushions out to the backyard to sleep on."

Gumps smiled. "Your grandmother had a heck of a time getting the mildew and grass stains out of those cushions . . ." His smile faded. "But when I watched you run out into the desert like your life depended on it, I knew it wasn't about stargazing."

My stomach dropped to my toes thinking about poor Gumps watching as I ran from him in the middle of the night — all in my sleep.

6

"I cut up my feet pretty badly," I admitted.

"I imagine you did."

I put my hand on the arm of his lumpy old brown cardigan. "Gumps, don't look so sad. It's just the ACES. It happens to everyone. I'll go to Barton and everything will be fine. I'll be back before you know it."

Gumps sighed, then drained the dregs of his cup, grimacing. "I don't know how you can stand this poison," he said. "I'll make a call. You get ready for school."

"But—"

"But nothing. I have deliveries to make and you won't be any worse off this evening than you are right now."

*

Walking to school without my best friend felt like strutting through town with no clothes on — just plain wrong. When I passed Saren's house, it was shut up tight like a store gone out of business. I wondered what her mother was up to now that Saren was at Barton. Mrs. Silver had been fun until her son — Saren's brother — Lex died from complications during the winnowing last year. After that she was never the same, understandably. But then her sadness turned into something else, something erratic and scary, and she went a little bonkers.

At first she wouldn't let Saren out of the house except for school. Before she died, Grandma would go and sit with Mrs. Silver, making tea and letting her talk about Lex, so Saren and I could go off on our own to the park or the corner store. When Saren started to sprout in the way that all girls do, Mrs. Silver talked about taking her away, someplace where they didn't winnow children.

"Now I know she's really crazy," Saren had said. "Where in the world *don't* they winnow children?" But Mrs. Silver talked about her plan the way some people talk about winning the lottery.

When Saren got her period, Mrs. Silver locked her in the bathroom. Saren banged on the door until her knuckles ripped, and then escaped out the window and ran all the way to my house. She spent the night, and the two of us stayed up watching movies, playing Scrabble, doing anything we could to keep her from falling asleep and going ACES. The next morning, Gumps called Mrs. Silver and convinced her to take Saren to Barton. All the while I was in class, trying to stay awake, worrying about Saren. That was only yesterday.

Maybe I shouldn't have been surprised that Saren would go ACES first. A little part of me was jealous. Of the two of us, Saren usually did things first. She was the first to get her ears pierced, the first to shoot up two whole inches, and she was always, always the first to think of the perfect comeback. Her smart mouth was the reason we became friends in the first place. Back in year one, Kamal Beck shouted across the lunchroom, "How come Marivic Stone hasn't got any parents?" and Saren shouted back, "How come Kamal Beck doesn't have any manners?" And just like that, she and I were friends.

A door slammed. I looked up to see Suki Ray coming out of her house in a skirt that was short enough to raise a few eyebrows and a paint-spattered denim jacket. She was a year ahead of me. We weren't friends, but I knew her the way you know everyone in a small school. Her glossy black hair was long on one side, tucked behind her ear in a shiny black wave. The other side was short, still growing in from where it had been shaved during the winnowing. Most kids just had their whole head buzzed and let it grow back. But not Suki. She always did things a bit differently. On anyone else that hairstyle would look weird, but on her it looked cool.

Saren thought Suki was amazing. When Suki had showed up at school wearing two wildly different earrings, Saren was impressed. "It's like she doesn't care what anybody thinks," she said. Saren could pull off a hairstyle like Suki's no problem. In fact, I bet Saren was making sure the doctors at Barton knew to shave only one side of her head. Thinking of Saren alone at Barton gave my heart a tweak and emboldened me to catch up to Suki.

"Hey, Suki!"

Suki turned. "Yeah?"

I blushed. Now that I had her attention I wasn't sure what to say. "Um, I'm Marivic. You don't know me. I'm in year six."

"I've seen you around. What's up?"

The idea that Suki Ray had registered my existence made me ridiculously happy. "Can I walk with you?"

Suki shrugged. "I'm not going to stop you."

I fell into step beside her, trying to find something to say. "Your hair looks great."

Suki ran her hand through the short prickles on one side, her knuckles decked out in big metal rings. "I'm thinking of bleaching this side and then dying it something bold, maybe green."

I nodded. "Cool."

"Did you call my name just to tell me how cool my hair looks?"

I flushed, ashamed at being caught out. "N-no. I had a question. You don't have to answer it, if you don't want to."

"I know I don't. So what is it?"

"Saren, my friend, went to Barton yesterday and I just started going ACES last night, and I guess what I want to know, I mean, what I'm thinking is, what's it like? The winnowing?"

What a mess of a sentence. I tried to get my breathing back to normal, Suki walking along in silence beside me. Her face was tough, inscrutable. As each second passed I regretted opening my mouth at all.

"It's like a dream," she said.

"A good dream?"

"No, I mean an actual dream. I know I was there — obviously, look at my hair — but it doesn't feel real. All I have is an impression of Barton . . . the doctors, a cafeteria, this buzzing noise I still hear in my sleep sometimes . . . but all the details are fuzzy. Weird, right?"

I tried not to shiver. "Yeah."

"I wouldn't worry about it, though. Even if it's terrible, it's not like you're going to remember it."

"I guess."

We arrived at the school.

"Well, this is where we split. Good luck at Barton, M."

She was already walking away by the time I managed to mutter thanks.

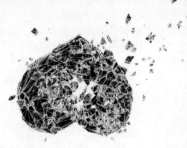

CHAPTER
TWO

Gym was my least favourite class on the best of days, but without Saren to keep me laughing, it was worse. I felt exposed without her beside me, especially when Quin narrowed her eyes, flipped her hair over one shoulder and fake-smiled at me. Quin was sneaky-mean, the kind of girl who said *interesting* when she meant *weird* and smiled sweetly while telling you that you were not invited to her birthday party.

Usually Quin was accompanied by her partner in crime, Tavi. Tavi I didn't mind so much, but she was nowhere in sight. These days it wasn't unusual for kids to be at school one day and gone the next. Chances are Tavi went ACES in the night and was whisked away to Barton, like Saren. I remembered her wearing sunglasses over the past week, a sure sign that something — like the imps — was affecting her eyesight. Maybe Quin was missing Tavi like I was missing Saren. Maybe it would soften her up a bit.

"Hey, Marivic, it's so weird to see you without Saren.

Is it true she had to be taken to Barton in a straitjacket?"

Maybe not.

"No," I said between gritted teeth.

Quin looked surprised. "No, she didn't go to Barton?"

"No, she did. Just not in a straitjacket."

"Now *there's* a person who needs as much fixing as she can get. Too bad they can't go in there and make a few other adjustments. Personality for one." Quin laughed, a few other girls joining in with her.

Before I could respond, Mrs. Cole blew her whistle. "Group two, please take your places for the two-hundred-metre dash in ten, nine, eight, seven . . ." Mrs. Cole couldn't be bothered to spit out the whistle she had clenched between her teeth, so all of her Ss were replaced with shrill noises that made my ears shudder. She was in fine Darby form, dressed in every single piece of school-issue gym clothing, from her fraying baseball cap to the yellow socks pulled up to her lumpy knees. If Saren were here, she'd say she was school spirit personified. The thought made me smile.

"Marivic Stone, what are you smiling about? Stop dawdling! Tie those shoes nice and tight and get to the starting line."

I made my way to the end of the line, stomach churning. I never had any desire to run on the best of days, but today I had even less. My feet were still a bit tender, and the smell of burnt flesh and the sensation of sinking into hot lava were still fresh in my mind.

"On your mark—"

I leaned forward, fingers in the dust, looking ahead to the finish line, trying not to listen to the boys sniggering behind me. I'd like to think they were laughing at something totally unrelated to the sight of all of our butts in the air, but I knew the boys in my class too well.

"Get set—"

Someone — probably Kamal, champion runner and first-class pain in the butt — whistled and the boys laughed again.

"Go!"

At the bleat of the whistle I shot forward, surprised at how smoothly my body moved from a crouch to a full runner's stance. The sound of the dry earth under my feet was encouraging, like a steady drum urging me on. My arms started pumping like it was the most natural thing in the world.

I forgot about Kamal laughing, I forgot about Saren and just enjoyed the feeling of my lungs, heart and legs working together. In what seemed like moments, the finish line, a thick white stripe spray-painted at the edge of the field, loomed up and the whole thing was over. I wasn't even sweating, which was surprising, but not as much of a shock as when I turned around and saw the rest of the runners weren't even at the halfway mark yet.

Mrs. Cole jogged toward me, whistle still gripped between her teeth, making tinny noises as she huffed and puffed toward the finish line. "Very impressive, Marivic! I think that's a school record."

Kamal found this amusing. "You mean a girls' record, right Mrs. C.?" he asked.

Mrs. Cole shook her head. "No, Kamal. I mean a school record. I can't be sure until I check my records book, but I think she even shaved a second off your time." Mrs. Cole beamed at me. "Keep this up, young lady, and you'll be on the podium at state."

Me? A champion runner? The only thing I had ever won was a couple of card games.

"Good racing, everyone. Now start those cool-down routines. I'm going to nip back to the office and check that book. Marivic, I have high hopes for you!"

I fell into a deep hamstring stretch, still dazed by the sudden turn of events.

"You should race Kamal."

I don't know who said it first, but the idea caught on and soon people were nodding and egging me on.

"I don't race girls," he said. "It wouldn't be fair."

Some of the girls protested, but he held up his hands in defence. "Don't get mad at me, get mad at science. No girl has ever outraced a boy before."

I hadn't seriously been thinking about racing him, but Kamal's comments made my skin prickle. "Where does it say that?" I asked.

Kamal shrugged. "I don't know, everywhere?"

Some of the boys laughed. The sound of their laughter got under my skin. "So what are you afraid of, if you're so sure you're going to win?" A chorus of *ooohs* followed. Even Quin looked impressed.

Kamal laughed, not the least bit annoyed. "I didn't say I was afraid. If you want to race, I'm all for it. Just don't be mad when you're choking on my dust."

The group divided into boys versus girls.

"Do it, Marivic, show him he's not the best."

"Someone has to put him in his place."

With the girls begging me to challenge him, I couldn't have backed down if I wanted to. I wished for the hundredth time that morning that Saren was there with me.

"Okay, fine."

The crowd scattered, boys on one side, girls on the other, whooping and hollering insults at each other. Kamal and I both stepped up to the groove in the dirt.

He grinned down at me from his full height, smiling toothily like a wolf. "You ready for this, Stone?" Kamal tried to look intimidating, but he pulled at his earlobes and shook his head like maybe he had water in his ears. Was I imagining things or was he nervous?

"Ready." My calves were screaming *move* and my lungs were already expanding like balloons in my chest.

Quin stepped up to the line, taking control. "On your marks," she said. I leaned forward, resting on the tips of my fingers. They felt electric, like they were pulling a current out of the earth and charging my muscles like a battery.

"Get set." My hips lifted, and out of the corner of my eye I could see Kamal in perfect form, looking graceful and powerful like a panther, built to run. *I can take him*, I thought.

"GO!" I shot ahead like a bullet, pumping my arms and letting my feet take over.

I kept my gaze in front of me and watched, amazed, as the blur of people at the finish line grew closer and closer, the mass of hair and faces and legs morphing into familiar people, their mouths open, yelling silent encouragement. Slowly the noise of the crowd rushed in. I looked back and saw Kamal had stopped a few feet behind me, doubled over, his hands pressing into the sides of his head, almost like he was in pain.

"*Now* what do you have to say about girls running?" someone asked him.

"I call foul," Kamal said between ragged breaths. He lifted his head, and I saw that he was in pain, his dark skin glazed in sweat and his shoulders heaving with effort. I couldn't remember the last time he had lost a race.

The crowd was outraged. "We saw it!" they shouted. "You're crazy!"

Kamal pointed a finger at me. "No, something's up. If you ask me, this one's running a little *imp*aired."

The jeering came to a dead stop, like a field of insects before the rain.

Mrs. Cole had returned. She didn't look thrilled anymore. She looked nervous. "Marivic, that was . . . something." It wasn't a compliment. My cheeks flamed, even though I hadn't done anything wrong. "Speed isn't the most common Adolescent Physical Impairment, but it is in the guide," Mrs. Cole said gently.

Suddenly no one was looking at me.

I swallowed. "I know."

"Does your grandfather know?"

"Yes."

"Perhaps you should go home at lunch today. Take some time off. Get ready for Barton."

I nodded and slunk off toward the girls' change room.

Nobody was cheering anymore.

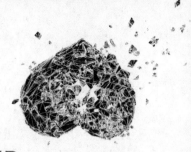

CHAPTER
THREE

Gumps was sitting at the kitchen table when I got home, the remains of an unidentified appliance spread out in front of him. He stared at it over the tips of his tented fingers.

"What did that used to be?"

"A toaster."

"Cause of death?"

"It's not a repair," he said. "I dissected this one myself. It's an oldie, haven't come across a model like this in ages. I wanted to see if I could still do it."

Gumps was a retired repairman, at least he was retired in the sense that he no longer worked at a regular job. He still liked to keep his skills sharp by practising on old appliances that people left at the side of the road for pickup or, worse, that he had scavenged from the scrapyard. Nowadays he made a few bucks delivering fridges and TVs.

"Is it just me or are you home a full half day early?"

"They sent me home," I said.

"Learned all there is to learn already?" Gumps said lightly.

"You know why. We had gym today and I won a race."

"They're sending kids home for winning races now? What is our education system coming to?"

"Gumps! Please! I shouldn't have gone to school today. My imps are setting in. I should be at Barton!"

With Saren, I added silently.

Gumps turned from his toaster innards and smiled sadly at me. "And you will be. Tonight. I happened to deliver a TV across town today, to a Mrs. Beck. She used to pal about with your mother once upon a time. I believe her son is in your class?"

I swallowed all the nasty things I could say about her son. Kamal. "Yes."

"Seems she's taking her son in after dinner. She's offered to drive you."

An image of Kamal, bent over in the field holding his head after losing his first race in years, flashed through my mind. Of course. His imps were setting in; he must have bog ears. As imps go, they were pretty common. Sometimes bog ears manifested as hearing loss, or dizziness, or imagining noises and sounds that no one else could hear. Anger flared in my chest. How dare he accuse me of being impaired when he was also going ACES? And now Gumps was abandoning me and sending me to Barton with him.

"You're not going to take me?"

Gumps looked down at his hands. "I have a delivery."

"You deliver things all day! I only go to Barton once."

"I'm sorry, Marivic. I'll make us something special. Breakfast for dinner, your favourite!"

"I don't want breakfast for dinner. I want you to take me to Barton!"

My face stung. I rubbed at my cheeks but the feeling wouldn't go away. They couldn't hurt any more if he'd actually reached out and slapped me.

"I don't understand. This morning you were in such a hurry to get there."

"You're seriously not going to take me?"

"Mrs. Beck offered. She's a nice person. She knew your mother."

"So? Lots of people are nice. Lots of people knew my mother."

Gumps turned back to his toaster. "You should take a shower. I'll get started on that French toast."

*

When I got my first pimple, I moved my Barton Guide from the back of my sock drawer to my nightstand, where I could consult it regularly. The closer I got to going ACES, the more curious I was. I became a devotee of the guide, underlining sections and learning them by heart.

Every kid in Darby gets a copy of the guide in year one, when the Barton nurses come to school to give out the SuperGen shots. The guide includes a brief history of the Infertility Crisis, caused by the use of experimental technology and chemical weapons during the Second World War. These toxins were also responsible for the Adolescent Physical Impairments (which everyone shortens to imps) — everything from changes in sight and hearing to increased strength and speed to temperature numbness. Their symptoms were listed in the Barton Guide alongside the RED test, which was used to distinguish between regular nightmares and going ACES.

Once you started, the ACES took over every night. Hence the R, for "Recurrence." If unwinnowed, the ACES got worse ("Escalation") and led to dangerous incidents, or "Destruction."

Destruction was the scariest part of the RED test. In the guide they included true stories about accidents that occurred when kids went ACES. One ran into the street and got hit by a car. Another fell into a pool and drowned. Not long before he left for Barton, Lex told Saren and me about a kid who had strangled his own mother to death when he went ACES because he thought she was someone else. That story was not included in the guide. Most people called Barton at the first sign of any change. There wasn't any need for a RED test. Now that I had experienced the ACES for myself, I could see why.

On the last page was a packing list. I had already packed an old purple gym bag months ago, but I wanted to go through the checklist to make sure I hadn't forgotten anything: pyjamas, toothbrush, my favourite coconut shampoo. After some consideration I also included Patches, my old stuffed giraffe.

I'd never spent the night anywhere but Saren's house, and who knows what was waiting for me at Barton. I hadn't slept with Patches in years but this seemed like the kind of situation where his fuzzy presence could be comforting. If I was going to be running through that lava every night in my dreams it would be nice to wake up to his soft fur and familiar smell. I made sure he was at the very bottom of my bag, shoved under socks and pyjamas.

*

Forty minutes later I sat at the table, ready to refuse all offers of food in protest. But Gumps kept threatening to feed me airplane-style, like a baby, so I ended up eating one bite of everything to get him off my case: scrambled eggs, French toast, fried tomato. He'd even found a package of hash browns hiding in the far corner of the freezer. He kept offering me more food, more salve for my feet, more orange juice. I knew I was being mean, but I couldn't bring myself to say anything nice or reassuring. If he cared that much, then he would be the one taking me to Barton.

"Mrs. Beck will be here any minute. I've got to go. Please, Marivic, aren't you going to say goodbye?"

I stared at my plate as if the meaning of life was written somewhere in the swirls of cinnamon on my French toast. I kept my eyes down, even though there were tears in them and I wanted more than anything to look at Gumps. But I knew that if I did I would not be able to restrain myself from throwing my arms around his neck and weeping into his bony old shoulder.

Gumps patted my head and gave my shoulder a squeeze. "That's okay, I'll say it for both of us. Goodbye, Marivic! Goodbye, Gumps!"

There were so many tears in my eyes that my French toast looked like it was underwater. My neck hurt with the effort of keeping still but I didn't move until the screen door squealed, the truck wheezed and then sputtered to life and disappeared down the street. Then and only then did I push my plate away. My dinner was spoiled. The tears made everything too salty.

I dumped the dishes in the sink, enjoying the sound of something — maybe a plate — breaking. Something for Gumps to clean up later when I was gone. I finished the chocolate milk and put the empty carton back in the fridge. Another nasty surprise for when he came back. I wanted him to feel as rotten as I did.

That's when I spotted my mother's photo on the fridge. It wasn't a great photo of her, but it was one of my favourites. She was standing in the kitchen — this kitchen — wearing Grandma's apron, white with broad blue stripes. It had a big pocket in the front and in the pocket was a baby: me. She had both hands under my armpits, holding me in place like a baby kangaroo in its mother's pouch. There were dirty dishes piled on the counter behind her, the sun coming through the window behind her was too bright, blotting out an entire corner, and my mother had laughed at the last moment, blurring her features. But I loved it anyway. It looked real. I had stared at this photo so many times I could almost remember being there.

My mother was one of the one hundred teachers and five hundred and eighty students who died when Darby Public School burned to the ground eleven years ago. I was just over a year old. I don't have any memories of her, only the stories my grandparents told me. Every year on her birthday, we have coconut cupcakes — her favourite — and Gumps brings out a photo album and tells me the stories behind all thirty-six photos. I know them by heart.

I know the reason she was smiling with her mouth closed in her eighth birthday picture is because she had lost three of her front teeth and she thought it made her look like a pirate. I know the big glasses she was wearing in the Christmas photo when she was twelve actually belonged to Gumps and that she put them on to make the photographer (also Gumps) laugh.

I know enough about her to know that she would have been a fun mom. It was only fair I have a memento of her while I was at Barton. I slid the magnets off the photo, peeled it from the fridge and carefully placed it between the glossy pages of the Barton Guide for safekeeping. Gumps had a whole album and a lifetime of memories. Surely I deserved one flimsy little picture.

Before I could change my mind, a horn sounded nearby. I went to the front door to see a sleek silver car with dark windows pulling into the driveway. My dinner threatened to make a reappearance. The horn bleated again — an angry sheep — and I hauled my bag over one shoulder and shuffled out to the car.

Kamal was slumped in the back seat, hugging an old pillow. I braced myself, waiting for a sarcastic comment, but he was too tired to care.

"Marivic Stone," Mrs. Beck said. She was as immaculate as her car, hair smoothed back into a business lady helmet, lipstick perfectly applied, crisp white shirt with no sweat stains or wrinkles. "I knew your mother. Better buckle up. I promised your grandfather I'd get you there in one piece."

"Yeah, before they cut us into pieces," Kamal muttered.

His mother looked at him in the rear-view mirror and said sharply, "Kamal. That's enough. Not today, please."

Beside me Kamal sighed and burrowed his head into the pillow like an overgrown puppy. I rested my forehead on the windowpane as we drove through town, past the sign that said, YOU ARE NOW LEAVING DARBY,

NEW MEXICO, THE CRADLE OF AMERICA, and out into the burnt desert. All that running — in dreams and in real life — caught up with me and I felt as worn out as an old shoe.

The drive was long and dusty. Mrs. Beck followed the signs shouting 15 MILES! 10 MILES! 5 MILES!

Eventually Barton appeared in the distance. It rose out of the desert, shimmering slightly like a mirage in the dying light of the day. As we got closer Barton became more solid: walls, windows, shrubbery and two sets of fences. The first was a perimeter fence, stretching back so far behind Barton that I couldn't see where it ended. It also stretched up — at least one storey high, ending in snarls of barbed wire, like overgrown metal thorns. It gave me the creeps. No matter what kind of plants they stuck out front or how many exclamation marks they had on the welcome signs, Barton felt like the military base it had once been. We passed an abandoned checkpoint, located just outside the second fence, and I shivered as we drove by, as if the ghost of a soldier was staring right at me.

Mrs. Beck drove us to the front entrance, put the car into park and said, "Here you are, front door service."

"You're not coming in?" I hated myself for the quiver in my voice. It wasn't like she owed me anything. I wasn't her daughter.

Kamal snorted as he let himself out of the car. "From here on out it's every man — and woman — for himself, right, Ma?"

I stumbled out of the car, shifting my bag. I looked away when Mrs. Beck wrapped Kamal into a big hug and kissed the top of his head, saying affectionately, "See you in a few weeks, kiddo."

To me, she smiled and nodded. "Good luck, Marivic."

Maybe I shouldn't have been so angry with Gumps. I didn't even hug him goodbye. There was a hole in my heart that kept getting bigger until it felt like it would take over my whole body and I would disappear into it, like a black hole. Mrs. Beck got back into the car and I watched it glide away, practically without a sound.

"Do me a favour and wait a few minutes before you come in," Kamal said. "I don't want people to think we came, like, together."

I looked around at the deserted driveway and up at the windows. "There's no one around. Who do you think is watching us?"

"Are you kidding?" Kamal snorted. "We're at Barton now. They're always watching us."

The Barton Center for Adolescent Health

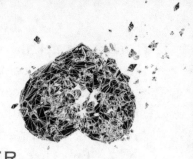

CHAPTER
FOUR

I counted to thirty before I entered, squatting on the sidewalk, pretending to search through my bag in case anyone spotted me from a window and wondered why on earth I wasn't going inside. Thirty seconds was all I would give that arrogant jerk Kamal.

There were two sets of doors, each sliding open silently as I approached, leading to a bright, breezy waiting area with cacti in red clay pots and sleek couches to sit on. Nurses in bright scrubs buzzed behind a glassed-in area with the words CHECK-IN painted in giant letters on one of the windows.

Kamal was nowhere to be seen. Where had he got to so fast? Music — loud enough to hear, but too soft to tell what the song was — floated through the lobby. I was deciding whether to sit on the couch or go up to the check-in desk when one of the nurses slid open the glass partition and asked if I needed help.

"I'm checking in. My name is Marivic Stone. My grandfather called this morning."

"Here you are!" the nurse chirped, peering at her computer screen. "Welcome, Marivic! That's a pretty name."

"Thanks. It's a combination of my grandmother's and my mother's names, Maria and Victoria. Mari-Vic. Something Gumps — I mean my grandfather — made up." I felt my cheeks flaming as I rambled on about my name to the nurse. She was smiling at me but it was probably part of her job to smile at nervous kids when they came in.

She passed me a clipboard and a pen. "I'm just going to get you to sign the Surrender Form then we're all set."

"Surrender Form?"

"Yes, you need to surrender your health and well-being to the Barton Center. It gives us permission to act in your best interests if there are any complications during the winnowing. You can't very well make decisions if you're under anesthetic or going ACES." The nurse smiled as she explained the form, as if it was no big deal. Still, the idea of surrendering my life to Barton made me feel uneasy. Not that I had any choice. I read the first paragraph, which was full of so much legal mumbo-jumbo it might as well have been written in Swahili. I signed my name and handed her the form.

"Perfect! Take a seat and an intake coordinator will be with you in a sec."

I perched on one of the couches, clutching my old bag, feeling shabby in the pristine lobby. The building was air-conditioned, which was a nice change from my sweaty old house. As Barton staff came and went they smiled at me, asked me my name and welcomed me. It started to feel less like a hospital and more like a hotel.

Eventually a woman with apple cheeks and lustrous

dark hair swept back in a ponytail came to speak to me. She was so pretty she looked like an actress playing the part of a nurse in a movie.

"I'm Roya," she said. "I'm the intake coordinator. Technically I'm a nurse, but think of me more like a camp counsellor. And you are?"

"Marivic."

Roya smiled even wider. "Welcome, Marivic! It's too late to start your intake exam today, so I'm going to take you straight to the residency floor to get you settled."

Roya chattered all the way to my room on the intake residency floor, the next floor up from the main level. I tried to pay attention as she told me about the intercoms in our rooms and lights out and what I could expect from the assessment tests, but there was too much to take in and I was anxious to see Saren.

"Here we are, your very own room."

We stopped at an open door with my name typed out on a card and slipped into a metal frame. Maybe it should have made me feel welcome, but I felt uneasy. Like the room itself was waiting for me.

Inside, there was a crisply made bed, a small sink, a desk and an intercom built into the wall by the door. Roya showed off the features of the room like a real estate agent, opening a narrow closet, flicking the light switch and pointing out a pile of folded towels sitting on the bed.

Everything was starched and white, so crisp and clean that I knew I wouldn't ever be totally comfortable. I missed the slightly funky smell of our old carpet and the warped doorways that swelled when it rained so you couldn't properly shut the doors. It wasn't a prison cell, but the room reminded me that despite the music and the cacti in the lobby, Barton wasn't a hotel, it was a medical centre.

"Is there anything you need?"

"Actually, I was wondering if I could see a friend of mine. She came yesterday. Her name is Saren Silver?"

Roya smiled. "She's just down the hall to the left, across from the boys' washroom. I'll take you."

"Thanks!" I wanted to run down the hall but resisted the urge. When I saw Saren's name on a door it almost felt too good to be true. I knocked and listened for any sign that she was inside.

Roya looked at her clipboard, frowned and said, "She should be in there. Maybe she's already asleep. Knock again."

I did, more insistently this time. I pressed my ear to the cold surface of the door and heard shuffling.

"She's in there!" I cried. "Saren, it's me!"

Then, figuring she wouldn't mind, I let myself in. We were always barging into each other's rooms un-announced back home in Darby. Why would it be any different here?

Saren's room was exactly like mine, blindingly white and full of crisp corners. She was sitting up on the bed, pressing her knees into her chest. Her knuckles were so pale I could see them from across the room, glimmering in the semi-darkness.

Something was wrong.

"Saren, are you okay?"

She didn't seem to hear me. She was panting with her whole body, like a dog, the sheets trembling around her knees. Her eyes were completely white, with not even a hint of a pupil or the warm dark brown of her iris.

"What's wrong with her eyes?"

Roya was at my elbow. "Marivic, we should go."

I jumped as a violent stream of gibberish poured from Saren's mouth, her voice swooping over a range of pitches I didn't know she had. She blinked, and suddenly her eyes cleared of the white film. Her pupils were so dilated they blotted out the brown of her eyes. She screamed, tendons in her neck popping and her voice breaking. She scrambled out of bed and started fumbling with the latch on the window. The sound of her nails scrabbling against the wood made the hair at the back of my neck stand on end. When she couldn't get the latch to work, she started tearing at the screen itself and screaming, "HELP!"

"Marivic!" Roya yanked hard on my arm, pulling me into the hallway. She shut the door and the sounds of Saren screaming disappeared, as if locked away in a deep vault.

"What are you doing?" I cried, trying the doorknob and finding it locked. "She needs us!"

Roya quickly ushered me down the hallway back to my room, my elbow trapped in her firm grip. "I'm sorry you had to see that."

"What happened?"

"I'm afraid you walked in on the middle of an episode."

"An episode?" I tried to remain calm, but the squeak in my voice said otherwise.

"What you refer to as 'going ACES.' It's a frightening thing to witness, but I promise you she's safe in her room. It would be more dangerous to wake her."

"Why?" I asked.

"You're never supposed to wake someone when they're going ACES."

I knew that, I had read it in the Barton Guide, but after watching Saren try to escape I had doubts. "But why? What happened to her eyes?"

Roya turned down the sheets on my bed. "I know it seems impossible, but you should try and get some sleep. You'll see Saren in the morning and see that everything's fine. You're at Barton now. We're going to take care of you." She smiled like nothing had happened, but I noticed she hadn't answered my question.

Thinking of Saren, locked in her room in the middle of a nightmare, I wasn't so sure. I waited until Roya had left, then found my mother's photo between the pages of my Barton Guide. I stared at it, letting the familiar shapes and sizes and colours calm my nerves before tucking it into the frame of the mirror hanging over the sink. I fell asleep with the hope that somewhere my mother was rooting for me.

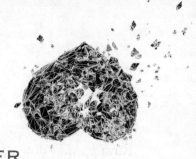

CHAPTER
FIVE

By the morning, I regretted all those times I had prayed to go ACES. I had been plagued by nightmares all night, getting sucked thigh-deep into whorls of lava, running from an enemy I couldn't see, waking exhausted and dehydrated and with torn fingernails. I stared at them, ragged and bloody, thinking of Saren scrabbling at her window. Is that what happened to me? Had I been trying to escape in my sleep and broken my fingernails in the process? There hadn't been anything like that in the Barton Guide.

I wanted check in on Saren first thing, but Roya insisted I go to my intake exam first.

"Now, lots of kids get worried when they hear the word 'exam,' but I think you'll find it's more like a checkup."

Once again, Roya avoided my questions and proceeded to talk about Barton as if it was no big deal, as if bloody fingers and night terrors and potentially deadly procedures were normal. I guess at Barton they are. The thought made me shiver.

We took the elevator back to the main floor then continued down a hallway of offices. A banging in the ceiling made me look up.

"What's that noise?" I asked.

Roya frowned. "Sounds like the A/C is acting up again. Nothing to worry about."

She paused and gestured to a series of black-and-white portraits in gilded frames on the wall, each one lit from above. "You may recognize these men and women as the Barton Five, the five scientists who discovered SuperGen and basically changed the world. Before the discovery of SuperGen, there hadn't been a baby born in America in ten years. Like the rest of the world, we were at the mercy of a pandemic infertility crisis."

Roya stopped at the final portrait, of a small man with light eyes. "And this of course is Dr. Roddenberry." He wasn't particularly handsome, or even all that distinctive, but I knew his face like I knew my own. It was all over Darby — in my textbooks, in the newspaper; some people even kept framed pictures of him on their walls, like a saint. "He's the reason you're here today. The reason we as people are here today."

I knew the story. Everyone did. How after the Second World War, women couldn't get pregnant. How babies died before they hit two years old. Until Dr. Roddenberry and his team came to Barton, discovered SuperGen and saved the human race from extinction. Roddenberry was long dead but his legacy lived on at Barton, in those working to unravel the mysteries of adolescence and perfect the winnowing.

"Here we are. Please change into a paper gown and Dr. Leathers will be with you in two shakes."

Intake room four looked like any old doctor's office: an examination table with a thin sheet of paper pulled across the top, a desk and swivel chair and a computer. I stuffed my clothes into my bag and sat on the table, trying not to make any sudden movements and rip the paper.

The only thing I'd left on was my necklace, a midnight-black charm in the shape of an upside-down heart on a thin silver chain. It had belonged to my grandmother. After she died I wore it every day, to keep her close to me. Surely it wouldn't interfere with anything. I felt better wearing it, like a part of her was nearby and watching over me. I was adjusting the paper gown over my knees when the door opened and a doctor with a big smile and floppy hair breezed in.

"Good morning, Marivic. I'm Dr. Leathers, but the Intakes call me Dr. Dad."

I couldn't imagine calling anyone that, but Dr. Dad went on. "I'm head of the intake program here, but that doesn't mean I shut myself away in the lab or spend all my time at big fundraising meetings. That's not why I came to Barton. I came here because I care about kids. I care about you and making your life better. You have any problems, you need anything at all, you let me know. I'm the big guy around here, they have to listen to me. Okay?"

Dr. Dad seemed more like a guy on TV who had something to sell, but if I didn't say anything at all he might go on and on and I'd never get out of there. I bet Saren had a few choice things to say about Dr. Dad. The thought made my lip twitch. No one was safe from Saren's impressions, even the head of Intakes at Barton. Was she awake? Was she okay?

"Okay, Marivic?"

I blinked. "Okay."

Dr. Dad leaned forward, cupping one ear as if he hadn't heard me correctly.

"Okay, Dr. . . . Dad."

Dr. Dad beamed. "That's better! Now let's get started. I'll give you a routine physical then ask you some questions about your imps — and your Adolescent Chronosomniatic Episodes, or what you kids call the ACES. Sound good?"

"I guess."

But before he could get started, there was a knock at the door.

"Well, now this is unusual. Are you expecting anybody?" Dr. Dad asked. He was being goofy, but I noticed the furrow in his brow, suggesting he was definitely not expecting anyone.

I shook my head dumbly.

"Come on in!"

An older man, completely bald with pencil-thin eyebrows and perfectly round spectacles, entered. Like Dr. Dad he wore a lab coat, but instead of jeans he was wearing khaki pants with a crease that looked as sharp as a razor's edge down the middle of each leg. Dr. Dad jumped up to greet him.

"Dr. Abrams," he said. "What a surprise!"

Side by side, Dr. Abrams towered over Dr. Leathers. He looked like a grizzled rugby player dressed up as a doctor for Halloween. Was I imagining things or did Dr. Dad look nervous?

"Good day, Dr. Leathers. I hope you don't mind, but I've elected to help with the intake exams this morning.

I hear we're understaffed and I consider myself the kind of leader who pitches in when needed." Dr. Abrams smiled. His voice was quiet and very precise, as if he had grown up at a fancy boarding school.

"Of course! I'll just head down to reception and see where else I'm needed." I hadn't been imagining things; Dr. Dad was definitely flustered. "Marivic, you're in excellent hands. This is the head honcho here. Dr. Abrams has been in charge of Barton for over ten years now."

I had heard of Dr. Abrams before. He was the doctor credited with perfecting the winnowing. Sometimes he was consulted as an expert for news reports on ACES and the imps, which was why he looked vaguely familiar — like an actor you've seen in a few movies but can never remember the name of. I never expected to meet him. It was like going on a tour of the White House and running into the president.

"Welcome, Marivic. I do hope you're not nervous," Dr. Abrams said. He smiled and I felt a bit better.

"Just a little," I admitted.

"I think you'll find the process completely painless. Shall we begin?"

The first part of the exam felt like a regular checkup, just as Roya had said. Dr. Abrams checked my ears, nose and throat, shone lights into my eyes and tapped each knee with the little rubber hammer. He leaned close with his stethoscope to check my heart, and paused.

"And what have we here?" he asked, two fingers on the chain of my necklace.

"It was my grandmother's," I explained. "Should I have taken it off?"

"No, that's fine. I'll just move it to the side here while

I check your heart. That's an unusual stone. I don't think I've seen one like it before."

I looked at the dark spade resting in the smooth palm of his hand. Today it seemed more midnight blue than black. "Thanks. I don't know what it is. It's just something she always had."

"Very nice. Now this will feel cold against your skin, but I promise you it won't take a second."

After Dr. Abrams checked my heart, he pressed the stethoscope into my abdomen and told me to take deep breaths. Going through these regular motions of a regular checkup helped me calm down.

Until he moved on to my feet. I held my breath as he examined the cuts and scrapes.

"What happened here?"

"I was running . . ." Dr. Abrams raised his skinny eyebrows at me, waiting for me to continue. They were so thin they looked drawn on. ". . . barefoot."

"I see. And do you usually run barefoot?"

"No. I didn't know I was barefoot. I didn't know I was running. I was dreaming about running and then when I woke up . . ." I looked down at my mangled feet and wiggled my toes.

"Were you having a nightmare or going ACES?" Dr. Abrams put finger quotes around the words "going ACES." He continued, "I know both of these terms are commonly used to describe the Adolescent Chronosomniatic Episodes, but at Barton we refer to them simply as episodes. Nightmares are not an accurate term."

"Why not?"

"Nightmares and episodes are fundamentally quite different. Nightmares, like dreams, typically occur during REM sleep. They are neither as intense nor as consistent as the Adolescent Chronosomniatic Episodes. These episodes, or ACES for short, indicate a deeper-rooted problem that is stimulated by the release of a mutated hormone from the pituitary gland." Dr. Abrams smiled at me. "I'm sure you've learned all this in school and I don't need to go on about it. Why don't you tell me about this barefoot running instead? Were you in the midst of an episode?"

"Yes. At least, I think so."

"In your academic file there is a note about sudden increased athletic ability. Can you elaborate on that?"

I was surprised that such recent information would already be in my file. "I won a race at school."

"Have you won races before?"

"No, usually I don't place at all."

Dr. Abrams smiled again. "I'll bet it felt good to win. Your speed might seem like a good thing now. But the fact is you've gained the ability through a genetic mutation, and uncurbed that mutation will grow until the ability gets out of control. Muscles can overdevelop, joints can be stressed, your heart can be overworked. You'd become a running machine instead of a person. Not that you need to worry about that. We're going to make things better. That's what we do here."

He licked a finger and turned the page in my file. "Now for a brief family history. Your father died in a car accident before you were born and your mother died during the Darby Fire?"

I nodded.

"I'm very sorry for your loss," Dr. Abrams said. "I remember that day well. What a tragedy."

There wasn't a person in Darby who wasn't affected by that fire, but I had lost my only mother, Gumps his only daughter. I shifted, looking for something to say to break the awkward moment.

"Thank you," I said. "But I had my grandparents. Although my grandmother died last year, which leaves just me and Gumps."

Dr. Abrams frowned. "Gumps?"

"That's what I call my grandfather," I explained.

"Ah, yes, Humphrey Stone. Maternal grandfather," he read. "Are you close?"

Not close enough that he would drive me to Barton, apparently. I had to swallow hard before I could answer the question in something that resembled my normal voice. "Yes."

"Is he in good health?"

"Fit as a fiddle, that's what he would say."

"No history of heart disease, migraines or asthma?"

"No."

"Your grandfather never complained of high blood pressure or allergies?"

"No."

"Did he ever talk to you about his job?"

"Sometimes he talks about his customers or the houses people live in. He delivers appliances, some repairs on the side. He's mostly retired now. I help him out a bit."

Dr. Abrams smiled kindly. "I mean before. Did he talk to you about his work here at Barton?"

I blinked, thinking maybe I had misheard the question. "Pardon?"

"Did your grandfather, Humphrey Stone, ever mention the nature of his work here at Barton?"

"No." I leaned forward, as if getting closer to the file would help me process the crazy things it said. "Does it say he worked here in my file?"

I couldn't believe it. Gumps had worked at Barton? When? And why hadn't he ever spoken about it?

Dr. Abrams ignored my question in favour of his own. "He never spoke about it to you or to anyone else in your presence?"

I said nothing, still shocked. Dr. Abrams paused, waiting for more. When it became clear I had nothing to say, he continued, speaking very slowly: "In the twelve years you have known your grandfather, you were under the impression that he worked as a delivery man his entire life?"

I felt like an idiot. Gumps was one of the smartest people I knew. How could I not have wondered why he chose to deliver appliances?

"Yes." The admission felt shameful. "Why, what did he do?"

"I'm afraid that's confidential."

"But you just asked me if I knew."

"It's important that we know what he may have told you." Dr. Abrams was definitely not smiling now. The tone in his voice meant business.

"He never told me anything," I said. Suddenly I was aware that the only clothing I had on was made of paper. My skin was chilled and I hugged my arms to my body for warmth.

Dr. Abrams stared at me for a second, then sat back and smiled with lips as thin as his eyebrows. "That's it for today. That wasn't so hard, now was it?"

I couldn't smile back at Dr. Abrams. I was too full of questions about Gumps.

"You've done very well, Marivic. Roya will be back in a moment to escort you to your room. I do hope you'll be comfortable here. I know it's a frightening time in your life, but we're going to take care of that as soon as we can."

Dr. Abrams smiled at me, bowed a little and left me shivering in my paper gown, my head reeling.

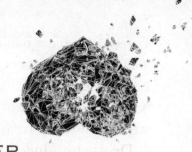

CHAPTER
SIX

I didn't see Saren until much later that afternoon. I was in my room flipping through a Barton welcome brochure, not really reading it, but trying to wrap my head around the idea of Gumps working at Barton, when I was totally side-swiped, knocked onto my bed by a running hug.

"Saren!"

"You're back!" she cried. "You were gone for ages!"

"Get off me!" I rolled over onto my back, pinning Saren underneath me on the bed. She struggled to break free and we rolled back and forth, giggling, until eventually it was me smushed on the bed, Saren laughing triumphantly from on top.

"I win!" she said between gasps. When she raised her arms in victory, I took the opportunity to roll out from under her and pull myself to a normal sitting position.

"I guess this means you're feeling better?" I asked.

"Sooo much better. I'm sorry about before. I think I was still half-asleep or something. Here you are, an eager little Intake, and I don't even give you a proper welcome."

Saren pressed her hands to her chest and added in a dramatic southern accent, "Will you *ev-ah* forgive me?"

She seemed like she was back to her jokey self, but I knew something was still off. She was talking a mile a minute and her gaze never once settled on mine.

"Obviously," I said.

Saren fell back on the bed in a pretend faint. "Well, thank heavens."

I lay back next to her and rested my head on my hands.

"Tell me everything I missed," she said.

For the next hour, I brought Saren up to speed on all the strange things that had happened in the last two days. It felt good to get everything off my chest. Saren was the perfect audience. She hooted with laughter when I told her about beating Kamal in the race. We tried to think of all the reasons why Gumps would have kept his job at Barton a secret. We agreed that Dr. Dad was annoying but basically a good guy. When I was finished, I felt exhilarated and less alone. My grandmother always said that sharing a burden lessened its load, and she was right. Nothing was that bad when you had your best friend beside you.

*

At dinner, I was surprised to see Quin in line with Tavi. She must have arrived sometime during the day.

"Hey, girls!" She waved us over as if we were long-lost friends. "Us Darby girls ought to stick together, don't you think?" Saren snorted but Quin didn't flinch. We walked over to the serving window, picked up our trays and listened to the options the kitchen staff had prepared.

"Chicken," Quin said.

"Lasagna," Tavi said.

"Eww, Tavi, don't get the lasagna! The cheese is all burned and the vegetables are mushy! She'll have the chicken," Quin told the cafeteria lady.

"Chicken," Tavi agreed, but she didn't look happy about it. Neither did the cafeteria lady, who had probably spent all day preparing the lasagna that Quin had just trashed.

I got the lasagna.

Kamal was seated at a corner table, next to a mousy-looking boy who wouldn't look up from his plate. Kamal was stretched out over two whole chairs, taking up as much space as possible. "What's wrong, girls? You don't want to sit with us? Having a private girl talk?"

Quin laughed. "Let's go over."

"We're not sitting with them too, are we?" I asked Saren.

"It won't be so bad," Saren said. "Besides, I haven't told Kamal he's an idiot in at least a week. That boy needs to be put in his place regularly."

We fell in step behind Quin and took seats at the boys' table. I smiled at the nervous-looking boy but he did not smile back.

"So. You guys settling in? You heard the Roddenberry ghost yet?" Kamal asked.

"Who?" Tavi asked.

"You've never heard of the Roddenberry ghost?" Kamal taunted. "He's famous!"

"He's an urban legend," Quin corrected. "Just a story people tell about Barton."

"Nah, it's true. Simon and I heard him today, right, Si?"

The boy, Simon, seemed to shrink as we all turned to look at him. "Well, we heard something. In the ceiling."

"I heard it too. Roya said it was the air conditioning," I said.

Kamal's eyes practically glittered. "Nah, it was the ghost!"

"Don't ghosts only come out at night?" Saren pointed out.

Kamal shook his head. "Amateur," he said. Saren bristled. "Ghosts don't care what time of day it is."

"Do you mean Roddenberry as in *the* Roddenberry?" Tavi asked.

"As in founder of the Barton Five, demigod, saviour of the modern world Roddenberry? Yes." Kamal leaned forward with a delighted look in his eye that made me nervous for what was coming next. "You know he was murdered by a former patient, right?"

"That's just a rumour," Saren said sharply. "You're so full of it, Kamal."

"It's true!" Kamal insisted. "It's all a big cover-up. I read about it."

"Where, in one of your tabloids?" Quin joked.

"Roddenberry died of a heart attack," I said. "It's in the textbook." I knew because I had read that textbook about fifty times.

Kamal laughed. "Oh, please. That textbook was produced by Barton. You think they're going to include the part where one of their experiments went bananas and killed their star scientist at a conference? You're so naïve, Stone."

Quin laughed. "What a great story! All we need now are some marshmallows and a campfire."

"Can we talk about something else please?" Tavi asked.

Kamal grinned. "All right, Tavi — what's with the shades?"

"It's my imps. My eyes are all wonky."

"And Ms. Quin, what's wrong with you?"

Quin smiled and tossed her braid over her shoulder. "Wouldn't you love to know?"

"Well we know what's wrong with Marivic. How did it feel to finish a race for once?"

Saren stared him down. "Man, what I would've given to see Marivic leave you in the dust."

Kamal glowered at me. "It wasn't a fair race. I don't like cheaters."

"Oh, but ghosts are okay," I said. Quin and Saren laughed and I felt that surge of power that came with saying the right thing at the right time. Being with Saren had recharged my batteries. I felt like me again.

Kamal was less impressed. He narrowed his eyes and I braced for his comeback, but instead he nodded toward Simon. "Simon here is having trouble with hot and cold."

"Really?" Tavi asked, looking at Simon with new interest. "That's supposed to be really rare."

Simon shrugged, wilting under the attention. "I guess."

"I want to see!" Quin said.

Simon looked to Kamal for support, but Kamal was nodding, agreeing with Quin. "Yeah, dude. Let's see what you got."

Simon sighed. "What do I have to do?" he asked.

"Nothing," Saren said. "You don't have to do anything you don't want to."

"C'mon, Simon, let's go." Kamal got up, carrying his tray to the far corner of the cafeteria and a pair of deep sinks meant for rinsing our dishes. Quin followed, grinning.

"You too, Tavi," she said over her shoulder. Tavi stood and followed, leaving Simon with Saren and me.

"You don't have to go," I muttered, but Simon looked from us to Kamal. He knew that the cool thing to do was go along with it. I wasn't surprised when he got up and made his way to the sinks.

"This is stupid," Saren said. "The imps are dangerous. It's not show and tell."

With a sigh, Saren pushed her tray away and went to join everyone else. "Come on. We can't leave that poor kid alone with those idiots."

Kamal was pointing to the hot and cold faucets. "We'll let them each run for a bit, and then you tell us which is which."

Simon was nodding. "Okay," he said, looking relieved.

"But first, we have to blindfold you."

"Oh." Simon appeared to be having second thoughts, but before he could say anything, Quin untied a long-sleeved shirt from around her waist.

"Will this work?"

Kamal winked at her, which made Quin's smile widen and her dimples deepen. "Perfect. Simon, you're a lucky man, having the shirt of the prettiest girl in Barton wrapped around your ugly little mug."

Quin giggled as Kamal knotted her shirt around Simon's forehead. Behind me, Saren gagged loudly. Once the blindfold was secured, Kamal grabbed Simon by the shoulders and spun him around, first one way, then the other. "Are you ready, Si-man?"

All this time the faucets had been running. Steam rolled off the hot faucet and billowed up over the sink.

Simon lurched forward one step at a time, holding his hands out in front of him.

Beside me Tavi sucked her breath in through her teeth. "This is a bad idea," she muttered, turning away. "I can't look."

"Okay, buddy! Here we go." Kamal had Simon's wrists in his hands and he guided them so that both hands hit different streams of water at the same time. Simon jumped at first, surprised at the sensation of the water on his fingers. After the initial shock he wiggled his fingers in the streams.

"Well? Which is which?"

Simon cocked his head to one side like a blind bird. "I'm not sure," he said. "They feel the same to me."

Quin gasped and clapped her hands, delighted. "Wow!" she said. "That is pretty freaking cool!"

Simon grinned too, but I couldn't help but notice the steam growing thicker in the hot sink. The faucet had been running for a few minutes now and the metal was starting to fog up.

Saren saw it too. "Okay that's enough," she said.

"It's not hurting him," Kamal said.

"You don't know that," she protested.

"Hey, man, are you in pain?" Kamal asked.

Simon shook his head. "I told you, I can't feel temperature anymore."

"Just because he can't feel it doesn't mean it isn't hot. That water must be boiling now! It's been on for too long!" I was practically shouting.

Beneath the hot water, Simon's left hand had turned bright red. At my shoulder, Tavi whimpered. "Can we turn the water off, please?"

"I told you this was stupid," Saren said.

Quin frowned at Simon's hand, the skin starting to pucker under the rushing water. "Okay, maybe he should switch them or something, so the cold water can cool the other hand down."

"Just turn it off!" I stormed forward, pushing through Quin and Kamal to turn the faucet off. I gasped as my hand made contact with the metal, burning hot. When I pulled my hand away I could see the impression of the faucet in white, the skin red and tender around it. I plunged it under the cold faucet and tried to keep from crying. Maybe Simon couldn't feel temperature, but I certainly could.

"Oh my god, look at his hand!" Tavi shrieked.

Simon stumbled back from the sink, pushing Quin's shirt off his eyes with the hand that had been under the cold faucet, which was bone white except for his knuckles, which were red. He held his other hand in front of him in wonder. The skin looked angry, puffed up and blotchy.

"You idiot, he's burned his hand!" Saren yelled.

"Get a nurse!" I said, meaning for Simon, but looking at my own angry welt and thinking I could use one too.

Saren bolted for the intercom.

"It's okay, Simon," I said. "It'll be okay."

Simon nodded, staring at his hand as the skin puckered, burst and began to peel. The scared look in his eyes sent spiders skittering over my shoulders and down my spine.

"I can't even feel it," he whispered.

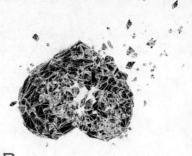

CHAPTER
SEVEN

A team of nurses came to fetch Simon. They made the rest of us sit at a table and wait for Dr. Dad to come and give us a lecture. Someone looked at my hand, gave me cream and placed a bandage over it. I stared at the weave of the gauze, wondering what my skin looked like underneath. Or what Simon's skin must look like now.

Tavi couldn't stop sniffing.

"Cut it out, Tavi. It's not like *you* burned *your* hand," Quin said savagely.

"Can you believe that? He didn't even *feel* it," Kamal said, shaking his head. "Crazy."

"This whole thing was stupid," Saren muttered. "If it wasn't for Marivic, Simon might not even have a hand left."

She smiled at me and I felt the tiniest bit like a hero. Even though what she said was probably not true — there was no way the water would have boiled his whole hand away, was there? — it made me feel good.

Dr. Dad came in, looking serious. He pulled a chair

out from the table and sat on it backwards. I suppose he thought it made him look cool. "Hey guys, I know you're worried about your friend but we're going to take good care of him."

"Will his hand be okay?" Tavi asked in a small voice.

"Yes. It was good that Quin here thought to call the nurses in when she did." Dr. Dad squeezed Quin's shoulder and gave her a grateful smile. Quin blushed and looked down bashfully, as if she had nothing to do with Simon burning his hand in the first place. I glared at her but she was too busy taking credit for something she didn't do to notice.

"It's great that you're having a good time but don't forget you're all here because of a serious physical condition. Not everyone's imps are as dramatic as Simon's, but it doesn't mean they are any less dangerous." Dr. Dad looked at each of us in turn. "Untreated you could go blind or deaf or become so developed in certain parts of your body that enormous physical strain is put on your joints or spine. Tomorrow we'll determine a personal range of imps, and how advanced they are, for each of you. Once we know what we're dealing with, we can go in there and fix the problem. That's the winnowing in a nutshell. Now I've asked Roya to give you each a little something that will help you get some rest. I'll see all of you tomorrow."

Saren and I waited for everyone else to file out of the cafeteria before heading back to our rooms.

"How's the hand?"

I flexed it carefully, feeling the skin stretch underneath. "It stings."

"You're my hero."

"Cut it out."

"You're definitely Simon's hero. He's probably dreaming about you right now."

I nudged her with my shoulder. "Stop it."

I couldn't get the image of Simon's blotchy, misshapen hand out of my mind. Where would he sleep tonight, I wondered. In his own room, or hooked up to a machine somewhere else?

"Wanna come hang out in my room?" Saren asked.

Lying on Saren's standard Barton bed, our feet dangling off the edge, wasn't exactly the same as hanging out on my porch or in her backyard, but it was as close to normal as something could be in Barton.

"It's weird being here. I keep thinking about Lex."

"Oh?" I was careful not to say too much in case I said the wrong thing. Since his death, she rarely talked about her brother. When my grandmother died I wanted to talk about her all the time. I found ways to bring her up in conversations that had nothing to do with her. But Saren never wanted to talk about Lex. Until now.

"I think about how shy he was, and how he would have hated answering all those questions in the intake exam. Mom always said I talked for the both of us, but who did the talking when he was here alone?"

Saren stopped, staring straight up at the ceiling. Tears leaked out the corners of her eyes and ran down her cheeks. I looked at her hand and thought about taking it in my own, but I felt suddenly shy.

"I miss him so much. I even miss the stupid things, like how much noise he made when he ate cereal, remember?"

I smiled and smacked my lips loudly. "Who could forget?"

Saren laughed a little. "He used to leave socks everywhere. You couldn't go into a room without finding a sock. It drove my mother crazy. I hate being here, knowing this is where he died. I look at the doctors and nurses and I wonder, did you do his intake exam? Did you run his assessment tests? Were you there with him in the operating room? How can I trust you with my own life, knowing that you let my brother die?"

"You can't think like that."

"I can't *stop* thinking like that."

There was a knock at the door. We both looked up to find Roya smiling at us. I wondered if she had heard what we were saying about the staff. Surely she wouldn't be smiling like that if she had.

"Hi, girls. Time to say good night."

"It's not that late," Saren protested.

"No, but you've had an eventful day and you need to be rested for your assessment tests tomorrow."

Saren sighed, making it known that she thought Roya was being a bit too parental.

"It's fine," I said, sliding off the bed. "I'm pretty tired."

Saren rolled over, hugging her pillow, and smiled at me. "'Night, Marivic."

"'Night, you big old softie."

Hearing Saren laugh as I walked back to my room made me feel as warm and delicious as hot chocolate. I tried desperately to hold on to this feeling, knowing sleep was coming and with sleep came the ACES.

"You guys are close, huh?" Roya said. "That's nice."

Roya smoothed her hair back and I caught a flash of a plastic tube hooked over her ear. She saw me looking and tapped it with a fingernail. "Hearing aid," she explained.

"Oh. Sorry. I wasn't staring," I said.

"It's all right. I've had it since I was twelve. Back when I was a kid the winnowing wasn't as sophisticated as it is now. It wasn't even called the winnowing yet. Doctors did whatever they could to curb people's imps, sometimes with drastic consequences. You're lucky you live in a time when the procedure has been perfected."

I thought of Lex Silver dying on the operating table. "Almost perfected," I said.

Roya's smile slipped a little. "Almost perfected," she agreed.

"So you had bog ears?" I asked.

Roya smiled. "First-rate bog ears. It's been a long time, but I still remember what it was like. I grew up in an apartment building in New York City. I was on the tenth floor and my best friend, Leila, was on the third. Leila had a cat named Boots and I knew before anyone else that Boots was going to have kittens."

"How?"

"I could hear their heartbeats. All the way up on the tenth floor, I could hear them ticking away inside Boots."

"Whoa. That's cool. A little creepy, but kind of cool."

Roya smiled. "It *was* cool. At first. But you can't live like that, with all those sounds fighting for space inside your head. It's overwhelming." Her smile had disappeared and she was frowning slightly, as if the memory had gone sour.

"Now. Take one of these, doctor's orders." She took a bottle from the pocket of her scrubs and offered me a single pill. "It's called Somnease. To help you sleep. It blocks the part of your brain that triggers the episodes and allows you to enter a regular sleep pattern, no going ACES!"

I looked at the little pill in my hand. It was bright purple, like grape Popsicles, my favourite flavour. Still, I had never heard of Somnease before. It sounded too good to be true. "Is it safe?"

Roya laughed. "Of course it's safe! Somnease is not addictive, if that's what you're worried about. Plus it only works for six hours. Think of it like an allergy pill; it soothes the symptoms, but only temporarily. After the winnowing you'll never need to take one again. But it's important to be well rested for your assessments tomorrow."

"All right." I slid the pill under my tongue. Roya ran the tap at the sink in my room and handed me a little paper cup of water to help wash the pill down.

"How long does it take to work?" I asked.

"Not long. Just lay back and go to sleep."

My mind was racing. I was thinking about Simon's hand, the assessments tomorrow and why Gumps had never told me that he had worked at Barton. At the moment, sleep felt like a foreign country.

"I'm not sure I can fall asleep," I admitted.

"Sometimes it helps me to think of all the things I'm thankful for," Roya suggested. "Then you go to sleep thinking good thoughts."

"Like what?"

"Roddenberry, SuperGen, my job, a good hair day." Roya smiled to let me know she was making a joke. After a moment she added, "Sometimes I think of those kittens. Good night, Marivic."

"Good night." Roya flicked the light switch before she left, closing the door behind her. It shut with a soft click. I dug around in my gym bag and found Patches.

He smelled so much like home that I was knocked off my feet by a tidal wave of homesickness and I had to sit on the edge of the bed with my nose buried in his matted fur.

If I was home, I would be at the kitchen table with Gumps, a jug of sun tea between us, me studying a textbook and him studying the Scrabble dictionary I got him two Christmases ago. I missed him so much even the hairs on my arms ached, but it was a complicated kind of missing.

I was still mad that he hadn't driven me here himself. And I was mad, confused and hurt that he hadn't told me about his work here. Maybe he didn't drop me off at Barton because of something that had happened when he worked here so many years ago. If that was the case, things must have ended pretty badly. But what kind of work did he do here? And why was it secret?

People are desperate to share good secrets with at least one other person. It's only the bad ones that stay secret.

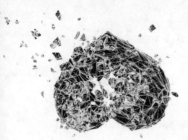

CHAPTER
EIGHT

Something was beeping. I blinked my eyes, which felt gummy, and saw white. White sheet, white walls, white sink gleaming across the room. I felt like I was underwater. I swam toward consciousness, little things coming back to me. I was at Barton. That beeping was the wake-up call, coming from the intercom on the wall by the door. Today was the assessments.

The beeping got shriller and louder until I thought I was going to scream. Then, suddenly, it stopped. A smooth voice said, "Good morning. Breakfast will be served in the cafeteria in fifteen minutes."

I forced myself to sit up and rubbed the sleep out of my eyes. I wasn't tired, but I didn't feel rested, either. I saw the white paper cup on the edge of the sink and remembered the Somnease. Maybe that's why I felt strange. I fumbled out of my pyjamas and put on the Barton-issue T-shirt and shorts with an elasticized waistband. They looked and felt exactly like the Darby gym clothes, only these ones were stamped with the Barton logo.

There was a knock at the door.

"Come in," I said, my voice rough and gravelly. Another side effect of Somnease, I supposed. I cleared my throat and tried again. "I said, come in."

Saren slipped into the room wearing an identical uniform, only her T-shirt was too small, riding up over her stomach, and she had rolled the waistband of her shorts down. Her arms and legs looked impossibly long.

"When did you get so tall?" I asked.

"It's called a growth spurt, maybe you've read about it in your beloved Barton Guide?" she said.

"Some girls have all the luck," I muttered, glancing down at my own flat-chested, vertically challenged form. Some girls got long and shapely, while others — like me — seemed to chub out, but not in the right places.

Breakfast was a lot more subdued than dinner had been. We were a room full of zombies, rubbing our eyes, slow to respond to simple questions and stumbling through the line as if we were new to walking. Most of that was likely due to the Somnease, but nerves and memories of last night may also have had something to do with it. I scanned the room for Simon, who was nowhere to be found.

"Where do you think Simon is?" I asked.

"Maybe he's too injured to do his assessments," Saren said.

"Poor Simon," I said. I spotted Kamal across the room, shovelling eggs into his mouth like it was his last meal. It made my skin prickle all over with anger.

"Look at Kamal. He doesn't even look guilty. I hate him."

"Yes, you've mentioned that before," Saren said.

After we finished, Roya came in and split us up. Saren and Quin were in the first group.

"You'll be headed to the sleep labs for dream mapping," she explained. "Levi here will take you there now."

An unsmiling nurse with the ghost of a moustache on his upper lip stepped forward to acknowledge his name. Saren was rotating her wrists, cracking every bone in a way that set my teeth on edge. I recognized that gesture. It was something she did when she was nervous.

"You'll be fine," I said.

"Yeah, I'm sure that's what they said to Lex too."

I couldn't think of anything else to say, so I watched silently as my best friend clenched her fists and walked away.

"The rest of you will be coming with me to sublevel two for your assessment tests."

I made my way toward Tavi, who was wearing a new pair of sunglasses, perfectly round circles of dark glass perched on her nose. She looked like a political revolutionary. "Nice shades," I said.

"Quin hates these ones," Tavi said. "She thinks they make me look like an old man."

"You do look a little like my grandfather," I admitted. "But he thinks he's very stylish."

Tavi smiled, but only with one side of her mouth. "Do you think this will be like a full day of phys. ed.?"

"I hope not," I said, picturing an endless series of track-and-field events performed in front of doctors with clipboards and blank faces.

Sublevel two looked less like a hospital wing and more like a school. Some of the rooms were equipped with industrial-sized sinks and lab equipment, and others were outfitted like a typical gymnasium, with climbing equipment and a track painted on the floor in red and white lines.

We cycled through various labs and stations one at a time. Some of the tests felt like regular checkup-type stuff, such as blinking at images through thick eye drops and straining to hear sentences at various decibels. Some of the tests felt more like games, like arranging heated porcelain stones from hottest to coldest or pushing various levers to test our strength.

A new team of Barton staff met us at each station, polite but not overly friendly, speaking only to give instructions and hook us up to a series of monitors, and then retreating to observe. It was impossible to know how you were doing because no one gave any indication if you had passed or failed.

Occasionally we passed each other as we moved from station to station. Kamal raised his hand for a high-five, gloating as I passed him on my way out of the eye exam. "Nailed it!" he said.

When I passed Tavi heading toward the gymnasium, she grimaced and muttered, "After this, the winnowing will be easy." Her old-man sunglasses were fogged up and her bangs were damp, like she had been sweating.

My last assessment was in a large gymnasium, a freshly painted racetrack gleaming under high, bright lights. Dr. Dad was waiting for me. "Ah, Marivic. Now you can finally show us what all the fuss is about."

"Us?"

Dr. Dad pointed to a window, high up. The glass was dark, but I could see the shapes of two more people and computer monitors in the shadows.

"The observation team will be watching from up there."

I wondered if that included Dr. Abrams. I suddenly had an urge to impress him. I wanted to impress all of them. "What am I supposed to do?"

"Run."

"For how long?"

"We'll tell you when to stop."

Dr. Dad slipped a bracelet made of cold plastic over my wrist and pushed it up my arm until it fit snugly against my bicep. "This will monitor your heart rate, acceleration, speed and distance," he explained. Smiling, he stepped back off the track and spread his arms. "Whenever you're ready."

I took a deep breath and started to jog. After a single lap my mind felt clear, the foggy effects of the Somnease all gone. As I picked up speed, I imagined I was leaving all my worries and questions behind: Gumps's secrets, Simon's hand, Saren curled up on her side, thinking about Lex.

With a clear head, I felt for that running sweet spot. When I found it, my body eased right in. It was like a musical chord and I let myself be carried away by it, enjoying the way I felt it sing in every part of my body. Suddenly the light changed. It was darker, and when I looked up I was surprised to see not the fluorescent panel lighting of the track but pot lights, hazy moons of light hanging in unexpected darkness. The rest of the room, including the observation team, had disappeared behind two high walls.

Where was I? What had happened to the racetrack? Under my feet, the springy track had hardened into unevenly poured concrete. Each step jolted my knees.

I struggled to maintain my place in the chord as I ran through a narrow hallway, which turned abruptly every few seconds. I had to slow my pace and run with my hands out to stop me from slamming into the walls that seemed to come from nowhere.

I was in a maze.

I tried not to think about how I had ended up there. It was all part of the imps. It was important for the Barton staff to observe me running at my fullest potential in order for them to properly assess me. But my panic dial had been turned way up, and as I skidded into wall after wall I wondered if I would ever get out. The lights seemed to be getting dimmer and I had to squint to see what was ahead of me. I was jogging at a slower pace now, keeping an eye out for the turns.

Then I heard the dogs.

There seemed to be a lot of them, snarling from somewhere nearby. I stopped, trying to suss out their location. Saren and I used to walk by a house on the way to school that had a bulldog chained in the front yard. He sounded exactly like these dogs. Once a kid antagonized him by running a stick across the chain-link fence. In a heartbeat the dog had the stick in his jaws and snapped it clean in two. I'll never forget how fast it moved or how easily that branch had snapped. It could just as easily have been a leg or an arm.

The snarling stopped. It was eerily silent. Maybe the dogs were listening for me too. I heard the click of a lock, followed by the whine of a metal door, and suddenly the room was full of the sound of excited, barking dogs.

They were in the maze with me.

The realization should have pushed me forward but

instead I stood there, not sure which turn to take. One thing I knew for sure was they were hungry. I knew it the way you know the alarm is going to go off the second before it does. I wasn't sure if dogs ate people, but I didn't want to be around to find out.

I ran blindly, my mouth open, breathing jagged. The sound of them snarling and barking echoed through the maze. It was impossible to tell how close they were.

Go left.

The suggestion appeared in my head, as clear as if someone had spoken it aloud. I felt the words rather than heard them, a voice invading my brain. I gasped for breath, suddenly aware of the heaving of my lungs and the ache in my legs.

Hurry, go left! They're coming!

I fell out of the chord and was blinded by harsh light. I tried to listen for the dogs, but they were gone. It felt like my ears were full of water.

Dr. Dad was shouting to me from the sidelines. I could tell by the deep red colour in his face and the veins popping in his neck. But compared to the voice in my head, his words felt distant, unimportant. Every breath I took shredded my dry throat.

Where was the maze? Where did the dogs go? Had they really been there, or was it part of the ACES?

Dr. Dad, Roya and two other Barton staff were running toward me. I saw their mouths moving and sensed their panic, but I couldn't stop. I ran on shaking legs until they gave out beneath me and I crumpled to the floor.

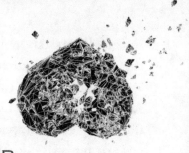

CHAPTER
NINE

Something was beeping. Not shrill and insistent like the beeping from the morning; this sound was low and steady. I held on to the sound like a rope and let it pull me back to reality. I opened my eyes and found I was lying on an examination table in a dimly lit room. An IV had been hooked up to my left arm and was dripping fluids into my body. Two figures in lab coats were staring at a monitor across the room with their backs to me. I had to swallow a few times before I could get any words past my parched throat.

"What happened?"

Dr. Dad whirled around, smiled broadly and advanced toward me, holding a cup with a bendy straw. "Sleeping Beauty awakes! Drink this, you'll feel better."

Dr. Dad held the cup in front of me. I sat up slowly and pressed the straw to my lips. The water felt so cool and delicious I closed my eyes and sighed through my nose.

"That was quite the show. You clocked some incredible

speeds. I don't know if any Intake has ever maintained that speed over such an extended amount of time."

The other doctor turned, and I was startled to see Dr. Abrams. Unlike Dr. Dad, he was not beaming.

"Can you describe what happens when you run, in your own words?" he asked.

"Let's give her a minute to recover, boss," Dr. Dad said.

Dr. Abrams blinked at me. "Are you feeling recovered, Marivic?"

"I guess," I said, feeling oddly disloyal to Dr. Dad. He might have had a lame sense of humour, but he wasn't a bad guy.

Dr. Abrams smiled. "Well then, when you're ready."

"At first it's just running, but then there's this current."

Dr. Abrams was hanging on my every word. "What do you mean, a current? Like a wind tunnel?"

"No, not exactly. It's more like a musical chord, but I don't just hear it, I can feel it. I run until I slip into it and the chord changes, like I was the missing note or something. Once I'm in it, I don't feel like I'm running anymore. It's like a moving current of music, pulling me along."

Both doctors were looking at me with patient expressions. Even though I was telling the truth as well as I could explain it, I knew it sounded crazy.

"Fascinating. Absolutely fascinating! Once you were in the chord, what happened next?" Dr. Dad asked.

"I was in a maze."

"A maze?"

"The room disappeared and I was in a maze. The light was different and there were these dogs."

Dr. Dad whistled. "That's really something. No wonder you were running so fast."

Dr. Abrams was staring at me as if he was trying to read my mind. "This maze," he said. "Can you describe what it looked like? Were there other people around?" I could tell he was picking his words carefully. I couldn't decide if that was because he thought I was crazy or not.

I was about to say no, but then I thought of that voice. There must have been someone there, otherwise where did the voice come from? It was crazy enough that the room had disappeared and I had hallucinated a pack of hungry dogs. What would the doctors think if I told them a voice had told me to go left?

Sensing that he was not going to get anything else out of me, Dr. Abrams changed the subject. "I want to show you something." He adjusted the monitor so it was angled toward me, showing a graph with a series of coloured lines.

"We monitored your heart rate, blood pressure and brain activity during your assessment test." Dr. Dad pointed at a dip in the purple line. "Right here you appear to slip into a brain pattern not unlike REM sleep."

"You mean I fell asleep? While I was running?"

"Not exactly. You fell into a state that is *like* sleep. It is a state of consciousness referred to as the suspended cycle. What you have described — feeling the chord and becoming a part of it — that is the suspended cycle. During this state you feel conscious and aware — in fact, some Intakes feel hyperaware of their surroundings — but in actuality, your awareness is hindered. You saw what happened to Simon last night. He boiled his own hand because he couldn't feel it. He might have boiled it down to the bone and never felt a thing. In your state you could have run for miles and ended up lost in a strange town or run right into traffic and then—"

Bam!

Dr. Abrams smacked his hand against the counter, making me jump. "I didn't realize how advanced your imps were until I saw it for myself. It's dangerous, and you're a danger to yourself. But we're here to help. I'm going to recommend moving your procedure up."

"Okay," I whispered.

I must have looked as scared as I felt, because Dr. Abrams softened his voice. "I'll let Dr. Sun know all of this before your dream mapping session tomorrow. Take a double dose of Somnease tonight. You need your rest." He patted my shoulder once before he left.

As usual, Roya was waiting for me. I felt like Roya was always waiting for me. She smiled and put a hand on my shoulder, steering me to the elevator and, eventually, my room.

"You're drenched," she said, lifting my damp ponytail off the back of my neck. "And your muscles must be aching. You need a hot shower. Everything looks better once you've had a hot shower."

*

The residence floor was deserted. Everyone must still have been in the bowels of Barton, completing their assessments or napping them off behind closed doors with the help of Somnease.

I stood in the shower, cut off from the world by hot water and clouds of steam, until I felt my muscles sigh and my fingers pucker up and get wrinkly. My grand-mother's charm still hung on the chain around my neck. I had forgotten to take it off. I picked it up and realized it wasn't wet. How was that possible? I held the charm away from my body, directly under the stream of water. Water pounded down around it, but it stayed dry.

I let the chain settle back around my neck. If it could stand up to water, it probably wouldn't get damaged. There were bigger things to think about. Like the fact that I was going to be winnowed soon. How different would I be? What were the risks? I tried to think about the positive side of things. Maybe if I asked Roya or Dr. Dad they would put me in a room close to Saren in the readjustment centre. Hadn't I been through enough? Hadn't Saren?

The water started to turn cold. Reluctantly I turned it off and wrapped myself in a towel. I rubbed furiously at my arms and legs, then wrapped my hair in a second towel. My knees and the soles of my feet were still throb-bing, but it wasn't nearly as bad as before. In fact, it had felt good to be able to run. Except for the part with the endless maze and the wild dogs. Maybe they would let me go for a run again.

I walked out of the bathroom, wondering who I should ask for permission, and ran right into a red-haired boy outside my room. He jumped back as if I had burned him.

"Oh! Sorry!"

"Were you just in my room? What are you doing here?" I said, holding my towel tightly across my chest.

"I'm just getting back from my assessment tests. I'm going to . . . change."

I looked at his clothes, which were shabby but not drenched in sweat like mine had been. His hair looked like it had been parted with a ruler and there were no telltale roses on his cheeks to suggest any kind of physical activity. Plus, I didn't remember him from this morning. There were a lot of people in my assessment group, but surely I would have spotted that hair. Something was wrong.

"What's your name?" I asked.

"Abbot."

"Abbot what? What school are you from? I'm—"

"Marivic, I know. Look, I should get back to my room. Maybe I'll see you later?"

Abbot had sidestepped around me and was already walking away. He was practically running. If I hadn't been decked out in only a towel I might have followed him. Instead I stepped into my room, locking the door behind me.

*

I quickly changed into my own clothes, throwing the Barton gym clothes in a damp pile in the corner. I considered running after Abbot, but he had been in such a hurry he was probably long gone by now. Maybe he *was* a new Intake. He wasn't old enough to be a staff member. I thought of the assessments and how real that maze had felt. Was it possible to hallucinate people and conversations? Was I imagining him? If that was the case then my imps were even worse than Dr. Abrams had suggested. The sooner I was winnowed the better.

I wandered down the hall and knocked on Saren's

door. I really needed to talk to her. I had to tell someone about the voice telling me to go left. I also wanted to tell her about Abbot.

There was no answer. I didn't know how long dream mapping lasted, but there were still a few hours before dinner. Maybe a nap would clear my head. There was the chance that I could go ACES, but maybe if I just dozed for a bit I wouldn't enter the suspended cycle. Even after the world's longest shower, my body still ached from all the running and lifting and other physical tests for the assessments.

Back in my room I pulled down the ribbed white comforter. It wasn't threadbare, but it wasn't exactly top quality, either. There were two flat pillows. Together they were approximately the thickness of one normal pillow. I went to fluff them some more and caught a glimpse of something underneath. An old photograph. And not just any photograph: a picture of Gumps.

My heart almost stopped. There was Gumps smiling at me from the past in black and white. His hair was thick and wavy and he had an impressive beard to match his wild eyebrows, which were darker and less wiry than the eyebrows I knew and loved. But it was him, jug ears and big smile caught mid-laugh, from the looks of it. He was wearing a Barton lab coat and leaning against something that looked a little bit like a washing machine, only longer and deeper and with a series of dials lined up along the front. He was holding one hand toward the camera, the fingers wrapped in a bandage. On the back of the photo someone had written, "Stone versus Bertha: Stone 2, Bertha 1. 1965." I guessed that Bertha was the machine and Gumps had injured his hand trying to fix her.

Here was the proof that Gumps had worked at Barton, but in what capacity? A repairman or a mechanic? Did Dr. Abrams leave this? It seemed like an odd thing for the head of Barton to do, especially since he had been so cagey about what it was that Gumps had done here. But if it wasn't him, who was it? Maybe he gave it to Roya to pass on?

I slid my hand under the pillow and found something else. It was the Barton brochure I had been reading the day before, only someone had added "Dis-" in red pen next to the heading so it read "Dis-orientation." The first paragraph was also crossed out and a message was written in the margins: "Disorientation. Sublevel three, the old pool. 11:00 p.m. Tell no one."

No one was underlined three times. Something told me that Disorientation was not an officially sanctioned Barton activity. Whoever left the photograph knew who my grandfather was and that he had worked here. They were using it as bait to get me to go to disorientation. It wasn't something that Dr. Abrams or Roya would do. It was the work of someone sneaky, someone who didn't belong at Barton.

Someone like Abbot.

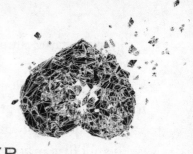

CHAPTER
TEN

The note had said to tell no one, but those words didn't apply to Saren. I told her everything. There were no secrets between best friends. I made sure we sat alone at dinner, away from any nosy Intakes.

"Look at what I got." I laid the photograph between our plates, angling our drinking glasses so no one could see what we were looking at. As far as anyone else was concerned, we were dissecting our sloppy joes.

"Is that Gumps?"

"Yep."

"Look at his hair!"

"Never mind his hair, Saren! This picture was taken at Barton in 1965. It proves he worked here. Apparently he did something with the equipment."

Saren read the message on the back. "Well, Abrams did tell you he worked here."

"But now we know for sure. And I got this." I pulled the brochure from my back pocket, smoothing it out over the photograph. The colour drained from Saren's face.

"I got the same thing," she whispered.

My heart sped up. "Really?" I was surprised that Saren had received an invitation. I assumed since it had come with the photograph and said to tell no one that the message was specifically for me.

She nodded and took a conservative bite of her salad.

"What do you think it means?" I asked.

"I don't know, but I'm going."

"You are?"

Saren nodded. "I had my consultation today. It was scary. It's a six-hour surgery. There are so many things that could go wrong."

"What does that have to do with anything?"

"What if there's another option?"

"What do you mean?"

"Think about it. Disorientation is the opposite of orientation. Maybe this person, whoever it is, has more information. Maybe there's something other than the winnowing."

We had entered murky waters. Saren wasn't thinking straight. In fact, she was starting to sound like her mother, a woman we both agreed had definitely gone off the deep end.

"Like what?" I asked, trying to keep my voice as neutral as possible. I knew Saren was afraid of the winnowing, but it was a necessary part of life, like losing your baby teeth or getting your period. There was no other option.

Saren flushed, frustrated. "I don't know. I'm not a doctor! Don't you want to know what this person has to say?"

I hadn't thought too much about what disorientation meant. Mostly I wanted to find out everything I could about Gumps and what he had done here.

"Who else do you think got one?" Saren asked.

We looked around the cafeteria, trying to figure out if other Intakes were having the same conversation at different tables. As far as I could tell, no one else seemed to be whispering about a secret meeting in the middle of the night.

"I'm not going to mention it to anyone else," I said. "*No one* is underlined three times."

"You told *me*," Saren pointed out.

"You don't count."

"Aww, thanks. That means a lot to me."

"You know what I mean! Wait, were you going to tell me? If I hadn't told you first?"

Saren busied herself with eating. "Of course," she said.

"You're lying," I realized. "You were going to keep it secret. From me."

Saren sighed. "I didn't think you would be interested. You've always been so gung-ho about the winnowing. You practically have the Barton Guide memorized and you've been keeping a dream journal for ages . . . It's like you couldn't wait for it to happen."

I felt as if someone had reached into my brain with a big eraser and rubbed out all the words in my head. I couldn't think of a single thing to say.

"Plus sneaking around after lights out, breaking the rules, that's never really been your thing."

I desperately reached for something to say. Something about how wrong she was, how I was just as brave as her, how I wasn't some silly kid who couldn't wait to grow up. But in the end all I could come up with was, "You were going to go without me?" I hated how pathetic I sounded and I hated the burning in my chest that meant I was seconds away from tears even more.

Saren sensed how hurt I was because she put down her fork and gave me a rib-crushing side-hug. "Oh, Marivic, don't cry! Why are we even talking about this? You brought it up and we're both going, it's fine!"

"Exactly, I brought it up and we're both going. That sounds a lot like breaking the rules to me, something that — apparently — is not 'my thing.'"

Saren gave me the full power of her don't-fool-with-me eyes. "Can we just hug this out and move on?"

Now it was me who was busy eating and avoiding eye contact. I told myself it was the chili and the extra hot sauce in the sloppy joes that were making my eyes water.

"So we're agreed. We'll meet up and head down to the old pool, whatever that is, for 11:00 p.m.? See what Mr. or Miss Disorientation has to say?"

"That's the other thing," I said. "I think I know who it is."

I told her about running into Abbot in the hallway.

"He was in your room?"

"I don't know for sure. He was outside my room moments before I found the photograph."

"And you're sure he doesn't work here?"

I shook my head. "He's too young. I can't tell how old he is, but he can't be older than us. He's too short and too nervous."

"Maybe he's just nervous around you," Saren said. "You were in a towel."

"Could you be serious, please? Why would someone not much older than us be at Barton if he isn't working here and isn't an Intake?"

Saren considered this. "The bad news is, I have no idea. The good news is, tonight just got a whole lot more interesting."

Saren and I agreed not to take our Somnease and to meet in the girls' bathroom at 10:45. When Roya came by with my pill, I tucked it into my cheek and silently prayed it was the kind of pill that didn't dissolve easily. I wanted her to say good night and get out of there so I could spit it out, but by the way she was lingering in the doorway, I could tell she wanted to talk.

"That was some running you did today," she said.

I nodded, not sure whether it was a compliment, and also unsure of whether I could speak without spitting out or swallowing the pill.

"It must make you feel invincible."

I tilted my head to the side like I was considering this. The truth was it *did* make me feel invincible. Believe it or not, I, Marivic Stone, avowed Couch Potato and Champion Sitter, was becoming a runner. And I liked it. No one was more surprised than me.

"Well. I'm sorry it ended so poorly. They really shouldn't have let the test go on that long . . ." Roya put a finger to her lips. "But don't tell Dr. Dad I said that."

I nodded, so much saliva collecting in my mouth I was sure the pill would dissolve like sugar in water. Either that or I was about to start drooling. Thankfully Roya winked at me, flicked the light and shut the door. I spit the whole mess into my hand, relieved to find the hard coating on the pill mostly intact. I put the pill in a cup for safekeeping and rinsed my hands in the sink, then tried not to think about running until it was time to meet up with Saren.

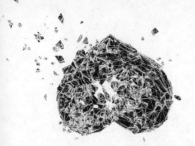

CHAPTER
ELEVEN

Barton was eerie at night. The lights were reduced and without the bustle of Intakes and Barton staff trekking from room to room, it felt like an abandoned laboratory, the kind haunted by ghosts of experiments gone wrong. I thought of Kamal's story about the Roddenberry ghost and reminded myself that, to Kamal, lying came as easily as breathing. Sublevel three was particularly desolate. I expected security or night nurses, but as Saren reminded me, no one lived on this floor, so why would they need anyone posted here?

"Unless they really are hiding something," she said.

I wished she hadn't added that part.

According to the map in the welcome brochure, the pool could be accessed by the change rooms. The girls' change room was at the very end of an especially dark hallway, as if they had cut the lights completely to the parts of the floor they weren't using.

"This is creepy," I whispered.

"This is exciting," Saren whispered back.

I pushed on the door and it opened soundlessly into an even darker room. Saren held on to my elbow and together we inched our way through the blackness. I held one hand out in front of me, swinging it back and forth to check for obstacles. After a few minutes of blind stumbling, our eyes adjusted and I noticed a thin strip of weak light stretched across the ground in front of us.

"That must be the door," I whispered. I stopped, wondering if it was a good idea to burst out of the darkness into a huge open space at the request of a stranger.

"What are you waiting for?" Saren whispered.

"We don't know what's waiting for us out there."

"Don't you want to know about Gumps?"

It was exactly the right thing to say. Plus, if the stranger who had summoned us here really was Abbot, he didn't look like a homicidal maniac. I was pretty sure even I could take him, if I had to.

Still, I really hoped I wouldn't have to. We moved forward again, perfectly in sync, like a two-headed creature.

"We'll do it together," Saren said. "On three. One, two, three."

We pushed the door open and stepped out onto the pool deck. Someone had turned on the emergency lighting, which washed the deck and the pool in a poisonous green glow. Flutter boards and an imposing backboard criss-crossed in a complicated series of straps hung on the walls above wooden benches like you'd find in a school gym. At either end of the pool stood two empty lifeguard chairs, each with a fat orange lifesaver ring looped around the rungs of the ladder.

We appeared to be alone, but Saren pinched the skin of my arm and said, "Look, over there."

I peered across the pool, where, within the shadows, I saw the outlines of more shadows, people-sized ones. It looked like at least three or four other Intakes had received the same memo we did.

A door slammed open to my right and I jumped, clapping my fingers over my mouth to keep from screaming.

"Helloooo?" Kamal strode out from what I assumed was the boys' change room, heading right for the lip of the pool without an ounce of caution. "Someone said something about a disorientation party?"

"Figures," I muttered.

Saren stepped out of the shadows. "Shh!" she hissed. "Are you trying to get us caught?"

"What's up, Saren? I see you got the same invite? Is that Stone hiding back there? Come on out, Stone!"

I clenched my teeth and walked out to meet them. There was a rustling beside me and a flutter board came crashing to the floor. Simon appeared, looking guilty.

"Simon!" I said. "How are you feeling?"

He held up a hand so swaddled in bandages it looked like he was wearing a white mitten. "Fine. I have to wait a few days before I can take the assessment tests, though."

Across the room the shadow figures shifted and came forward. Quin was in the lead, with Tavi and a few other girls I didn't recognize behind her. She sat at the edge of the pool and let her feet dangle over the cavernous empty space below. She looked as comfortable there as she did on a summer afternoon, sunning herself at the Darby pool.

"So what is this exactly, like a secret society or something? This seems like something you would be into, Kamal." Quin flashed a smile from across the empty pool.

Kamal held his hands up. "Not guilty," he said. "I'm just as ignorant as you."

Quin's smile faltered, unsure if she was being insulted. "So who gave out those brochures then? Saren?"

"Not me," Saren said.

"Well it definitely wasn't Marivic," Quin said.

Did everybody think I was a boring, predictable lover of rules?

"Maybe it's part of orientation," another girl suggested. Quin shot her a disgusted look and the poor girl shrank back into the shadows.

"I'm only staying for five more minutes and then I'm out of here," Tavi said. For once she was without sunglasses, but I noticed she was playing with her hair so her bangs kept falling into her eyes.

"Sometimes you can be no fun," Quin said.

My cafeteria conversation with Saren was fresh enough that it still stung, and I recognized a similar feeling in Tavi as she hunched over the pool, pretending not to care. We were both supporting characters in other people's lives. Only Tavi had it way worse than me. Quin was an evil queen who enjoyed having minions to order around; Saren was an avenging warrior princess who always spoke the truth, even when it hurt.

Suddenly, a new voice cut through all the muttering and whispering: "Welcome to disorientation." It was distorted and full of reverb, like Mrs. Cole speaking into her megaphone.

"Where is that voice coming from?" Saren said.

"Um, hello? Who are you?" Quin demanded.

"Before we begin, I need your solemn vow that no matter what happens here tonight, you will not tell anyone about it. No friends, no parents and no Barton staff."

"I'm not promising anything until I know what this is all about," Quin said. A couple of the others agreed.

"What you are about to learn will change the way you look at the world."

"Okay, this guy is a little much," Saren whispered. "Does he sound like your guy? The redhead?"

"I'm not sure," I admitted. I had shared only a handful of words with Abbot, and he had been desperate to get away from me.

"Who are you, the Wizard of Oz? Come out and let us see you!" Kamal said.

There was no response. We were looking at each other across and around the pool, waiting for something to happen, when Tavi gasped and pointed at the bottom of the pool. "RATS!" she squealed.

Quin shot up and backed away from the pool. Saren grabbed for my arm and we both looked down and saw something much bigger than a rat push the grate away and crawl out of what must have been the drainpipe.

"That's not a rat, it's a kid!" Kamal said. "Dude, where did you come from?"

I watched as Abbot stood up, rubbing unidentifiable muck out of his hair. It looked less red in the greenish light. In his hand was a small red megaphone. I noticed one just like it strapped to one of the lifeguard chairs. The other chair was missing one. He must have swiped it to make his voice sound more impressive.

"I can't tell you that," Abbot said. "But I can tell you that what you've been told about the winnowing and Barton is a lie."

Kamal narrowed his eyes. "Wait, are you the guy who sent us those brochures?"

Abbot stood a little taller. Somehow it made him seem even younger. "Yes," he said solemnly.

Kamal clapped his hands and hooted with laughter. "You? You've got to be kidding! What are you, like nine years old? Are you, like, the janitor's kid or something?"

"My name is Abbot and I am a member of People for a Winnowing Free World, otherwise known as Winfree."

Kamal stopped laughing. "I've heard of Winfree."

Quin scoffed. "Oh, great. You're one of Kamal's crazy lizard-people-killer-robot theories come to life. Are you telling me that I came all the way down here in the middle of the night to listen to a bunch of conspiracy theories? How did you even get in here?"

Abbot ignored her questions. "The members of Winfree believe that it is possible to live in a world without winnowing. Barton is not what you think. Some of the things they've done here are . . ."

"Illegal?" Saren suggested.

Abbot looked very sombre. "Worse. Immoral, wrong."

"Immoral?" I repeated.

"They've been experimenting on children for years. That's what the winnowing is, experimenting. They've convinced the world that they're helping you, but did you know that of the thirty-five winnowing centres in America, Barton has the highest death rate?"

Across the pool, Tavi paled. "Is that true?" she asked.

Abbot looked directly at her. "Yes. What they're really doing is butchering you. They restrict your abilities—"

"—impairments," Quin said haughtily.

Abbot would not be discouraged. "—*abilities*, and then they mess with your memory."

"But without the winnowing people go crazy. You get sick, you *die*," Tavi said.

"Only because you haven't been taught how to deal with your abilities. What if they spent all their time and resources teaching people to live with these so-called impairments? What if the ACES are telling you something?"

"Like what?" Saren asked. She was sitting forward, eating up every word he said. I was worried she was going to fall right off the edge and down to the cracked tiles below.

"I don't know, no one's taken the time to really study them. No one but Dr. Lowry."

"Dr. Elizabeth Lowry?" Kamal said. "As in member of the Barton Five, creator of dream mapping Dr. Elizabeth Lowry?"

"The one and only," Abbot said. "If you come with me, I'll take you to her. She used to work here. She knows what goes on and she wants to make things right."

"Wait, come with you where?" Quin asked.

Abbot hesitated. "I can't tell you. But if you want to live life fully intact, as nature intended you to, meet me tomorrow night and your new life with Winfree can begin. The only thing is, you can never return to your old life. If you join Winfree you'll be saying goodbye to your friends and family, maybe for good."

Quin laughed. "Okay, this is a joke, right?"

"No," Abbot said.

"You seriously expect us to just run away with you to a secret location? What I should do is pull that fire alarm over there and let Dr. Dad know there is a rat in the building."

Even in the pale light, I could see Abbot blanch. "You promised you wouldn't say anything," he said.

"I promised no such thing!" Quin said, her voice full of ice. "I came here tonight because I thought there was going to be a secret pool party or kids telling ghost stories or something, not a shrimpy little conspiracy theorist who wants me to run away with him." A few people sniggered. Abbot shifted his weight from foot to foot and Quin gloated, visibly pleased at how uncomfortable she was making him.

"It's not about me; it's about Winfree. Don't you want to know the truth?"

"You have to admit, dude, you don't really look the revolutionary type," Kamal said.

"I can prove it," Abbot said.

Quin snorted. "Prove what?"

"That Barton is hiding the truth."

"About what?"

"Dr. Roddenberry's murder."

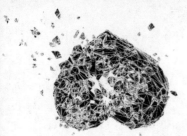

CHAPTER
TWELVE

The silence was heavy, like the sky before a storm. Quin was the first one to find her voice. "Not this again. Dr. Roddenberry died of a heart attack," she said.

"Wait, let's hear the little dude out," Kamal said. "Okay, you got my attention. How can you prove it?"

"Just a minute." Abbot disappeared back into the drain and returned lugging a bag of padded envelopes. He dumped them on the floor and started sifting through them. "Any of you guys want to give me a hand?"

Tavi pulled her feet up and tucked them underneath her, physically recoiling from the idea.

Saren hopped down into the pool. "I'll help," she said.

"Me too," I said, not wanting to be left behind.

Abbot smiled at me. "Marivic, grab the projector over there by the ladder."

"Um, how does the weird little guy know your name, Marivic?" Quin asked.

I ignored her as I walked over to retrieve the bulky projector.

"What are those?" Simon asked, peering at the envelopes.

"These are the confessions of Barton60," Abbot said.

"Barton60?" Tavi repeated.

"That's what they called the group of children born to the women injected with SuperGen in 1960." Abbot pointed at the padded envelopes at my feet. "Marivic, pick one."

I selected an envelope at random. Inside was a film canister. It was labelled *Delacourt, Jean. Barton 031860. Confession, 08/21/76.* Abbot slipped the film out of the canister and threaded it through the projector. The ancient machine came to life with a whir, and two figures appeared on the wall of the deep end. The images were bumpy and distorted by the tiled pool wall, but it was clear enough to see a teenage girl with long, wild hair sitting across the table from a police officer.

"Showtime," Abbot said.

The police officer spoke first. "Please state your name and age for the record."

"Jean Elizabeth Delacourt. Sixteen."

"Miss Delacourt, can you tell us, in your own words, why you are here?"

"I wish to make a confession."

"Would you like a lawyer present?"

"No, thank you." Jean's voice was calm but she sounded impossibly young. Too young to be sitting across from a police officer about to make a confession.

"Let the record show that Miss Delacourt has refused her right to legal representation. Go on."

"On the afternoon of August 20, 1976, I entered the Desert Rose Hotel in Las Vegas, Nevada, at 3:30 p.m.

I told the concierge that I had a letter for Dr. Richard Roddenberry, and would he mind ensuring that he received it. He said he would take care of it, and I saw him make note of the letter next to an entry with Dr. Roddenberry's name. It said he was staying in suite 1920. I followed a maid to the fifth floor and stole the ring of keys off her cleaning cart. Then I made my way to suite 1920. I let myself into Dr. Roddenberry's suite. There was a bottle of orange juice on the table. I crushed six Somnease and six Paxocet into the juice. I went back to the fifth floor and dropped the keys for the maid or someone else to find them. I caught the 8:05 bus home."

"Were you aware that combining those particular drugs would likely lead to death?"

"Yes."

Someone up on the pool deck whimpered.

"Why, Miss Delacourt?" the police officer asked.

Jean responded in a cold voice. "I only did to him what he did to us."

"Are you referring to the medical treatments Dr. Roddenberry provided for you at the Barton Center?"

"Yes."

The interview ended but the tape continued to crackle like paper on fire. Armies of goosebumps popped up along my arms. "She sounds so . . . dead inside."

"I know," Abbot said. "According to the medical records she was on a lot of heavy drugs, prescribed by Roddenberry himself. Antipsychotics, sleeping pills, probably to help her cope with the ACES. They didn't have the winnowing back then."

"I don't understand. If they have her confession, why wasn't she arrested?" Saren asked.

Quin snorted. "Oh, come on, it's obviously a phony tape. These conspiracy types fabricate their own evidence all the time."

"Pass me another one," Abbot said.

I ripped open another envelope and passed the second film reel to Abbot. The name on the canister was Douglas Cope. Abbot threaded it into the machine and we waited for the images to appear on the wall of the pool. This time the cop had a thick moustache and was sitting opposite a young man with a shaggy haircut.

"Please state your name and age for the record."

"Douglas John Cope. Sixteen."

"Mr. Cope, can you tell us, in your own words, why you are here."

"I wish to make a confession."

"Would you like a lawyer present?"

"No, thank you."

"Let the record show that Mr. Cope has refused his right to legal representation. Go on."

"On the afternoon of August 20, 1976, I entered the Desert Rose Hotel in Las Vegas, Nevada, at 3:30 p.m. I told the concierge that I had a letter for Dr. Richard Roddenberry, and would he mind ensuring that he received it. He said he would take care of it, and I saw him make note of the letter next to an entry with Dr. Roddenberry's name. It said he was staying in suite 1920. I followed a maid to the fifth floor and stole the ring of keys off her cleaning cart."

"It's the same," I realized.

Abbot nodded. "Word for word. I checked the transcripts." He gestured to the envelopes on the floor. "All of them are exactly the same."

"But Jean never mentioned Douglas or anybody else?" Saren asked.

"Nine people confessed to the murder of Roddenberry. They gave identical confessions. They're all here, in these envelopes; you can see them yourself. The police were stumped. They called in Barton to try and get to the bottom of the murder, but there were no fingerprints, no witnesses, no signs that anything criminal had happened. In the end they said he died of natural causes. There's nothing out of the ordinary about a heart attack."

"But these films prove that the heart attack was caused by drugs," Kamal said.

"Yes, but no one could prove that he didn't take the drugs himself. He certainly had access to them. He died of a combination of drugs he prescribed regularly to Barton60."

"What happened to the nine people who confessed?" Saren asked.

"All dead. Five from drug overdose. Two from gang-related violence. Jean was committed to a mental institution and died of food poisoning and Douglas died of a massive heart attack at twenty-one."

"Twenty-one? But that's so young," Tavi said.

Abbot nodded. "I know. He was an athlete too. A runner. That's how he died. His heart gave out one day during a run."

My blood ran cold in my veins. Dr. Abrams's warning about turning into a running machine came rushing back at me. Is that what happened to Douglas? Is that what would happen to me without the winnowing? But if that was the case why was Abbot so dead set against the procedure?

"So they're all dead? Doesn't that seem—"

Abbot looked grim. "Convenient? Yes. But I don't think Barton had anything to do with their deaths. It's odd that they all died so young, but that has more to do with the drugs Barton was feeding them and the fact that they never learned to manage their unique abilities. I know this is all crazy. I couldn't believe it myself."

"Even if your little home movies were real, what does any of this have to do with us?" Quin asked.

"Don't you get it? After Barton60 went crazy and killed Roddenberry, Abrams panicked. When Roddenberry died, Dr. Abrams became director at Barton. He's the doctor who made the winnowing mandatory. Now every kid who comes through here gets their brain sliced up so there is absolutely no chance of something like that happening again."

"But without the winnowing, people went crazy. You said so yourself. They had to take all those drugs, they couldn't cope," Tavi said. "You just showed us that with the videos."

"Children die during the winnowing. It's an imperfect process that Barton created to cover their own mistakes."

Beside me, Saren stiffened. I knew she was thinking about Lex. "What do you mean, their own mistakes?" I asked.

"Why do you think people develop these so-called 'impairments'?" Abbot asked.

I blinked at him. This was in the Barton Guide; they'd been drilling it into us since year one.

Quin spoke up. "Wow, you really are dumb. Environmental factors, exposure to toxins left over from the war, there's a whole list. Where have you been living?"

Abbot shook his head sadly. "Those things are all bad, but that's not what causes your vision to suddenly go haywire or makes Marivic run like some kind of human cheetah," he smiled at me hopefully, but I couldn't smile back. I wasn't sure I was on his side just yet. "It's SuperGen."

Quin laughed. "SuperGen is why we're alive. Without SuperGen there would be no babies. We'd be well on our way to extinction."

Abbot shrugged. "Maybe we would be. But these strange physical anomalies started with the first group of children born to women who had been injected with SuperGen."

Quin wasn't the only one who was having trouble digesting this new information. Saren was full of questions too. "But everyone gets the SuperGen shot. It's mandatory. You're trying to tell me that parents, doctors, the government — basically everyone — is injecting children with something that they know causes them to go ACES."

"Not everyone has made the connection. Barton is very good at convincing people that toxins in the environment are at fault. It's been so many years since a child was born who didn't eventually develop the symptoms that people have accepted them as part of growing up now. Remember that there had been no babies born between 1946 and 1955. Even after SuperGen was given to the first few test groups, a lot of those babies died. Barton60 was the first real group of children to grow up seemingly healthy."

Everyone fell quiet. It was a lot to take in. And if Abbot was right — if what he said was true — it was the kind of information that changed everything. Barton created SuperGen. SuperGen caused children to go ACES and develop the imps. Barton created the winnowing to get rid of these less attractive side effects, which had possibly led to the murder of the very man responsible for SuperGen. I was full of questions, but the biggest one was what did Gumps have to do with all of this?

Quin stood up. "Well. I've heard enough. Thanks for a very entertaining evening. This was better than a ghost story."

"You don't believe me," Abbot said. He looked crest-fallen. "I chose you, all of you, because I thought you would want to know. I thought you would believe me."

"So you've been spying on us this whole time? Creepy!" Quin gave an exaggerated shiver. "Not only do I *not* believe you, but I think you need to work on your delivery. Those movies were not very good quality and you crawled out of a drainpipe." Quin wrinkled her nose. Somehow, on her, even this gesture looked pretty. "I can practically smell you from here."

Quin looked pointedly at Kamal. "Kamal, are you going to walk me back to my room?"

Kamal got to his feet and took a bow. "At your service. I wouldn't want anything to happen to you ladies on the way back."

Abbot looked at Saren and me. "What about you?"

"I don't know," Saren said, looking at her feet. "It seems pretty farfetched."

"Are you two coming with us?" Kamal called down.

Saren looked at me with her eyebrows raised. I shook my head. I still had a few questions I wanted to ask Abbot, but I'd rather do it without Kamal and Quin around.

"No, go on without us," Saren said. "We have a few more questions."

"I never took you for a conspiracy theorist, Silver," Kamal said. "Are you sure you don't want to come with us so those two lovebirds can be alone?"

"Get lost, Kamal. Shouldn't be too hard for you," Saren said.

I waited for the sound of the others traipsing through the change rooms to fade before looking up at Abbot. I hoped he hadn't taken Kamal's comments about lovebirds to heart, but the pink in his cheeks told me that he probably had.

"He's an idiot," I explained. "I don't have, I mean I'm not in . . ." I stumbled, looking for a way to say I didn't have a crush on him without making him feel bad.

Luckily Saren came to my rescue. "She has a few questions about her grandfather."

"Yes," I said, relieved. I pulled out the picture from my pocket. "Where did you get this?"

Abbot looked extremely satisfied with himself. "I knew that picture would convince you to come."

"How did you know to give it to me? What do you know about my grandfather?"

"Not much. I know he was a mechanical engineer who worked here from the beginning, back when Barton was a military base, even before Roddenberry took over in 1947."

"But what did he do? What's Bertha?"

"My guess is it was a machine he built. It looks a little like the neuroimaging machines they use in dream mapping, but a really early version of one."

"Let me see," Saren said. "I've already been to dream mapping but Marivic hasn't." She held the picture at an angle and scrutinized it up close. "Oh yeah," she said. "I can totally see that now."

"But what did he actually do?"

Abbot shrugged. "I don't know. There is almost no record of him in the files. At least the ones I've found."

"So maybe he wasn't all that involved," I suggested. "Maybe he was a repair guy. That's what he does now." Try as I might I couldn't wrap my head around the idea of Gumps building neuroimaging machines.

"Maybe," Abbot said. "Or maybe whatever he did here was so top secret that those files are hidden or possibly destroyed. Why did he suddenly leave a job he had been at for thirty-five years? Did he even mention to you that he worked at Barton?"

I didn't answer. I had asked myself similar questions over and over again since discovering Gumps's secret. I came here to find out what Abbot knew about Gumps and it turned out he knew almost as little as I did.

Beside me, Saren cleared her throat. "So. This Winfree thing. Is it the real deal?"

Abbot perked up like a daisy in the sun. "Yes. I swear. My family has been involved from the beginning. It's my life's work."

"Life's work?" I muttered. "You're a kid."

"I'm fourteen."

"Four*teen*?" I repeated.

Abbot looked miffed, but he must have been used to people having trouble believing he was fourteen years old. He barely came up to my shoulder and I wasn't exactly tall.

"And if we wanted to join, what do we need to do?" Saren asked.

"Well, we'll need to get you out of here. Soon. Before the winnowing. The process is irreversible. Plus, you may not even remember this conversation."

"Why not?" I asked.

"Haven't you noticed that when kids come back from Barton they can never seem to remember any of the details of what happened?" Abbot asked.

I thought about Suki and her hazy memories.

He continued. "It's part of the winnowing. They mess with your memories so you can't really describe what goes on. It keeps people ignorant and a little scared."

"That's terrible," I said.

"That's Barton," Abbot said.

So far my Barton experience had been fine. There were some scary moments, but that was to be expected. Going ACES was scary and the winnowing would put an end to it. The staff were friendly; nobody had asked me to do anything I didn't want to do. I had a hard time recasting them as evil. Part of me believed Abbot's story — why would he have any reason to make it up? — but if it was true, that meant everything I had been told, everything I believed about going ACES, about Barton, about growing up, was a lie.

"I have my final dream mapping session tomorrow," Saren said.

"Then we need to get you out of here soon. Tomorrow night," Abbot insisted.

"*Tomorrow night*? Saren, are you serious? Don't you want to think about this?"

My words fell on deaf ears. All Saren cared about was the plan. "Where do I meet you? How do we get out of here?"

"Meet me in the boys' bathroom on the residence floor at midnight. We'll go from there."

"Whoa, whoa, whoa, Saren. Seriously?" It was like I wasn't there. Neither of them was paying any attention to me.

"Okay. I'll think about it," Saren said.

Abbot's eyes were shining. "I promise you, you won't regret it. Winfree is the future."

"We should probably go," Saren said. "Thanks, Abbot."

I turned and followed Saren up the ladder and onto the pool deck. I was so numb with shock I was worried I wouldn't be able to climb the ladder properly. Saren never once looked back.

"Are you serious?" I hissed as we felt our way through the girls' change room. "You're just going to run off with him?"

"You make it sound like I'm eloping," Saren said. "It's not like that. I believe him."

"But you can never go back. You'd never see your mother again."

"My mother is not exactly all there, in case you forgot. She went crazy when my brother died. And he died because of the winnowing. For all I know I might die, or you might. But if I can be part of this Winfree movement I could change things. I could make it so no one died because of the stupid winnowing again."

"Saren, I know you're scared, but you aren't your brother. Just because his surgery went wrong doesn't mean yours will."

Saren's eyes flashed. "I'm not scared, Marivic! I'm angry! I want to make things different! I thought you of all people would get it."

"What does that mean?"

"You know what it's like to lose a family member. You grew up without a mother and then your grandmother died. If you could do something to change that, wouldn't you?"

"You can't bring someone back from the dead."

"I know that, but I can make it so no one has to feel the way I did. Maybe I can do something so some other little girl doesn't have to watch her own mother turn into a crazy person."

Saren stabbed the up button by the elevator. The door opened immediately with a loud ding. It seemed especially loud in the deserted hallway. I cringed, wondering if the whole building could hear us. We hurried into the elevator. I waited until the door closed before continuing.

"But, Saren, I'd never see you again."

Finally I hit a nerve. Saren grabbed my arm, gazing beseechingly into my face. "Then come with me. I saw your face back there. You believe him, I know you do."

"I don't know what I believe. I admit it's weird, but that doesn't mean I'm going to drop everything and run away. What about Gumps?"

"Exactly. What about Gumps? I mean it doesn't look good for him, does it?"

I pulled my arm away from her claw-like grip. Her fingers left little red dents in my skin where she had been squeezing my arm. "What do you mean?"

"It's like Abbot said. Why would a man work someplace for years and never mention it to his granddaughter unless he wasn't proud of the work he had done? Why is there no mention of what he did anywhere in the files unless Barton or whoever doesn't want anyone to know what it was?"

I couldn't have been more hurt if Saren had physically thrown me down a flight of stairs. "You think Gumps did something wrong? You think he experimented on children like Roddenberry did?"

Saren threw her hands in the air. "Maybe! Or maybe he helped make the machines that they used to experiment on them. Even if he didn't do the experiments himself, he must have known about it. That makes him guilty in my book."

"Gumps has never been anything but nice to you. He loves you! He treats you like his own granddaughter. He looked after you when your own stupid mother locked you up like a criminal."

"Don't be so naïve, Marivic! I know it's hard but imagine he wasn't your grandfather for one second and take a good hard look at the facts!"

"There are no facts! Just crazy ideas!"

"I'm going, Marivic. Whether you like it or not. I'm sorry your grandfather isn't the person you thought he was. I really am. I thought he was a great guy too! But it doesn't change the fact that something is seriously wrong at Barton and he clearly was a part of it. And if you can't see it, maybe it's best to let them cut up your brain so you can go back to living in ignorance like another stupid sheep."

The elevator doors slid open to the residency floor. It was brighter on this floor, moonlight streaming through the large glass windows, softening the shadows and the edges of the corridor. I watched Saren storm off to her room, too flabbergasted and hurt to follow. It wasn't until the doors closed and I had to hit the open button that I was able to bring myself to move.

I let myself back into my room and salvaged what was left of the Somnease pill I had left on the sink. I climbed into bed fully clothed and waited for the medication to quiet the roaring in my mind and send me into the deepest, darkest oblivion.

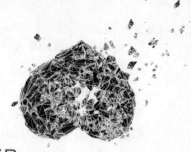

CHAPTER
THIRTEEN

"Marivic, wake up." Roya was standing over me, frowning. "Didn't you hear the alarm? Breakfast is almost over. You'll be late for dream mapping."

I tried to mumble something but found my lips and tongue too dry to make any sound. Roya got me a cup of water and held it out. "Here. Drink this. Somnease is dehydrating." I drank the entire cup of water and Roya immediately gave me another one, along with a granola bar and a banana. "You won't have time to go down and grab breakfast, but you can eat these on the way. I'll wait outside while you get dressed."

Thankfully she hadn't noticed that I was already dressed, having slept in my clothes from the night before. I changed shirts and scarfed half the banana before joining her in the hallway.

Roya talked brightly about nothing — the incredible heat, tonight's movie in the common room, her new shoes — as we ventured down to sublevel two in the elevator. My heart ached as I remembered Saren's hurtful words.

I couldn't believe she could judge Gumps so harshly with barely a second thought. I was glad I had slept in and didn't have to face her, or anyone, at breakfast. I wondered if they had whispered about disorientation or if they had decided to honour Abbot's wishes and never bring it up again. I wondered if anyone else had decided to run away and join Winfree.

"Here we are. Marivic, I'd like you to meet Dr. Sun."

Roya gestured to a kind-looking doctor wearing a Barton lab coat over raspberry-coloured scrubs.

"Hello, Marivic." When she smiled, her cheeks dimpled. They looked deep enough to swallow your thumb.

"Hi." I smiled back, even though there were splinters in my heart. Roya was frowning at me from the corner. Why was she still here?

"Dream mapping is really very simple," Dr. Sun explained. "This first part doesn't even require machines, just talking. I'll ask you about your episodes and take some notes. After that we will hook you up to a series of monitors that will measure brain activity during your episodes."

"What if I can't fall asleep?"

"We can give you a small dose of something to help, if necessary. Now, can you remember the first time you experienced a dream that felt different? More vivid or violent than usual?"

"It was four nights ago, the night before I came here. I was running and the ground got hot and then melted into this burning, molten lava . . ." Remembering it made my heart beat faster, as if I was still in the dream, running. "There was nowhere to go, I had to keep running and my feet were sinking."

Dr. Sun touched my arm and smiled gently at me. "That sounds scary. Thank you for sharing it with me. I have a few questions and then I promise I won't make you talk about it again, okay?"

I blew out all my air in an unsteady breath. "Okay."

"Was there anyone else with you?"

"Not that I could see, but I could feel other people around me."

Dr. Sun nodded and wrote it down, free of judgment. "What about the lava? In the episode did you have a physical sensation of pain or burning?"

I swallowed, remembering the hot splashes against my calves. "Yes."

"What about other senses? Could you smell or taste anything?"

"I smelled burning."

"And did you hear anything? Voices, music, other sounds?"

"Footsteps, screaming and the sound of the lava. It sort of pops every now and again."

"You're doing great, Marivic, really great. We're almost through. Have you ever experienced this episode a second time?"

"Yes, my first night here."

"And what other episodes have you experienced?"

I hesitated. "Just that one, really."

Dr. Sun looked up from her note taking. "Nothing else in the past few evenings? How much Somnease have you been taking?"

"Just what was given to me," I said, feeling defensive. "I had an episode, I guess you would call it, during the assessment tests yesterday. I don't know if that counts.

I wasn't asleep but Dr. Dad told me that I accessed the suspended cycle, which I guess is what happens when you go ACES?"

"Yes, there's a note here on your chart. Why don't you tell me about it in your own words."

I told her about the maze and the dogs. This time I mentioned the voice telling me to go left.

"Can you describe the voice?"

"Not really. It came from inside my head."

"But it wasn't your own voice?"

"No, it was like someone had hijacked my thoughts."

"And you're sure it wasn't your own instinct or intuition telling you what to do?"

"No. I don't think so." I was beginning to feel crazier and crazier. "Does this count? Is it helpful?"

Dr. Sun smiled reassuringly. "Everything counts. Now let's move on to part two."

I changed into a paper robe and a nurse wiped my arms, forehead and chest down with rubbing alcohol before attaching small circular electrodes to my skin.

Dr. Sun and a nurse returned with a gurney. They helped me lie back, rearranging all the wires so I could be as comfortable as possible, and then they both wheeled the gurney down a hallway to another room. It was dark and there was a low hum.

"Try to stay calm, Marivic. Dream mapping doesn't hurt. We're going to slide you into the neuroimaging machine and turn on the monitors. It's a tight fit, so some Intakes prefer to close their eyes before they enter, especially if they're a bit claustrophobic."

I strained my neck, trying to get a glimpse of what they were about to stuff me into. I wouldn't describe myself as claustrophobic, but I wasn't exactly thrilled at the idea of being enclosed in a small space and then having Dr. Sun induce the ACES. The machine looked like Bertha, the machine in the photo of Gumps, only it was much leaner and modern looking. Did Gumps make this machine? Or an earlier version of it? There were too many coincidences; I was starting to feel unhinged, panicked.

"Please keep your head still," Dr. Sun said. "I can tell you're nervous, your heart rate is elevated. We're going to give you a shot of something to help you sleep, then all you need to do is close your eyes and dream. That's not so hard, is it?"

As Dr. Sun spoke to me in her gentle, lilting voice I felt the cold prick of a needle in the crook of my elbow. It was over in less than a second, and then I was being lifted onto another gurney. They strapped my wrists and ankles in and before I could ask why, I was being slid into the narrow mouth of Gumps's machine.

"Just close your eyes and remember that you're being closely monitored and the episodes can't hurt you."

I did as I was told, shutting out the curved walls just inches from my face and the sight of wires sprouting from my arms and chest. I wasn't sure which freaked me out the most: the restraints on my wrists and ankles, or the fact that I was about to pass out in a narrow box that closely resembled a coffin. I could feel the pull of the drugs, drawing me toward sleep.

Don't panic, I told myself. Don't panic, don't panic, don't panic—

The muscles in my legs twitched, remembering what it felt like to be free and running, not strapped down in a lab. I took shaky breaths and tried not to think about

Gumps or the fact that Saren was going to run away with a rebel group later that night. Instead I imagined that I was running. Footsteps falling at a steady, even pace; arms swinging, propelling me forward. The more I thought about running, the calmer I became until I could feel the chord waiting for me. Impossible, I thought. It's the drugs — but still I reached for it and, sure enough, found my place among the vibrations.

*

When I opened my eyes I was still lying on my back, enclosed in a tube. The walls were made of thick glass or plastic and they were so close I felt like if I exhaled I would be able to see my breath clouding the surface. Only there was a giant tube in my mouth. For a moment I panicked — I couldn't breathe with this tube jammed between my teeth — but then I realized it must be helping me breathe. It was just one of many tubes I was sprouting — yellow, red, clear. There were tubes in my arms, in my chest, on my head. There was movement down by my toes. The shapes appeared to be people, but the light above me was so bright and flickering it made everything outside its glare uncertain.

I was moving down a hall. Where was I? What had happened to Dr. Sun? Why wasn't I going ACES? Did I have a seizure or something and now was being wheeled to an emergency room? The voices around me were muffled. I had no hope of seeing the faces of these people, so instead I focused on listening to their words.

"A second one!"

"What are the chances?"

"Must be careful now."

"Shh, I think she's waking."

"I'll take care of that."

Take care of what, I thought. I shifted and found myself strapped in tightly. Now I really started to panic. I tried to spit out the tube in my mouth, but everything started to go wonky and even my heartbeat seemed to slow down. The voices were stretched out into meaningless sounds and eventually everything went black.

*

My eyes felt heavy, much too heavy to open. Someone was typing quickly. I heard the rapid clicking of fingers on keys above the hum of machines. Then someone — Dr. Sun, maybe — was talking in a low voice. I only heard her side of the conversation, so I guessed she must have been on the phone. I remembered seeing one in the lab when I was first wheeled in.

"Yes, very unusual. One of the highest I've seen. Did not respond to the stimulus. No, I'm alone. Are you sure? Yes, of course. Of course."

I heard the click of the receiver in the cradle and footsteps padding lightly away. I cracked my eyes open and saw I was still hooked up to the wires but I had been wheeled out of the medical coffin and was back in the first room, where Dr. Sun had asked me about my episodes. She was looking at a monitor near the foot of the bed, with her back to me. I glanced toward the phone and saw that she had left her clipboard with her notes beside it. It was my dream map, six coloured lines wiggling across reams of paper. I had no idea what it all meant, only that at the bottom, in bold letters and highlighted in purple, it said: *Level 4 ATP. Recommended action unknown.*

"You're awake." Dr. Sun smiled at me, all traces of worry that I'd heard in her voice on the phone completely gone.

"Did I pass?" I asked.

Dr. Sun laughed her charming, tinkly laugh. "We got what we needed. I have a few follow-up questions and then you're free to return to your room. Can you tell me about your episode?"

"I'm not sure that it was one."

"What do you mean?"

"I mean I dreamed I was in a tube with a bunch of wires attached to me. Only I wasn't in the neuroimaging machine, I was being wheeled down a hallway. I guess I woke up when you were bringing me back here."

Dr. Sun frowned at her chart.

"What is it?" I asked. "What does the chart say?"

"According to our chart you entered the suspended cycle and your brain activity here suggests that you definitely did experience an episode."

"Is it possible that I just don't remember it?"

"It's highly unlikely. Are you sure you don't remember anything else? Any running? The lava in the road? Any unusual physical sensation?"

"There was a tube in my mouth. I thought I was choking. Did you put a tube in my mouth?"

"No, there was nothing in your mouth."

"What does Level 4 ATP mean?" I asked.

Dr. Sun blinked at me. "Why on earth would you ask that?"

"I saw it on my chart. Is it bad?"

"It's nothing; it's medical shorthand for the surgeon."

"But it's not bad?"

"No, it's not bad. But your results aren't as clear as I would like them to be. We may do one more session tomorrow before we go ahead with a winnowing plan."

I felt like I had failed. Maybe two nights of Somnease had messed with my brain. Even though Roya had said it was safe, maybe I was the exception. But then how to explain the maze with the dogs? And if I wasn't awake when Dr. Sun wheeled me back to the room, why had I dreamt about another tube?

My stomach groaned loudly.

"Lunchtime!" Dr. Sun said brightly. "We'll get you cleaned up and out of here in no time."

*

There was a knock at the door.

"Come in," I said. I was expecting Roya with my lunch but it was Tavi who entered, carrying a lunch tray. Today she was wearing neon laddered sunglasses that were more fashionable than functional.

"Roya said you needed lunch."

"Yeah, thanks. You can just put it on the table, I guess."

Tavi set the tray down and then sat in the little chair tucked under the desk. She looked exhausted, all planes and angles, like someone had sketched a version of her in pencil. "Can I hang out in here for a while?" she asked, her arms crossed tight against her body, her hands cupping her elbows. "I don't want to be alone."

"Where's Quin?" I asked.

Tavi shrugged. "Still at her assessments, I guess."

I scooted over on the bed and made room for Tavi to join me.

"I guess the dream mapping was pretty bad?" I asked.

"I've been taking Somnease for a few nights now. I forgot how bad going ACES could be."

"What do you dream about?" I asked.

"It's the same dream, only each time it lasts a little bit longer. I'm laughing, happy about something, but I can't remember what. Suddenly there is this bang and blast of heat and I can't hear a thing," Tavi brought her hands to her ears as she remembered, as if she was there in the episode. "And then the laughing turns to screaming and the ground starts to move. When I look down I see that it's not the ground, it's this sea of lava, and there's nowhere to go, so I'm running in it."

"I've dreamt about the lava too!" I said, my heart hammering. That means two of us had the same dream. Surely that wasn't normal. How many other kids had the same dream? Why wasn't there any mention of this in the Barton Guide? "Only my dream starts with me running."

"That makes sense, with your imps and everything," Tavi said. "Why do you think we dream about the same thing? What does it mean?"

"I don't know," I admitted. "I used to be obsessed with dream interpretation. I had this dictionary that tells you what things mean when you dream about them. Like if you dream about losing teeth it means you're worried about what you look like."

"Did the book say anything about running?"

"Running in a dream usually means you're running

from something in your real life. I don't know that it makes sense with the ACES."

"ACES aren't normal dreams, so maybe you can't use a regular dream dictionary," Tavi suggested.

"Do you think any of that stuff from last night is true?"

"Shhh!" Tavi grabbed my arm as if she could turn down the volume of my voice by squeezing my wrist, and then looked up as if expecting to see a hidden camera blinking away.

"What are you worried about?" I asked, lowering my voice. Her paranoia was contagious.

"You don't know who's listening," she said.

"You think we're being monitored?" I whispered.

"You don't?" she whispered back.

"If you think we're being watched why did you sneak down to the pool last night?"

"I didn't want to go, but Quin thought it would be fun. As far as I'm concerned, last night never happened."

"So you don't believe all that stuff about SuperGen causing the imps, and Barton60."

"I don't know what you're talking about," Tavi said stubbornly.

"Saren believes it."

"Good for Saren. Where is she, anyway? I didn't see her at breakfast or lunch."

"I don't know," I admitted. "We got in a fight."

Tavi looked taken aback. "You did? But you guys never fight. What was it about?"

I lowered my voice. "Winfree."

"So is she going to . . . ?" Tavi didn't finish her sentence but I knew what she was trying to say.

"I think so."

"Whoa." Tavi sniffed and pushed her sunglasses up the bridge of her nose to wipe at her eyes. When she opened them I saw that the irises, normally a light green, were almost leached of colour and the whites of her eyes were silvery and thick, as if there was a film over them. I looked away quickly.

"I know, they're freaky, aren't they?" Tavi said. "It's okay. You don't have to look."

"Do they hurt?" I asked.

"No, mostly they itch. Plus I see weird shapes around certain things and I get colours all wrong."

"Shapes like shadows?"

"More like auras, around living things. I know, it sounds so ridiculous. I don't even believe in auras."

"Have you ever thought about what would happen, you know, if there wasn't the winnowing?" I asked.

Tavi shuddered. "No. I hate that my eyes look like this. I hate that when I look at something I've seen every day of my life it's a new colour or surrounded by this pulsing *thing*. I can't wait for everything to go back to normal." Tavi was so sure. She reminded me of myself only a few days before. "Plus I never ever want to dream about that lava again."

"Oh my god, there you are! Everyone is looking for you!" Quin stood in the doorway, her Barton T-shirt damp and clingy, ponytail hanging limply behind her. Somehow she managed to make physical exhaustion look pretty.

Tavi slid off the bed and went to join her. "Why?" she asked.

"Not you. Marivic."

"What's wrong?" I asked.

Quin looked genuinely flustered, not like she was play-acting. Her eyes were big and round. "You mean you seriously don't know?"

"Know what?"

Quin shrank back, stepping into the hallway. "I don't know if I should be the one to tell you."

"Tell me what?"

"What's going on, Quin?" Tavi asked.

Quin took another step backwards into the hallway. "Maybe I should get Roya."

"Just say it, Quin!" Tavi said.

"It's Saren. She was winnowed this morning, only — it didn't go well."

There were actual tears in Quin's eyes. Watching her tear up set off a whole fire station's worth of alarm bells in my head.

"No, you're wrong. She had another dream mapping scheduled this morning."

Quin shook her head, tears spilling over her cheeks. "They told us at lunch. There were complications, like with her brother. She died. She actually *died*."

Tavi gasped and then the two of them started to cry loudly. I felt numb, like I was watching a play about someone who had died, someone I had nothing to do with. Quin was genuinely upset and there was no way she would make something like this up. She wasn't that mean. But if it wasn't a cruel trick, that meant it was true. Saren was dead.

"I'm sorry," Quin kept moaning. "I'm so, so sorry."

Tavi rushed to her side and the two of them fell into each other's arms, sobbing. "She died, Tavi. She actually died!" Quin said.

"Stop saying that!" I yelled.

Roya appeared in the doorway. "What's going on?" she asked.

"Sa-Saren," Quin said.

Roya looked right at me, her eyes full of regret, and the truth slammed into me like a fist to the stomach. It was true. Saren had died. My eyes and throat and lungs burned and I started to shake.

"I'm very sorry for your loss, Marivic," Roya said.

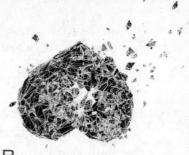

CHAPTER
FOURTEEN

I refused to get out of bed. I was trapped in a state somewhere between zombie and nightmare. Tavi and Quin
kept looking in on me but I couldn't bring myself to
speak to them. Kamal knocked on my door and told me
he was sorry. I didn't even look at him. Dr. Dad brought
a therapist up to talk to me about my grief but I barely
heard a word he said. In the end he patted my shoulder,
told me I needed some time and promised to come back
later. I heard Intakes going to and from their rooms,
whispering.

"Is she going ACES?"

"I don't think so, but something is definitely wrong."

But I *am* going ACES. I'm in the middle of the worst
possible nightmare. Only I'm awake and it's real. Saren
is dead. We never got the chance to make up and now
I'll never see her again. The tears came so full and thick
I thought I would choke on them. You were right, Saren.
Apparently the Silvers *were* unfit for the winnowing.

I skipped dinner. I couldn't imagine ever eating again.

My stomach had closed up shop. My tongue had shrivelled up. My arms and legs felt like stone. Marivic Stone, made of stone. Only my heart was working, and it was so painful I wished it would give up too.

Roya came to check on me. "Your friends are all in the lounge watching a movie," she said. "They're worried about you."

"They're not my friends," I said. "They're just people I go to school with. Saren was my friend. My best and only friend. And you let her die."

Roya looked uncomfortable. She glanced at the hallway like she wished she was anywhere but here, but at the last moment changed her mind and sat on the edge of my bed.

"How did she die?" I asked.

I wanted to hear the truth. It felt like punishing myself and I wanted to be punished for the way I left things with Saren. The arguing, the low blows . . . I deserved all the pain I felt.

"We aren't allowed to discuss the medical details of other patients," Roya told me.

I turned away, refusing to look at her. "Is death considered a medical detail?"

"It sounds callous when you put it that way, I know. These things happen, death happens. But what happened to Saren was rare. It won't happen to you."

I remembered saying the same thing to Saren when she had been worried about having the same fate as Lex. "You don't know that for sure."

"No," Roya admitted.

I turned my face back to look at her. "Is it true that the winnowing affects your memory? That when people come back, they don't remember the process? They forget little things, and not just about Barton, but things from before, like names, or how to tie their shoes, that sort of stuff."

I watched Roya respond. She chose her words very carefully. "Yes, in order to get rid of the imps and episodes once and for all, the doctors sometimes have to cut very close to the normal parts of the brain."

The ache in my heart was so big I felt it to the tips of my hair. How could I go back to my old life without Saren? How could I do anything when I felt this terrible?

"What if I want them to cut things out?"

Roya shook her head sadly. "It doesn't work that way."

"But they could, right? They have the ability to do it. I want to forget this whole stupid experience."

"When you go home, Saren will still be dead. You're going to find out eventually."

I knew she was right, but I didn't want to accept it. It hurt too badly.

"What if they cut out all my memories of her? Then it wouldn't hurt and I'd never know what I was missing."

Roya placed her hand lightly on my shoulder. She looked like she wanted to do more, maybe give it a pat or rub my back, something nice like a parent would do. Instead she hesitated, leaving it there. "I know you're hurting now, but that's a good thing. Mourning someone's death is the other side of loving them. You can't have one without the other. It means she was a true friend."

What a stupid thing to say. Since when did feeling this bad mean something good?

Roya shook out two Somnease pills from the bottle in her pocket and left them on the nightstand.

"Take two tonight. Good night, Marivic."

I couldn't be bothered to say good night back.

*

I was stuck in a strange place between sleep and awake. All I could do was cry. Every time I felt like I had dried up, I would remember something else, something stupid, like how Saren had once found a queen of hearts card on the ground and for three weeks she consulted the card before making any decisions because she thought it was lucky, and new tears would spring up from some inexhaustible source in my body. There were so many little things that made up a person; how could they just stop existing?

I wondered what Mrs. Silver would do when she found out. Maybe she already knew. Losing not one but two children to the winnowing was unbearable. It would kill her. She'd turn into a snail of a person, curled up inside that stuffy house.

If only they hadn't moved up her surgery, Saren would be alive and hours away from a new life with Winfree, where she'd never be winnowed and would not have died. The timing felt especially cruel. I hadn't wanted to lose Saren to Winfree, but at least I would know that she was alive, fighting for a cause. Saren was never more ferociously Saren than when she was standing up for what she believed in.

If Abbot was right that SuperGen was the cause of the imps and Barton was trying to hide the truth by cutting out the bits and pieces of us that they decided were unsavoury, then Barton was responsible for Saren's death.

Who was going to make Barton pay? And how could I let them do the same to me, knowing that they had killed Saren?

Abbot said it was possible to live with the imps, that Dr. Lowry could help control my ACES. I could live unwinnowed, join Winfree and get to the bottom of what was going on at Barton, like Saren wanted. She couldn't take up her quest but I could do it for her. I would find out the truth and make people pay for Saren's death. She was the brightest star in my galaxy and they had blotted her out.

Mrs. Silver could be sad for the both of us. I was going to be angry.

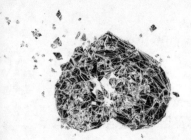

CHAPTER
FIFTEEN

Midnight snuck up on me quickly. I left everything behind except my grandmother's necklace, safe under my T-shirt, and my two photographs — the one of my mother and the one Abbot had left, of Gumps — both tucked carefully into my back pocket.

The hall was silent. Maybe everyone was given a double-dose of Somnease. I wasn't the only person affected by Saren's death. The Intakes were on edge and worried. It was in Barton's best interest to keep everyone drugged and sleeping. Maybe things hadn't changed all that much from the Barton60 days. I made my way toward the boys' bathroom, refusing to look across the hall, at the room that had once belonged to Saren.

The bathroom was dimly lit by individual lighting fixtures above the sinks and the urinals. I positioned myself in a dark spot between the sinks. I could crouch down and hide if anyone else came in. I really hoped nobody would. I never wanted to see someone use a urinal if I could help it. But I watched and waited, and no one came. Then I heard something ringing against metal. *Tap tap tap.* Then again, *tap tap tap.*

"Marivic, look up."

I did, blinking. Ten fingers were curled around the grate in the ceiling vent. "Abbot, is that you?"

"Yes. Are you alone?" His voice echoed strangely in the darkness of the vent.

"Yes."

"Just a minute."

The banging in the air vent was creepy but familiar — I realized it was Abbot we'd been hearing in the vents, not the so-called Roddenberry ghost. I made a mental note to tell Abbot to be more careful when he was crawling around up there.

There was the sound of scuffling, then the grate shifted with a tooth-aching squeal of metal on metal and Abbot slowly let himself down, landing on shaky legs like a newborn colt. He was wearing a Barton lab coat that was at least a size too big. It looked like he was caught up in a big white bedsheet. He righted himself, adjusted the lab coat and grinned at me.

"I'm so glad you're coming. You've made the right choice, Marivic. Just wait."

"You heard about Saren?"

The grin disappeared. "Yes. I'm sorry."

I took a shaky breath and found that despite hours of crying, I still seemed to have a few tears left in me. But I wasn't about to let them loose. Not in front of Abbot, and not when I had decided to pick up Saren's mantle. I had to be the brave one now. Who knew what was ahead of me as part of Winfree — living in tents in the woods, moving from one dangerous mission to the next? From this point on, I was Marivic the revolutionary. I needed to start acting like it.

"Now what?"

"Now we leave," he said. "We're going to sneak into the main-floor laundry room though the air vents. There's a truck that backs right up to the room at one a.m. to load the dirty laundry and take it into town for washing. You're going to be in that truck."

"We're going to the laundromat?"

"No, the delivery trucks always take the back road, which passes by the Barton Flats, in and out of Barton. The Flats is a housing development where the military families used to live back when Barton was an active base. There's a yellow flashing light that the truck will stop at. When the truck stops, you jump out the back and run to the Flats. Find number four and wait outside for pickup."

I felt a wild urge to laugh. Listening to Abbot talk made the whole situation feel absurd. I had to keep telling myself that I wasn't in a book or a movie. This was real life.

"You look weird. What's wrong?" Abbot asked.

"It's just all so crazy . . . I don't even know you and you're talking about a getaway plan like it's nothing more than a walk around the block."

"I know it seems unbelievable but when you meet Dr. Lowry, she'll explain everything to you. You have to trust me. Are you ready?"

Ready to crawl through the vent, jump out of a moving truck and join forces with a secret revolutionary group that until a few days ago I never knew existed? Not really. But what choice did I have? Gumps was hiding something, Saren was dead and if I stayed at Barton, I could be too. I wasn't going to wait around for things to happen to me. Marivic Stone was taking charge of her own life.

"Ready enough," I said.

"Ready for what?"

Abbot and I whirled around to find Kamal standing in the doorway, arms crossed. "You planning on making a run for it, Stone?"

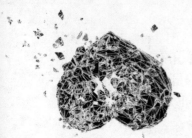

CHAPTER
SIXTEEN

I stood there opening and closing my mouth like a fish for much too long. Abbot recovered faster.

"I know what this looks like," he began calmly.

"It looks like a getaway." Kamal sauntered farther into the bathroom, eyeing Abbot's lab coat with a smirk. "What are you supposed to be, a doctor?"

"You're Kamal, right?" Abbot asked.

Kamal stood a bit taller, flattered at being recognized. "Maybe." Kamal pointed his thumb in my direction. "Why, has this one been talking about me?"

I had recovered from my shock enough to roll my eyes, which made Kamal laugh. "She loves me," he gloated.

Before I could protest, Abbot rushed on, "You're the one with the theories."

Kamal's eyes narrowed. "Yeah, I've got a few theories."

"What if I told you they were true?"

Kamal considered this. "I know about you Winfree people. I've read some of your anti-winnowing stuff. It's solid. I wondered if Winfree was behind that disorientation invite thing. That's why I went down to the pool last night."

I wanted to ask how on earth he had got his hands on anything written by Winfree, but Abbot didn't seem to care about these details. "Then come with us. We have a safe house not far from here. I can explain more there, but you have to be quiet and you have to come now."

"No, you don't even know him!" I said. It was hard enough leaving my life behind. The only good part of starting over was leaving the bad parts — like Kamal — behind. The boys didn't seem to hear my protest. Either that or they didn't care.

"It has to be tonight," Abbot said. I was impressed with how bossy he was. It didn't seem to bother him that Kamal was a full head taller and had muscles to spare. Next to Kamal, Abbot looked like a red-headed grasshopper. "But if you come with us you can never go back to your regular life."

There was a flicker in Kamal's resolve; I saw it run across his face the way lights hiccup during a power surge. Kamal had lots of friends and a legitimate athletic career waiting for him. His mom seemed nice. His best friend wasn't dead. His only guardian wasn't hiding something big and possibly terrible. Kamal had more to lose than I did. So it was a surprise when he rolled his shoulders, looked Abbot in the eye and said, "Yeah, I'm in. What next?"

"We get into that vent."

Kamal and I looked up. I swear the ceiling looked higher than it did five minutes ago. Kamal must have been thinking the same thing, because he swung his arms up and tried to brush the vent with his fingers. No luck.

"Exactly how are we supposed to do that?" he asked.

"Stand on that sink and jump."

The sink that Abbot was pointing at was a few feet to the left of the gaping hole in the ceiling. Even standing, I wasn't sure I could reach the opening. But there didn't seem to be another choice.

"You're kidding," I said.

"Marivic, you're stronger than you think. You're changing. Remember, you have the power of your abilities behind you." To hear Abbot talk about them, you would think the imps were something useful, like the power of invisibility or superhuman strength. I wasn't convinced my running skills were of much use in this situation.

"How are you getting up there?" Kamal asked.

"Same way," said Abbot.

Kamal snorted. "You've got, like, four inches and fifty pounds on this guy, Stone. If he can make it, you sure as heck can."

I'm not sure who felt more insulted, me or Abbot. But Kamal had a point. On the scrawny scale, Abbot was somewhere between drowned rat and starving puppy.

"This is crazy," I muttered.

"I'll go first," Abbot said.

We watched as he stepped up on top of the sink. He was surprisingly agile, like a cat. Carefully, he rolled up from a crouch to a standing position and gazed at the dark square cut out of the ceiling, as if visualizing what he was about to do. Then he took a deep knee bend and jumped. In one smooth movement, he caught the edge of the ceiling and pulled himself up and into the darkness.

"Wow," I said.

"Impressive," Kamal agreed.

There was a scuffling noise and Abbot's head appeared in the vent, grinning. "Who's next?"

"Ladies first," said Kamal.

I bounced lightly on the balls of my feet and felt my muscles flex in response. Abbot was right; I felt stronger than I ever had before. I wiped down the cold porcelain with the bottom of my T-shirt, ensuring the surface was dry. I steadied myself with my hands on either side and stepped up. I caught a glimpse of myself in the mirror, perched on the sink like a frog, knees jutting out on both sides. I blew out my breath slowly, fluttering my bangs, and stood to my full height. Even when I stretched my arms as far as they could go there was a foot between the ceiling and the tips of my fingers.

"It's too far," I said.

I was afraid of slipping and falling, but I was also afraid of looking stupid in front of the boys. I wasn't graceful or athletic, which was about to become glaringly clear.

"If you feel like you're going to slip, jump first," Kamal suggested.

"Easy for you to say. You can probably reach the edge just standing," I muttered.

I took one more deep breath, squatted deeply and leapt through the air, shooting my arms forward like Superman. When my hands connected with the edge, I used the momentum of my legs to swing myself upward and over the lip, launching myself into the darkness.

I lay there with my feet dangling over the edge, my palms tingling from where I had scraped them against the rough surface of the ceiling, catching my breath while Abbot laughed somewhere ahead of me in the darkness.

"I told you," he said.

*

Abbot led us through a maze of dark vents.

"Be quiet," he whispered. "Every little sound is magnified in these vents. We don't want to get caught."

The air tasted like dust and metal. I breathed with my mouth open to avoid panicking in the small, unknowable space. It was a tight fit and we had to crawl with our shoulders hunched and heads down. Kamal kept bumping his head on the ceiling with an impossibly loud clang, swearing under his breath. Each time, I felt my heart rate spike, expecting a doctor or a nurse to start banging on the ceiling and calling for someone to smoke us out. I bumped my own head a few times, but Abbot moved as gracefully as a fish through water. In the vents his small size was an advantage.

"There's a dead end here," Abbot whispered. His voice sounded hollow in the vent. "We're going down to the first floor. Watch what I do." Abbot braced himself by putting his hands and feet on the sides of the vent and shimmied down slowly. It was the sort of thing that normally made my heart race but my new muscles never let me down. I felt a little bit nervous but mostly exhilarated, like a singer about to take the stage. Even so, I was relieved when we reached the first floor vent system and could return to crawling on our hands and knees.

I was trying to picture what part of the building we were in and how far the laundry room was when Abbot stopped abruptly. I fell headfirst into his shoes and behind me Kamal stumbled right into my butt.

"You could have warned us," I hissed.

Kamal laughed under his breath. "Aren't you going to make some comment about me kissing your butt?"

"I think you just did it for me," I said through gritted teeth, relieved that it was too dark for either of the boys to see the blush creeping across my face and down my neck.

"Shh," Abbot said. "Our voices will carry. I'm going to take out the vent, then drop into the room. I'll call to you when it's your turn."

I nodded, even though I knew he couldn't see me. I heard the sound of metal protesting as Abbot slid the vent to one side, and then nothing. I watched, crouched on my knees, as Abbot turned around and dropped out of sight and into the room below. I crawled carefully over the vent that now rested on the floor of the tunnel and peered into the dim room below. Laundry bins that looked like large wheeled Dumpsters were parked against the wall, directly below us. Abbot was fighting his way through a mass of sheets and hauled himself out and over the edge. He waved at me.

"Come on!" he murmured.

Kamal shouldered his way in beside me to take a look. "Looks like we've got a soft landing. I hope nobody here wet the bed last night."

"Gross."

"What are you waiting for, the sheets to dry?"

"Move over," I said. "I need to rearrange."

Kamal backtracked into the vent while I turned around and lowered myself carefully, my feet pedalling in mid-air. Even though I knew there was six feet of soft, forgiving laundry waiting to receive me, letting go was hard. Even harder than jumping had been. My shoulders were beginning to ache and just before I could let go, Kamal grabbed my fingers and peeled them off the vent for me, sending me sailing down into the room.

I was too shocked to scream. I barely had a chance to breathe before I was engulfed in Barton-issue bedding. I thrashed my way back to the top, pushing aside towels and untangling my legs from the sheets. It didn't smell like urine, but you never know what nasty surprises are waiting for you in someone else's dirty laundry.

Kamal lowered himself through the open vent and let go, plummeting at an alarmingly fast rate. There was barely enough time for me to flatten myself against the edge of the bin as he cannonballed barely a foot from me, rattling the entire container, and me with it.

When he got to a standing position he was grinning. "Now that was cool."

"You could have landed on me," I said.

"But I didn't," Kamal pointed out. "So you have nothing to be mad about."

I couldn't believe I was having a stupid argument with my least-favourite person in the middle of the biggest night of my life.

"The laundry truck should be here anytime now," Abbot said. "They'll wheel these containers directly into the back of the truck and then take off."

"How do you know all this stuff?" I asked.

Abbot looked up at the hole where the air vent used to be. "I've spent a lot of time watching how Barton works."

Kamal smirked. "Dude, is that why you're so pale? Do you live in the walls, like some kind of Barton termite?"

Abbot blushed, but before he could respond there was a click and a buzzing noise. We all froze, recognizing the sound of the door just about to open. I resisted the urge to dive down into the laundry like a rabbit in a hole.

"Get in!" I whisper-yelled, but Abbot shook his head.

"Not enough time — I'll meet you there!"

"Where?" I hissed.

"The Flats! Just get to number four and wait!"

"Stone, we have to get down!" Kamal draped an arm around my shoulder. I stiffened and shoved it off.

"You're leaving me alone?"

Abbot hesitated, his gaze drifting over to Kamal. "You're not alone."

Then he slipped out of sight behind the row of bins, heading who knows where. Footsteps echoed in the room and my survival instincts kicked in. I took a deep breath before digging my way to the bottom of the bin. I pulled laundry over my head until I was satisfied that no part of me could be seen. Then I made myself go absolutely still. Somewhere in the bin, Kamal was doing the same thing, but I couldn't see him through the layers of linens.

I didn't hear Abbot slip out of the room, but I told myself he was safe, that he didn't look too ridiculous in the borrowed lab coat, and surely someone who had been navigating Barton by air vent for ages knew what he was doing.

There was a great shuddering of metal upon metal that set my teeth on edge, even buried in all those sheets. It was followed by a steady creaking noise, the sound of the garage door to the outside being opened. Next came a beeping sound that got louder and more insistent. The truck was backing up. There was a metallic clang and I imagined the ramp — like the one in the back of Gumps's truck, only bigger — connecting with the cement of the laundry-room floor. I heard whistling and heavy footsteps as the truck driver approached and started talking to whoever else had just entered the room. I started to get nervous as first one then another bin was rolled onto the truck. Kamal and I were hidden in the third bin, farthest from the door.

Don't be stupid, I told myself. The driver can't see through solid fabric! Still, when he grabbed the bin and spun it around, I had to dig my nails into the skin of my palms to keep from crying out.

Once I got over the initial shock, I felt myself start to relax. Somehow the cool night air made it through all those towels and sheets and touched my skin. It made me feel one step closer to freedom. It was almost fun being wheeled across the floor, up an incline and then into the truck. The driver pushed the bin into the others and we bounced off, like a super-secret version of bumper cars. Then the doors were slammed shut and the whistling disappeared.

The laundry started to shift and I knew Kamal was making his way to the top of the pile. I waited for the rumble of the engine to start up and then dug myself out as well. In the semi-darkness Kamal looked like a disembodied head floating on a sea of white.

"Phew! It's hard to breathe under there," Kamal said.

"You should have waited until the truck started," I said. "He might have heard us."

"Nah. That guy probably can't hear anything over the sound of his truly awful whistling."

"Shh. We should be concentrating on the route."

"It's not that hard. We just wait for the van to slow

down. I don't think we've even left the Barton grounds yet." Kamal gripped the edge of the bin and pulled himself out of the laundry and onto the floor just as we hit a bump in the road, which sent him flying into the side of the truck with a thwack.

We both froze.

"Do you think the driver heard that?" I whispered.

Kamal rubbed his shoulders. "If he did, he probably thought it was one of the bins. I'm fine, by the way. I guess I know where your priorities stand."

I refused to let his comment get to me. Instead I focused on the movement of the van. "Do you think we're slowing down?"

"It's too soon."

With every lurch or bump of the laundry bin, I was sure the truck had slowed down. I felt like a five-year-old on a car trip, asking, "Are we there yet?" Kamal suggested I get out of the laundry bin, which was constantly moving and making it harder to determine the acceleration of the truck.

I scrambled over the edge, trying to avoid getting crushed between two bins. It wasn't as awkward as jumping off a bathroom sink and into an air vent, but it wasn't the most graceful thing I've ever done. I wondered what other physical challenges were ahead of me now that I was officially on the run. Kamal was right, outside of the bin it was easier to feel the motions of the truck. When it did slow down, we both looked up at the same time. My heart kicked into high gear.

"This is it," Kamal said. "Are you ready?"

"How slow should the truck be going before we jump out?"

"There's no guarantee he'll stop at all." Kamal jiggled the handle and frowned.

"What's wrong?"

"It's stuck."

Kamal used both hands and put his full weight on the handle, grimacing with the effort. "Or maybe it's locked. Did Termite mention anything about this locking from the outside?"

"What are we going to do?"

The truck came to a complete stop.

Kamal started shouting and banging on the door. I dug my nails into his arm and wrenched him away from the wall. "What are you doing? He'll hear us!"

"That's the idea! Make as much noise as you can. He'll come back to check it out and then we run."

"Are you crazy? What if he's armed?"

"He's a laundry man, why would he be armed?"

"What if there're two of them?"

"Then I'll take the bigger guy. Look, Marivic, what choice do we have? Sit back and let them take us to the laundromat? We'd be stranded. How will we get word to Abbot?"

Kamal was right but it didn't make me feel any better. My heart was pounding so hard it felt like it was bruising me from the inside out. It was a simple plan, really. The door would open, we would jump out and run. Kamal was state champion; I was the fastest impaired runner Barton had ever seen. Surely we could outrun an old delivery man. Still, it would be nice to have something to guarantee us a head start . . . My eyes fell on a coil of rope near the door. It looked like a huge snake, lying in wait.

"Okay. But when he opens the door throw that rope

at him. It will keep him distracted while we make a run for it."

Kamal grinned. "Now you're talking."

"Hey! HEY!" I screamed, kicking and slamming my palms at the wall. Despite my fear, it felt good to hit something.

The door opened and night poured in. There was a moment of silence, the air in the van reverberating with the memory of all that kicking and screaming. Then Kamal let out a war cry and, with a running leap, jumped out of the van. I saw the rope leave his hands and smack into a dark shadow of a man. The man yelled and held his hands up in defense as the rope fell heavily upon him, knocking him to his knees.

This time I didn't need Kamal to give me a push. I jumped, bending my knees deeply to absorb the shock when my feet hit the pavement. I barely wobbled, like a champion gymnast who had just stuck a very difficult landing. I took off running, soaring across the uneven desert. My legs felt like they grew an inch with every stride as I ran for the cluster of houses to the left. The sound of my feet hitting the ground thundered in my ears, dried grasses crunching and pebbles skittering away.

I looked back only once to make sure the driver wasn't in pursuit. I was relieved to see the van was already gone, but the feeling passed when I realized the driver was probably en route to Barton, where he would alert the staff there what had happened. We needed to get to the safe house, and fast. I passed Kamal but kept going, my gaze trained on the houses that grew bigger as I came closer and forced myself to slow to a light jog. Only then did I look behind me again.

The moon was high. It cast a silvery light over Kamal, turning the white of his socks and sneakers almost fluorescent, like a glow-in-the-dark beacon. I waited at the end of a dark row of houses, no street lamps or lights from the houses to cut through the darkness. It was clear that no one had been in the Barton Flats for ages. The road was being reclaimed by the earth, weeds rising up through the cracks and splitting the asphalt into puzzle pieces.

"Whew," Kamal said, coming to a stop beside me. He bent forward and rested his hands on his knees, taking big breaths that shook his entire back. "You really are some runner."

I was too wound up to be flattered. "Do you think the driver has contacted Barton already?"

"Hard to say," Kamal said between breaths. "But I don't want to wait around here to find out."

"Do you think Abbot got out okay?"

Kamal straightened up, stretching his arms over his head and rolling his neck from side to side. "Only one way to find out. Which one of these houses is number four?"

"Second house on the right," I said.

"And straight on till morning!" Kamal crowed. I looked blankly at him. "What? It's from *Peter Pan*! I'm not just unbelievably handsome and a sick athlete, I've got brains too. I'm the full package."

Kamal had clearly recovered from his exhaustion.

"Let's go," I said.

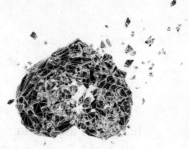

CHAPTER
SEVENTEEN

The houses in the Barton Flats were all one-storey buildings. They looked like something from a fairy tale, built out of the white pebbles from *Hansel and Gretel*. Some had tattered flags with dirty stripes and fraying stars hanging from leaning flagpoles. It felt like stepping back in time. Number four had an old lawn chair with a sagging seat of woven plastic left out to rust on the front lawn.

"Man this place is depressing," Kamal said. "It's worse than east Darby."

"I live in east Darby," I said stiffly.

"Not anymore," Kamal pointed out.

"I can still be offended."

"Should we wait inside?" Kamal asked.

"Maybe we should just wait here," I suggested, parking myself on the lawn of number four. The idea of going into that darkened house gave me the creeps.

"C'mon, where's your sense of adventure?"

"We just broke out of Barton and are about to join a super-secret group. That's enough adventure for me right now, thanks."

Kamal sat down beside me. "Fine. I don't want to leave you alone in case something happens."

For the first few minutes, Kamal and I sat side by side in silence. It was painfully obvious that we didn't have anything to say to each other. I had so much to think about that I was happy to be alone with my thoughts, but Kamal was the kind of person who couldn't deal with silences.

"So what do you know about Winfree?"

"Nothing, really." I admitted. "Only what Abbot told us at disorientation."

Kamal snorted. "I can't believe a little guy like that is involved in something as massive as Winfree."

"What do you know about it, then?"

"My uncle gets these magazines called *The Canary* that he passes on to me. They look like comic books and are full of crazy theories about the winnowing, human experiments during the war, all sorts of wacked-out stuff. Most people don't take it seriously but that's part of the genius. They only look ridiculous, when really *The Canary* is how the truth is spread."

"And you believe it enough to leave home?"

Kamal's confidence slipped. "That part hasn't set in yet. Maybe the revolution or whatever this is won't take very long and we'll be returning home heroes before year seven begins. So why are you here?" Kamal asked.

"Saren," I said. "And my grandfather. He used to work at Barton."

"Doing what?"

"I don't know. He never mentioned it. I didn't know anything about it until Dr. Abrams asked me during my intake exam."

"Abrams did your intake exam?" Kamal whistled. "That's crazy."

"Why?"

"That's low-level type stuff. Abrams is the boss-man. Most Intakes never even see him. He barely makes public appearances anymore. You know, there was a rumour that he was dead and they made a clone Abrams to replace him."

I laughed out loud. "A clone? That's ridiculous."

Kamal shook his head. "Go ahead and laugh. Stranger things have happened. Look at the Roddenberry murder. That turned out to be true, right? Your friend Abbot believes it. You must believe it enough to run away to join a group you've never heard of."

"A cover-up is one thing, but clones?"

"Clone or not, Abrams decided to descend from his throne to give you your intake exam. There must be something about you."

"Or my grandfather."

We fell silent, me thinking about Gumps, Kamal thinking about who knows what. It was a less awkward silence, but I couldn't help wishing I was sitting there with anyone else but him.

Suddenly, the sound of a screen door slapping closed echoed across the still night.

Kamal stood up. "Did you hear that?"

"Yes," I breathed, not daring to make more noise than absolutely necessary.

"Termite said this place was abandoned."

"Maybe it was the wind?"

Kamal didn't look convinced. "What wind? Come on, I'm going in."

"Abbot never said anything about going inside the house."

"He also said this place was abandoned. Do you want to wait around out here and find out if he was right?"

*

Even in the dark I could tell the house was not well made. It felt thrown together, like a shed-in-a-box from the hardware store, the kind you could assemble in a single afternoon. The furniture was flimsy and purely functional, no interesting patterns or cushions or embellishments at all.

Three pairs of women's shoes, old-fashioned with a low heel, and one pair of men's lace-up shoes sat on a mat just inside the doorway. An old-timey hat, the kind gangsters wear in black-and-white movies, hung from a peg on the wall.

"Who do you think lived here?" Kamal asked.

I pointed at the shoes. "At least one man and a woman," I said. "A long time ago."

Kamal and I wandered down the hall and peered into rooms. My senses were on high alert, waiting for another door to slam somewhere out there in the darkness. There were signs of the people who had lived there everywhere. A rumpled bedsheet, a book cracked open and left face down on a nightstand, a wastepaper basket with the mummified remains of what might have been tissues. A pantry full of canned milk and canned corn. In the kitchen, two place settings stood abandoned — two plates, two forks, two knives, two glasses painted with yellow flowers — a ghost of someone's breakfast. The dust was thick and the air felt stale; no one had been here in years.

"Creepy," Kamal said. "They must have left in a hurry. Why else would you leave your table set up like that?"

"I don't know," I admitted. "Don't you have one of your theories about this place?"

I was joking, but Kamal took the question seriously. "Not really. There are lots of rumours about Barton itself, back when it was a military base — that they were testing classified weapons like bombs and chemical warfare. I just figured that when Barton was shut down people moved out, but this is weird. It's like people got up and left in the middle of breakfast."

I peered out the window, careful not to get too close, wondering if perhaps someone was still living in the Flats, and if they knew we were here. Maybe they were watching us now. I backed away from the window and noticed a note had been left on the counter. The penmanship was spiky and old-fashioned.

"Listen to this." I read aloud: "'Dear Geoffrey, Tried to reach you at the base but in all the evacuation madness I could not get through. I wanted to wait for you but the Colonel said there wasn't time. Going to my mother's, please call me there. Love, Carol.'"

Kamal whistled softly. "Whoa. What's the date?"

"July 18, 1947."

"Sounds like Carol left in a hurry."

"I guess that explains why the table was set," I said.

"I told you, chemical warfare. Or maybe a radiation leak."

"You don't know that for sure."

"No, but why else would they evacuate immediately? I'm telling you, during the war, everyone was doing this stuff, not just us. The Germans, the Russians, the Japanese, the Brits . . . They were all looking for the perfect lethal cocktail. You can't mess around with major chemical weapons without the odd accident. Where do you think the Infertility Crisis came from? Crazy military scientists who were trying to make the weapon to end all weapons. And the hilarious part is it worked, just not the way they planned. What's the best way to wipe a species out? Make sure they can't have babies."

I knew all this. I had heard it before. Some people believed the Infertility Crisis was God punishing us for the war. Others, like Kamal, thought it was humans playing around with science who had contaminated the Earth and everything that lived on it. Either way, the cause was the same. War had led to the Infertility Crisis. We created our own demise. Until Roddenberry and the rest of the Barton Five saved the day.

"But they must have cleared it up, the leak or whatever, otherwise Roddenberry wouldn't have moved in."

Kamal shrugged. "Maybe. But who knows how long certain toxins can stay in the ground, or the water. People are different now. Adolescence is different. Our grandparents never had to be winnowed."

"I don't want to talk about this anymore." I walked quickly out of the kitchen and went to wait for Abbot in the front room. It was less stuffy and everything was touched with the cool blue light of the moon streaming in through the front window. It was calming. My knees felt wobbly again, as if they were islands floating in the middle of my legs. Dust motes puffed out as I sat down in a lumpy chair. I wondered if poisonous chemicals could live in a chair, and for how long.

A newspaper was folded on the coffee table. It was bigger than the newspaper that arrived on our front stoop every morning, and the paper, though old and brittle, was better quality. I opened it up carefully, feeling like I was touching something I shouldn't be, as if the house was a museum and the newspaper should be behind glass.

The paper was dated July 18, 1947, the same day as the note. The front page had a story about war tribunals over in Europe, but the story that caught my attention was about an unusual electrical storm: *Electrical Storm Causes Power Outage, Panic.*

Kamal interrupted my reading. "There's a car coming," he said.

I stilled my breath and listened for it. I heard nothing. "How do you know?"

Kamal tapped his ear. "I've got a sick pair of bog ears," he said. "Most stuff is just noise but I can recognize the sweet, sweet sound of a car in my sleep."

"How far away is it?" I asked.

"Maybe five minutes?"

"It must be the pickup. Where's Abbot? He should be here by now." I wasn't sure how much time had passed, but even someone who didn't have the benefit of impaired speed should have made it to the house by now.

"What do we do if he doesn't show?" Kamal asked.

"He'll show; he's just delayed. He comes and goes from Barton all the time." At least that's what he'd told me. I wondered how many times he had snuck in, and what the odds were of him getting caught. What if tonight was the night he got caught?

"But what if he doesn't show? Do we just get in the car with a complete stranger?"

"I don't know," I admitted.

We crouched by the bay window in the front room, which gave us a decent view of the dirt road and Barton off in the distance. Barton was all lit up. It seemed like too much light for the middle of the night. Had someone discovered Kamal and I were missing? Were they going room to room, looking for us? Had the delivery man already been in contact with them? I hoped Abbot had escaped and was on his way now.

A few minutes later, just as Kamal predicted, a shadowy car turned off the old service road. The lights were off and the car appeared to be in neutral, rolling slowly and soundlessly to a stop in front of number four.

Kamal and I both stood and waited. Eventually, a man unfolded himself from the front seat. I couldn't see his face very well, but he had eerily pale skin that appeared to shine in the moonlight. Even from a distance, I noted that he was unusually tall with spidery limbs. He leaned against the hood of the car and whistled. It was the same tune, only a few bars, whistled over and over again.

"Maybe it's a signal," Kamal whispered. He crept to the front door, cracked it an inch and, before I could tell him to stop, whistled the same tune back. Outside the man went very still then cocked his head to the side like a bird.

After a moment he called out, "You're not Abbot." His voice was startling in the silence. It wasn't loud, but it was deep and world-weary, even though from this distance he didn't look much older than twenty-five.

Kamal pushed the door open but didn't move out of the doorway. "We got separated," he said. The night was so still he didn't need to raise his voice to be heard. The man did not look bothered by this information.

"I see. Are you coming with me?"

Kamal looked at me. "Well?" he said. "Isn't this what we're supposed to do?"

"But Abbot!" I protested. "We can't leave without him."

"He breaks in and out of there all the time, you said so yourself. We can't stay here."

I was torn. I had no desire to stay in the creepy house, on that creepy street, but Abbot was the only connection I had to Winfree. Part of me yearned to sit tight and wait for him. But what if he never came? What if he found another way to get to the safe house and I waited here until someone came back for me or I starved to death? I knew nothing about this man in the car, except that Abbot had trusted him. That would have to do for now.

"All right."

Kamal and I walked over to the car. The man looked over at us but didn't get up to shake hands or anything. It was just a glance, but in that moment the whites of his eyes caught the light. They were cloudy and highly reflective. It stopped me in my tracks. What did I really know about Abbot or this man?

Kamal cleared his throat and introduced himself, holding out his hand to shake.

The man looked down at Kamal's outstretched hand through a mess of hair, amused. "Ren," he said. He was so skinny it looked painful; I couldn't imagine him folding those long legs into the car. Up close there was no doubt about it — his eyes had that same glassy, shimmering look that Tavi's eyes had. I knew it was rude to stare, but I couldn't look anywhere else. What did it mean?

"This is Marivic."

Ren offered me his hand to shake, but I keep mine at my side. I wasn't sold on him yet. *Welcome, little sister.*

The thought appeared suddenly in my head, drowning out any other thoughts, like brain freeze. It was just like before, during the assessments, when the directions "go left" had popped into my head out of nowhere. I stepped back, pressing my hands to my ears. Ren's expression hadn't changed, but he was looking at me instead of Kamal, his lip still curled up in that slightly amused way.

Cool trick, huh?

"How are you doing that?"

"Stone, what is wrong with you?" Kamal said. To Ren, he added, "She's wound a bit tightly, don't take offence."

Ren chuckled. He turned and opened the car door. "All right, let's go."

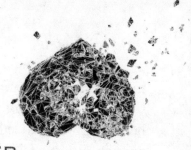

CHAPTER
EIGHTEEN

I sat in the front seat, hands in my lap, staring straight ahead as we pulled out of the Barton Flats. I resisted the urge to look behind me as we drove away, just to make sure we were actually leaving. Instead I stole little peeks at Ren. He looked like he was barely driving, one arm dangling out the window, the other resting lightly on the steering wheel.

In my head I heard Gumps saying "two o'clock and ten o'clock, at all times." I swallowed the lump that formed in my throat. I might never see him again. It was hard to imagine what *never* meant. I hoped I had done the right thing. I needed to know more about his past, about Barton, about why he lied.

People lie for all sorts of reasons.

Ren's thoughts made me jump, even though he hadn't physically touched me. I banged my elbow on the armrest and the throbbing just made it even more clear that I wasn't imagining things. I was hearing his voice in my head. I had the pain to prove it.

Sorry about that. The feeling takes some getting used to.

I wanted to respond but I didn't know how. Behind me, Kamal was staring out the window, silent for once. One thing I knew for sure: if I opened my mouth he'd be in my business and I didn't want him involved. Just because we were fellow escapees didn't make us friends. You had to earn that. In my heart I was all mixed up, mad and sad and confused.

I hear you loud and clear, little sister. Don't try so hard. Try to turn off your brain, or at least shut a few things down. Focus on your breathing; sometimes that helps.

I thought about running and slipping into the current.

That's it exactly.

Inhale for four, exhale for four. It felt good to do something familiar. I was still alert, but less tense. On my next inhale, I thought a question just for Ren: *How come I can hear you?*

We're both telepaths.

You mean mind readers?

Sort of. The Barton folks would say it was one of your imps.

But it's not on the list.

Ren laughed, but it wasn't like any other laugh I'd known. I could feel it. My head was light, as if someone stuck a straw in my brain and was blowing bubbles. My chest tingled, like the feeling that comes after a laugh. It was strange and exhilarating all at once.

No, it's definitely not on the list. Wouldn't want people to freak out, now would we?

I thought I was just a good runner.

We all have the same basic abilities, only some are more pronounced. You'll find you develop more as you get older.

Like bog ears?

Maybe.

"What kind of car is this anyway?" Kamal asked. I was annoyed, even though he had no way of knowing he had interrupted a conversation between Ren and me.

"A getaway car," Ren answered. It was jarring to hear him talk aloud. His voice felt different in my head, more gentle.

Kamal sniffed, disappointed. "I was expecting something a bit more . . . flashy, you know?"

"We don't want to draw attention to ourselves."

"Mission accomplished," Kamal said with a laugh. "Nobody's going to look twice at this junk bucket."

Can you read Kamal's mind?

No, he's not like you and me. Telepaths can only communicate like this with other telepaths. Give him time; he may develop the skill. You gotta have an open mind. Right now, he's closed tight.

How many others do you know?

Outwardly, Ren smiled. His face was put together in such an odd way that his smile didn't seem to get bigger, only more crooked. *Only you.*

I gasped, aloud. The sound caught Kamal's attention. "You okay up there, Stone? You're unusually quiet. You haven't insulted me in at least fifteen minutes."

Ren's smile got even more crooked.

I cleared my throat and reached for a lie. "Yes, I fell asleep for a minute and startled myself."

"How long is this going to take? Where exactly are we going, anyway?" Kamal asked.

"Not far," Ren said aloud. I was fascinated by his voice, drawn out like a cowboy's in an old western, but gravelly too. It was nothing like his thoughts in my head. They didn't have a sound, but more a sensation.

How did you know I would be able to hear you if there are no others?

I waited for Ren to explain but he didn't. It felt strangely empty in my head without him there.

Isn't it lonely?

Nah. Mostly I feel useless. What good is an ability if you can't use it?

Something didn't feel right. The thought felt light and hard to grasp. It was a bit sour, like a wrong note in a chord. He's lying, I thought. Then I worried that he had heard my thoughts. How much could he read? Would he always be there? How did I tune him out?

I'll teach you, little sister, don't worry. The main thing is, you have to be open.

How do I know if I'm open? I wasn't trying before.

That was different. You were in full-on panic mode. Panic leaves you wide open for anyone to poke around in there.

But you just said it was only you and me. Who else would be in there?

You're curious. Curious is good. You're going to fit right in.

Kamal thrust his head forward between the seats. "Hey. Is there any music? Or is that against the rules too?"

Ren smiled. "Great idea, little brother," he said, then he fiddled around under the dashboard until his long fingers closed around a cassette tape. He popped it into the deck and tinny music filtered through the speakers. Everyone in the car seemed to relax. The music was a distraction, something to think about other than where we were going, or what we had just done.

I listened hard to the lyrics, trying to anticipate the next line. I was tired of talking. I worried that Ren would sense it and be offended, but I felt alone again and I knew he was no longer in my head.

*

There was a stripe of light blue along the horizon, like lace edging on a dark curtain, when Ren finally pulled off the highway. A diner straight out of another era — one with roller skates and poodle skirts — squatted behind a gas pump. It was a low building with the words GAS COFFEE EGGS blinking in red lights by the door. It was too dusky to see much else.

"C'mon, weary travellers, we're home." Ren unfolded himself from the front seat, and again I was surprised by his height. It was like watching an optical illusion unfurl right before my eyes. "Welcome to the Starlight Diner."

"Wait, what? I thought you needed gas or maybe a bathroom break," Kamal said, frowning at the deserted restaurant.

"Three birds, one stone," Ren said, and he turned and ambled into the diner, hands balled in the pockets of his jeans.

"He's kind of a weird dude," Kamal said when Ren was out of earshot.

I shrugged. "What choice do we have?"

Inside, the Starlight Diner was divided into two parts, a sit-down restaurant on one side and a small convenience store on the other, stocked with on-the-road kind of items. A Slushee machine slowly churned toxically green lime-flavoured ice, and a grab-and-go counter with doughnuts and oily muffins glistened under a yellow lamp. There didn't appear to be anybody sitting behind the counter, but a giant bell had been left out. I guess to summon a cashier if anyone came in looking to buy something.

Ren walked into the diner and sat down on a stool by the counter. He had to twist his knees to one side because his legs were too long to fit underneath the counter.

There was a TV mounted above, playing an early morning show. Laughter floated out of the tinny speakers and into the diner. It was a pleasant, homey sound. After four days at Barton, I had forgotten how comforting the sound of TV could be. Kamal and I stood awkwardly in the empty diner, not sure where to sit.

"So what is this place?" Kamal said.

"Home," Ren answered, eyes glued to the TV.

"You live here?"

"There are rooms upstairs and out back. It used to be a motel. Technically it still is; we just don't rent the rooms out anymore." Ren pointed to a sign in the window that said NO VACANCY. "This is Daisy's place. She runs the kitchen and I deal with the gas station."

Before I could ask anything else, a woman in a greasy full-length apron came through the kitchen doors. Her hair was yellowish grey and smushed underneath a hairnet.

Ren nodded at her. "Morning, Daisy. This is Kamal and Marivic. Friends of Abbot's."

Daisy wiped her hands on her apron and came at us

with her arms open, looking for a hug. "Nice to meet you both," she said, pulling us forcefully into her bosom. She smelled like hot butter and cinnamon.

She released us and stood back to get a good look at us. "Now what have you done with my son?"

My jaw dropped. "Abbot's your *son*?" Daisy looked like she was well into her sixties. Wasn't Abbot a bit young to be her son?

"Adopted. But it makes no difference to the heart," Daisy said.

I opened my mouth to apologize, but the words were swallowed by a lion-sized yawn. I had so many questions but I was beginning to droop. Even my stomach was too tired to growl.

"I can see you're done talking for the night. Gosh, it's basically morning. Let's find you a bed. We can talk all you like after you get some rest."

I followed Daisy through the swinging doors into a kitchen, every surface covered in pots and pans. Daisy turned to her right and climbed up a rickety, narrow staircase. I couldn't hear Kamal or Ren behind me and I was too tired to care if they had come along or not.

Daisy whispered as we walked, "Take the room at the end of the hall. It's nothing special, but it is clean."

"You knew I was coming?"

"The Starlight Diner is always ready to welcome weary travellers."

A flimsy curtain fluttered in the window, about as useful as a hole in a bucket. Blue morning light, the sounds of cars belching down the highway and the stink of gas and rubber tires poured into the room. Half a bunk bed was wedged against the wall, four wooden pegs sticking straight out of each bedpost, as if the top half had been ripped off by a twister just moments before.

"Mind the ceiling. That angle doesn't look so bad now, but plenty of people have whacked themselves good in the morning."

Daisy pulled back a flowered sheet and patted the pillow. I managed to mutter a thank you before sinking onto the bed. I lost the battle against my heavy eyelids and I heard her murmuring and felt her tugging my shoes off my feet. Then she swung my legs into the bed and settled the sheet around my shoulders.

"You sleep tight, cupcake."

THE STARLIGHT DINER, ROUTE 66

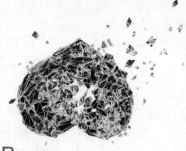

CHAPTER
NINETEEN

Smoke was curling under the door. It was thick and heavy, blacker than I had ever seen, as if it was full of grit. I was on my back, on a cold floor, a bay of sinks behind me and a row of toilet stalls in front of me.

I propped myself up on my hands and yelped in pain. My palms were rubbed raw. Gritting my teeth, I shuffled away from the billowing smoke toward the window, new tears springing up every time my skinned palms made contact with the floor. I got to my knees and shakily stood up, my head swirling.

I put my forehead and both hands on the wall. I couldn't stand otherwise. I took a few shallow breaths, trying to take in only clean air, but it was getting harder and harder to find pockets of it in the room. The window was at least a foot above me. When I raised my hands, my fingertips grasped the ledge.

Suddenly there was a break in the smoke and a person stumbled through it — a woman, with a scarf held over her mouth and nose, her other arm in front of her, cutting *a path for herself in the smoke. She lowered the scarf from her face to call out and I recognized her.*

It was my mother. Her face was streaked with soot and her hair was wild, but it was her. She had come to rescue me! I wanted to speak, but I couldn't get my mouth to work. She was patting me down, looking for injuries. Her mouth was moving, but I couldn't hear anything over the roar of the fire. Then, a voice started somewhere deep in my head: Come back, come back, come back.

It was slow and calm, the opposite of an alarm. I blinked through the sweat and tears in my eyes. Was it my mother who was speaking? She looked so panicked and the voice was so calm. I focused on it instead of my smarting palms or the sweat that ran down from my hairline and into my eyes. Stinging, everything was stinging.

Come back, come back, come back.

*

When I opened my eyes, the panic of the burning room was gone, but the voice was still there, murmuring those same words in my head: *Come back, come back, come back.*

I blinked, taking in the shabby angled ceiling, the window with its wimpy excuse for a curtain and the exposed pegs of the bunk bed. I wasn't home. I wasn't at Barton. I was at the Starlight Diner.

And someone was holding my hand. It took me a second to realize that I knew him. It was Ren, speaking directly into my head again. He smiled kindly at me as I put two and two together. I noticed bruise-coloured smudges underneath his eyes.

The next time he spoke it was aloud. "There you are. Welcome back, little sister."

"It was your voice, in my nightmare," I said.

Ren was in an old undershirt and a pair of striped pyjama bottoms, the kind Gumps wore. The old man pyjamas suited Ren. It was hard to say exactly how old he was, even in the full light of day. His skin was hairless, so smooth it looked polished, but his face was all planes and hollows.

"How did you know? Was I screaming? Did I wake you?"

"You didn't make a peep. At least not out loud."

"So you could sense my nightmare telepathically?"

Ren considered this explanation with a solemn face. "You could say that. Do you feel like talking about it? It might help."

"There was a fire. And I think . . . I mean, I *know* . . . my mother was there."

He nodded, encouraging me to go on, and I realized that it wouldn't sound so strange to him, a mother showing up to rescue a child. It was a typical mom thing to do. He didn't know I didn't remember her, that I had no idea how she moved or what her voice sounded like, that she was nothing but a collage I had created, made of someone else's memories and old photos.

The photo! I reached into my back pocket and retrieved it, a little wrinkled, but still in one piece. Looking at it now I was sure it had been her in the dream. I handed it to Ren.

"This is her. Victoria Stone. I never knew her; she died when I was little. But the woman in my dream looked like her and — I just *knew*. What do you think it means?

Is it normal, to have an — episode — like that?"

Ren considered the photo, his brow furrowed and his strange, silvery eyes dark and troubled. After a moment of contemplation he set it on the nightstand.

"You should ask Dr. Lowry that question. You're awake now. Why don't you come on down for some sticky buns? Daisy is dying to fatten you up. She believes there is nothing a little butter and sugar won't fix. I happen to agree with her." Bit by bit, Ren curled up out of the chair. I fully expected his bones to creak as he straightened up.

"You're so tall," I said. "I've never seen a person as tall as you."

"You been outside of Darby much?" Ren teased.

"No," I admitted, feeling dumb as a rock. Maybe there were tons of tall people in the world and I just didn't know it.

It takes all kinds.

I started as Ren's words slipped into my mind. He winked at me and turned to leave the room. "I'll catch you later, little sister," he said, and then he was gone.

*

Daisy was in the kitchen, humming. I hung back on the stairs until she waltzed over to the fridge to get more eggs. When she looked up, she smiled broadly.

"Well here she is now! Good morning, cupcake! Or should I say good evening? You slept all day, you poor thing. It's practically dinnertime! Are you hungry?"

"Yes."

"Good. I've got a batch of sticky buns browning in the

oven as we speak. In the meantime, go stand over there. I've got a job for you."

Daisy pointed me in the direction of an island dusted in flour. She handed me a big white apron with a scalloped edge. I looped it over my neck and tied it tightly round my waist. Next, she set a blue-and-white mixing bowl in front of me. I blinked at it, remembering the last time I had spent any time in the kitchen.

In February I'd decided to make Gumps a cake for his birthday, just like Grandma used to do when she was alive. I took the yellowed card with the recipe for red velvet cake, written in Grandma's careful handwriting, out of the flowered recipe tin, called up Saren for moral support and together we attempted our first cake. We had a lot of fun and made a huge mess, but I mixed up baking soda with baking powder, therefore rendering our cake inedible. Gumps had eaten a whole piece anyway, just to make me and Saren laugh.

There, in the unfamiliar kitchen of the Starlight Diner, I missed Saren so much I could taste it, as bitter as our failed cake. We would never make another cake together. I would never see her again. Never is such a cruel word. I gripped the edge of the island and tried to breathe through the ache in my chest.

Daisy must have noticed something was up, because she put a hand on my shoulder and asked gently, "Have you made sticky buns before, Marivic?"

I took a shaky breath and managed to reply in a somewhat regular voice. "No, ma'am, never."

"I give you two hours and you'll be able to put me out of business," she teased. "I'll roll them out and you wind them into spirals, like so. Got it?" I watched carefully as she took handfuls of dough from the mixing bowl and rolled them into big fat snakes. Next she wound each snake into a tight coil, then set them in a deep glass baking dish. "Mind they don't touch when you put them in, or it'll be murder to separate them once they've fluffed up in the oven."

I set to work, rolling sticky buns and setting them in the dish. Once the first dish was full, Daisy replaced it with a new one.

"How many are we making?" I asked.

"A couple dozen. These are my specialty. Many a weary traveller stops by the Starlight looking for one of Daisy's sticky buns. Can't very well disappoint them, now can we?"

I liked working with Daisy. She was a musical baker, sometimes humming, sometimes whistling, sometimes breaking out into a full song with words, ringing a spoon against a mixing bowl for emphasis. It was soothing to be surrounded by the smell of raisin-studded sticky buns toasting in the oven. It felt good to be busy, to have something to focus on other than missing Saren. Plus, I felt safe with Daisy, like I could ask her anything.

"What is this place? Is it part of Winfree?"

"Yes and no. The Starlight Diner is an old motel and restaurant my husband and I bought years ago when we were looking to get out of St. Louis. He passed on two years ago and now Ren helps me run the place. We get Winfree types passing through from time to time. With Bitsy here, it's become a base of sorts."

"Bitsy?" I asked.

"Ah, that's what we call my big sister, Dr. Lowry. You'll meet her shortly."

"I was imagining some sort of rebel camp in the woods," I admitted. "You know, tents, campfires, no running water . . ."

Daisy laughed. "No sirree, the only time we get close to roughing it out here is when Ren tries to make eggs. You can't find a tire as rubbery as his omelettes."

"Are you part of Winfree?" I asked.

"I suppose I am, though I don't do much but feed and shelter people."

"How did you get involved?"

"It was all Bitsy's doing. She came running to me and my husband after that bad business over at the Darby school. Poor thing was absolutely shell-shocked, could barely string two words together, babbling about purges and SuperGen. It was frightening. My famous big sister, big-time scientist, reduced to a few words, covered in soot, with a strange kid in tow."

"What kid?"

"Ren, of course."

I stopped rolling snakes to stare at Daisy. "Ren is Dr. Lowry's son?"

"Not by blood, but in every other way, yes. She pulled him out of what was left of that school and the two of them took off for New York City, never once looking back."

The muscles around my heart tightened. I couldn't believe what I was hearing. "What bad business? Do you mean the Darby Fire? That's impossible. There were no survivors."

Daisy clucked her tongue. "Well, that's the official story. The real one, as it so often is, is quite different. After the fire, New York City was the best place for Bitsy and Ren to hide: plenty big, plus they had a fertility test centre so no one would look twice at a kid in the streets. As far as anyone in Darby knew, everyone died in that fire, including Ren. Bitsy was worried if they ever found out he was still alive, they'd hunt him down."

"But why?"

"Because he was supposed to be dead. All those poor children were. Not only was he supposed to be dead, but Bitsy left him alone. She didn't tamper with his natural abilities or drug him up, like some of those other Barton children. I suppose officially you would say he was 'unwinnowed.'"

I felt like I was two steps behind. "Unwinnowed?" I repeated. "Ren is totally and completely unwinnowed?"

"We figure he might be the only one of his kind alive. Except for you and that young fella snoring away upstairs."

"Kamal," I said, but I was thinking about Ren. If what Daisy said was true and Ren was unwinnowed, then he must have been the person Abbot was talking about when he said it was possible to live as an unwinnowed person. Ren was that person. He was the proof.

"But why did they have to hide in the city? Why was he supposed to be dead?"

Daisy bristled. "That fire was no accident. The folks up at Barton thought something had gone wrong with the children. There was talk of wiping the slate clean. They fought long and hard about it, but eventually fear won out." Daisy clucked her tongue. "It pains me to say that fear usually does."

"The fire at Darby Public School was set on purpose?"

Daisy nodded, suddenly solemn. It was unsettling to see her so drawn. "They called it the Purge."

Despite the heat and the smell of sticky buns sizzling in the oven, I shivered.

"Bitsy was having none of it. She went to the school to warn the staff, but she was too late. Lucky for Ren she came when she did. He was half-dead, thrown out of the school by the blast and caught in a pile of debris."

"Why didn't she go to the police?"

Daisy shook her head. "What goes on at Barton is bigger than the police. Besides, there was Ren to worry about. No one could know he was alive."

A row of dough snakes lay in front of me, waiting to be coiled into sticky buns, but I couldn't bring myself to continue. Even my hands were in a state of shock. The Darby Fire had been set on purpose. An entire school of children and my mother had been killed. Except for Ren. I couldn't wrap my head around it. The situation was too big.

Suddenly Daisy was standing in front of me, both hands resting on my shoulders. "It's hard to take in, I know. It's difficult to fathom so much evil in the world. But I promise you're with the good guys. We're going to make it right. And now we have you on our side and we're tickled pink."

Daisy steered me toward the stairs, a plate of sticky buns in my hands. "Now. These are fresh from the oven. You go take a break and enjoy it. Think of it like a sort of breakfast in bed. Maybe offer one or two to that friend of yours up there."

Without thinking, I said, "He's not my friend," then felt a little guilty about it. Daisy was so nice. It made me feel extra mean.

"Well, your colleague then." Daisy smiled. "Look, cupcake, it's better the two of you stay out of sight for a while."

"You think the police are looking for us?"

Daisy hesitated. "Not the police."

"Barton, then."

She nodded, looking grim. The expression didn't suit her; hers was a face meant for smiling and singing. It reminded me how totally, completely crazy running away from Barton had been. "It's possible. I think it's just as likely they told your people you died from complications during the winnowing."

Even though I knew that me not coming home would be devastating for Gumps, somehow the idea of him picking up the phone and receiving the news that I had died felt worse. He would sit at his chair in the kitchen, staring at the floor for a long time. He would get lost in his thoughts and forget to eat. I knew this because it's exactly what he had done when Grandma died. Only I had been there to remind him about things like food and showering and funeral arrangements. Other people tried to get to him, but I was the only one who succeeded.

"Now you go on upstairs and enjoy those sticky buns. Food always tastes better if you've made it yourself."

*

I watched from my window as the odd person came and went from the Starlight Diner. It wasn't exactly hopping out here in the middle of the desert. It was the perfect place for a secret headquarters. I imagined the travellers ordering hungry man breakfasts even though it was well into the evening, pots of coffee and one of Daisy's sticky buns. Gumps would love this place. It hurt to realize I could never show it to him. That I would never again sit across the table from him and share a meal.

I blinked back tears and turned my thoughts to Abbot

and what had happened to him. Daisy hadn't been concerned, which in turn helped me to relax. Maybe he had decided to hide out in the vents until things calmed down and he could make his escape. Already my time at Barton felt like it was years ago. The efficient staff in their lab coats and the tests and the silver trays of food felt like they had happened in a dream. It wasn't as real as the worn wooden spoons in the kitchen or the fluffy sticky buns I was using to mop up as much gooey cinnamon topping as I could from my plate.

"Did you save one of those for me?" Kamal was leaning against the door frame, bleary eyed but otherwise upbeat. There were two sticky buns left. Reluctantly, I pushed the plate forward.

"You can have the rest."

Kamal came into the room and dragged the delicate scalloped chair away from the matching vanity, pulling it up to the bed where I was sitting cross-legged. He looked ridiculous on the chair, like a giant in a doll's house. I wondered briefly who had stayed in this room before me and what she had needed a vanity for all the way out here in the middle of the desert.

Kamal ate noisily, crumbs sticking to his lips and syrup dribbling on my sheets.

"Careful! I have to sleep here!" I muttered, rubbing at the syrup before it could set into the sheet permanently.

"You made these, Stone?" he asked through a mouthful of sticky bun. "Impressive." He tore the last bun in two and pushed half of it into his mouth with his fingers. "So what are you doing up here? Are we under house arrest?"

"Sort of. Daisy thinks Barton might be looking for us. She told me to stay out of sight."

Kamal swallowed. I swear the whole thing went down his throat in a solid lump, like a rat in a boa constrictor. "They can't expect us to stay cooped up here all day long. We need to do something. This is the revolution!"

"What did you think we'd be doing, exactly?"

Kamal shrugged. "I don't know. Tapping phone lines, going undercover, setting car bombs as diversionary tactics."

I felt my eyebrows jump into my hairline. "Diversionary tactics?" I repeated.

"Yeah, you know. You set an explosion one place to attract the police when really you're on the opposite side of town, breaking into a totally different place. What did *you* think we'd be doing?"

"I don't know. I hadn't really thought about it." The truth was, running away to join Winfree had been a snap decision, a choice I made when I thought I had no other choices. In that mixed-up state of grief and anger I had decided to do what Saren would do, but the differences between us had never felt more vast. I left to avenge Saren but now that I was here I didn't know if I had what it took to do the actual avenging. How could a kid take on a group of people who had heartlessly burned down an entire school full of people? "I guess I thought they would teach us to control our imps."

Kamal jumped up and rubbed his hands together, sending a fine dust of crumbs to the floor. "Well, I can't sit here all night, and I bet those imped-up runner's legs of yours can't either. Let's go explore."

"What part of 'stay out of sight, Barton is looking for you' didn't you understand?"

"We won't go out into the diner. There's a whole

motel back there." Kamal thumbed over his shoulder. "Ren said it was vacant."

"If there's no one there, then what are we looking for?"

Kamal grinned. "If we knew what we were looking for, it wouldn't be any fun! Come on, if this is headquarters or even just a stopover for Winfree, they've got to have files or information or something holed up in those old rooms. Why waste a perfectly good rundown motel?"

He had a point, and my curiosity was good and stoked, but I felt bad about ignoring Daisy's instructions. "But Daisy—"

"Won't even know. We're part of Winfree now, so it's not like we're snooping. What Winfree knows, we know. Doesn't that seem fair to you?"

It did. Plus exploring motel rooms felt much more manageable than going undercover or setting off explosives.

"Fine. I'm coming. But only because I don't trust you not to mess something up."

Kamal grinned. "Nah, you're coming because you're a revolutionary now." He held out his fist for a fist-bump, but I brushed past him without offering my own knuckles, not wanting to give him the satisfaction. We weren't a team yet. We weren't even friends.

But I was smiling.

*

Ren never told us how long the motel part of the diner had been closed down, but judging by the thick blankets of dust and the sour smell rising out of the old couches, it was a very long time. We searched the left wing first, walking down a narrow hallway with orange carpet thin as felt, worn down by years of people trodding back and forth.

"Can you hear anyone nearby? You know, with your bog ears?" I asked, dreading the idea of barging in on a sleeping revolutionary.

Kamal shook his head. "It doesn't work like that. There's a lot of white noise, like having a bunch of things on in the background. I have no idea what most of it is. I tune it out, otherwise I'd go crazy."

So much for an early warning system. We would have to proceed carefully without the aid of Kamal's bog ears.

It was getting dark, but I insisted we keep the lights off in case Daisy happened to look out the back window and see us silhouetted in the windows.

"It's hard to explore in the dark," Kamal complained. "Why don't we just pull the curtains closed first?"

I rubbed the holey fabric between two fingers. "A lot of good that would do. These curtains are so moth eaten, they might as well be made of lace."

Kamal huffed. "Fine."

We were both frustrated. We'd poked around three rooms, looking under mattresses and running our fingers along the wall looking for disguised seams that would indicate hidden compartments (Kamal's idea, not mine). So far we'd found nothing but mouse poop and ten different kinds of dust. An hour had passed. I wondered if Daisy or Ren would come check on us, and what would happen if they found us gone. I thought about sending Ren a message telepathically but I wasn't sure I could do it without him there to talk me through it.

"Just a few more rooms and then we should go back," I said.

"Chickening out already?"

"What if they're looking for us?"

"Fine, let's finish this hallway. We can check the other one out tomorrow."

Maybe it was because we had decided to call it a day, but the next room was different from the others. It was bigger than the other rooms — like a luxury suite, if such a thing existed in a motel like this — and the bed had been removed and replaced with filing cabinets. Three desks had been pushed up against the wall, creating a long workspace covered in neat piles of paper.

Beside me I could feel Kamal smiling. "Now this is what I'm talking about."

A corkboard covered in yellowing newspaper articles had been propped up over the desks. I recognized one of the headlines: *Electrical Storm Causes Power Outage, Panic.*

"Hey, this is the same paper I found in the pickup location."

I couldn't reach the corkboard without standing on the table. I moved two piles of paper, shifting them to the floor, and took off my shoes before stepping up on the desk. I was careful as a cat on a fence, but the movement disturbed another pile and a few papers fluttered to the floor. I made note of where they were so I could put them back exactly as they had been.

I unpinned the article, which had been neatly snipped from the paper, and handed it to Kamal. He read it aloud.

A *number of residents reported unusual activity in the night sky around 11:30 p.m. on July 17. Judy Hamilton described a series of white flashes, like heat lightning.*

"*I thought the big one had been dropped and the end*

was in sight. I gathered up my kids and we hid out in the cellar, like you're told to during a raid. But then nothing happened so I figured it must have been lightning. I kept waiting for the thunder, but it never came," said the forty-seven-year-old mother of two.

Across town, Officer Tad Turner was on duty when he saw a flash of light out of the corner of his eye. "I didn't see the first one, but I looked in the general direction and sure enough there were two more pulses and then everything went quiet. I thought we were in for a boomer for sure. Then I got a whiff of that smell and I thought maybe something had exploded over at the base."

At the military base, there were reports of smoke and a burning smell. General Duke confirmed that the lightning did indeed touch down, but that there were no injuries to report. "We have one less fern bush on the base," he joked, suggesting that it was the shrub that the base residents smelled burning.

Meteorologists confirmed that there was a significant atmospheric disturbance recorded at 11:31 p.m. but did not offer any explanation for the isolated lightning strikes. Hydro also reported that there was a seven-minute power outage across the county and the base, from 11:25 to 11:31 p.m. Power surges are not uncommon during electrical weather activity.

When he finished, Kamal said, "What a load of crap. Lightning strikes? Electrical storm? Isn't it obvious?"

I blinked at him. "Isn't what obvious?"

"Unusual activity in the sky?" Kamal stared, waiting for me to clue in. When I didn't, he rolled his eyes. "It was a UFO."

"Like a spaceship? You're kidding."

"There are lots of UFO sightings all over the country. I read about them in *The Canary* all the time."

I rolled my eyes. "But nobody really believes in them."

"People see something they think is lightning on the night of the seventeenth. On the eighteenth everyone is evacuated. What if they were evacuated because a UFO crashed?"

"Fine. Let's say your theory is right." Kamal's eyebrows shot up. I rolled my eyes. "I didn't say it *was* right, but if it is, they evacuate the military base so they can clean up the crash and keep it top secret. Then what?"

"Then the base is shut down and reopened as a medical centre three years later with Roddenberry in charge, and a few years after that, babies are born again."

We stared at each other for a moment, letting the reality of the timeline and what that might mean sink in.

"Maybe the crash did something to the water," I said, thinking aloud. "Maybe it boosted fertility or something."

Kamal shook his head. "No, because people would have been drinking that water for years. There were no births until Roddenberry introduced the SuperGen shots."

"Which is what, exactly? Some kind of hormone?" We knew all about hormones. They were what made men and women different. Hormones were responsible for puberty. I tried to remember what it said in the Barton Guide about SuperGen, but nothing in the guide had been very specific.

A voice from the corner made us both jump.

"You've figured it out."

Kamal bumped the desk. It shook and I lost my footing, kicking another pile of papers to the ground. So much for keeping track of where things went. Luckily

I caught my balance and managed to turn a fall into a jump, landing on the floor beside Kamal, bringing yet another avalanche of papers with me. I couldn't have made a bigger mess if I tried.

A door leading to an adjoining room was open and an old woman was standing there, tall but hunched over. She had thick white hair pulled back from her face, and glasses resting on the top of her head. She had the same heart-shaped face as Daisy, but was much taller and not as soft around the middle.

"May I ask what you're doing in my office?" she asked, taking in the empty desks and the floor strewn with what I imagined was her hard work.

"Your office?" I repeated weakly.

Kamal moved forward, recognition brightening his face. "You're Dr. Lowry, one of the Barton Five," he said. "You're like, famous."

Dr. Lowry bowed her head, acknowledging the truth. But she didn't look pleased or especially flattered by the comment.

"So you must know everything that goes on at Barton. You can tell us the truth," Kamal said. "What is SuperGen?"

"SuperGen *is* used as a fertility drug, that much is true. But what we don't talk about, what we all swore not to discuss, is what that drug is made from."

"Which is?"

Dr. Lowry smiled, but it was a sad sort of smile. "Haven't you guessed? SuperGen is a hormone derived from alien DNA."

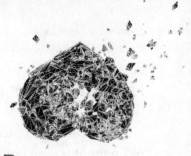

CHAPTER
TWENTY

I waited for the punchline, looking from Kamal to Dr. Lowry to Kamal again, expecting one of them to break into gales of laughter and tease me for being so gullible. It was the kind of joke Kamal would make. Only he didn't look smug or superior. He looked uneasy, like he couldn't believe what he was hearing either.

Because it couldn't be true. It was too unbelievable. SuperGen was made of alien DNA? But that would mean that *any* baby born with the aid of SuperGen would have alien DNA. It would mean that *I* had alien DNA. Everyone I knew — Kamal, Quin, Tavi, even Saren — we had little alien bits running in our veins and in our skin.

Dr. Lowry spoke first, calmly, quietly. "I know this must be shocking. Won't you come into my room? There is a couch you can sit on." Her concerned gaze fell on me. "Your friend looks quite faint."

I'm not his friend, I wanted to say, and I'm not going to faint, but I couldn't remember how to speak.

"I'm an alien?" Kamal said. I'd never seen him so sober. In any other situation I would have laughed at the look on his face, but I imagine my face looked exactly the same. Shocked. Scared. Skeptical.

"No." Dr. Lowry stepped farther into the room, determined that if we weren't going to come to her, she would come to us. "No, if anything you're a hybrid. Though I have never used that term. There's so little of their DNA in your system that that particular word doesn't seem accurate."

Kamal was full of questions, like me, only he was having no trouble getting his mouth to work. "A hybrid? How is that possible? How is that allowed?" he asked.

"Dr. Roddenberry's experiments were strictly off the record. He was part of the team that arrived after the UFO crashed on July seventeenth, a geneticist. He was there when they recovered the bodies and stayed on with a small, elite team to do further testing."

Finally, I found my voice. "The bodies?" I whispered.

"Alien bodies," Dr. Lowry confirmed, her voice gentle, like Daisy's. I was reminded that they were sisters. "There were three of them. They all died within seventy-two hours of crashing here."

The sticky buns I had consumed felt like cement in my stomach. Any lingering taste of cinnamon had turned to dust in my mouth. What she was saying was crazy. Unbelievable. Totally and utterly impossible. But why would she lie?

"So he used alien DNA to create SuperGen," Kamal said. He had started to pace across the room. "Wouldn't the government, like, freak out and shut the project down?"

Dr. Lowry remained calm, following Kamal's movements with her eyes. "When SuperGen worked, people were so thrilled they didn't stop to ask how he arrived at his discovery. There were certain individuals in our government who knew exactly what was going on but they agreed to keep it quiet. After all, babies were being born again. And now they had a drug they could patent and sell to the highest bidder."

"What do you mean, sell?" Kamal asked.

"The Infertility Crisis was a worldwide phenomenon. While there are more babies born now than there were twenty years ago, the United States is the only country that seems to have found a lasting, effective cure. Or if not a cure, an antidote."

"But if we have a cure, why don't we share it?"

"We do share it, with select allies who are willing to pay. England, for example, and Canada. As the populations of other countries die off, so do our enemies. Don't you see? The United States is one of a handful of countries in the world where babies are born. It is possible that in seventy-five years we will be the only country left in the world."

I thought of the map that was hanging across the back of my classroom in Darby. There were so many countries on that map, some of them with names I couldn't pronounce. They had jagged, irregular borders, like puzzle pieces that fit together to make the world. I realized that each of those puzzle pieces represented not just a country, but thousands and millions of people who lived there. How could all of those people just disappear? How could anyone let millions and millions of people cease to exist?

"That's evil," I said.

"That's war," Dr. Lowry said sadly. "In some people's minds, it is the best kind of war. No weapons have been used, no soldiers' lives have been put at risk. We will win simply by doing nothing."

Kamal had been silent for a long time. It might have been a record for him. I thought that he was just as horrified as I was about our government sitting back and watching the world's population dwindle, until he spoke up.

"Wait. Go back a second. You're telling me that our government knows that the children being born are part alien and they don't seem to think that's a big deal?"

"Very few people know the truth about SuperGen's origins."

"But someone must have wondered."

"Don't underestimate the power of a miracle. People were so thrilled that there was an end to the crisis that they didn't ask a lot of questions. When they did, Dr. Roddenberry told them it was a synthetic hormone, something created in the lab by experimenting and mutating existing hormones."

Kamal snorted. "You mean existing alien hormones."

Dr. Lowry did not flinch at Kamal's attitude. "Yes, that's a more accurate way to describe it. But the explanation made sense and it wasn't exactly a lie. It is a hormone that has been altered." Dr. Lowry looked rueful. "Just not a human one."

"How many people know?" I asked.

"Maybe a handful. Even at Barton today, very few doctors know SuperGen's true origins."

"So there are doctors injecting us with an alien drug and even they don't know it?"

"Yes. Originally Roddenberry injected SuperGen into healthy women of child-bearing age who wanted to conceive. But when Dr. Abrams became head of Barton, he introduced a mandatory childhood booster shot." Dr. Lowry frowned. "I'm still not sure why, exactly. Dr. Abrams kept his cards close to his chest."

"So the imps aren't side effects — they're normal?" Kamal asked.

"The imps are not impairments at all, but *abilities* you've inherited. We know next to nothing about the aliens or where they came from. But the imps have given us clues. Perhaps the weather is more volatile and so they developed a thicker skin to withstand greater temperatures. Maybe some people have a gift for running, because your ancestors ran from a predator."

I could barely grasp what I was hearing. "But why do we go ACES?" I asked.

"Why the SuperGen children 'go ACES,' as you say, is trickier to determine. I studied the sleep patterns of the SuperGen children, mapping their brain activity in various states of consciousness, for many years. But perhaps the most interesting part of my job was the least scientific." Dr. Lowry lowered her voice. "I began to collect accounts of the ACES."

I lowered my voice, just as Dr. Lowry had done. "And what did you find?"

"There are many different theories about the ACES and what they mean, but as far as I know, it's a mystery that has yet to be solved."

"But they're not even trying to, are they? Not at Barton. They just cut out all the bits that aren't useful." Kamal kicked at the papers on the floor.

"It's a lot to take in. I understand," Dr. Lowry said gently.

Kamal sneered. "Really? You understand? Are you part alien too?"

The room felt very close and very hot. My legs started to ping and more than anything I wanted to run.

"I need some air," I said.

"Of course," Dr. Lowry said, calm as ever. "You take as much time as you need."

*

I stumbled out of the stuffy room and hurried toward the exit sign at the end of the hall. At first the door stuck, but I threw all my weight against the metal bar and it gave way with a groan. I escaped into the cool desert air, finding myself in an unkempt courtyard walled on two sides by the wings of the motel. The grass had died and the only objects of note were a circle of old sun-bleached picnic tables and a green Dumpster with a cloud of bees humming over it.

Night was falling, dropping shadows over everything. Beyond the courtyard, desert stretched ahead of me as far as I could see. There was lots of room for running. Having never been a runner before, I never really believed it when people claimed that physical activity was a good way to clear your mind. That sounded like something athletes said to make the rest of us feel bad about our lack of athletic abilities. But now all I wanted to do was feel my heart, lungs and legs sync up to one rhythm that pounded all thoughts of aliens, Saren and Gumps out of my head.

With each step, I felt my heart rate increase and my

tension decrease. Soon I was breathing hard, the chord rippling through my body, urging me to fun faster, farther. Desert rolled out under my feet and I wondered how fast I was going, and how far I could run. Could I make it all the way back to Darby? Or Barton? What would happen if I just showed up now? I could pretend I had been sleepwalking, driven to run away during a particularly bad bout of the ACES. I had run into the desert before, at home. Would the Barton staff believe me?

If I went back now I might not remember any of this — Winfree, the Starlight Diner, the truth about SuperGen — after the winnowing. Not knowing would be so much easier. Mystery, intrigue, government cover-ups — those were the kind of things Saren always found interesting, not me.

Can you believe it, Saren? We're part alien — we're extraterrestrial! I tried to imagine Saren's half of the conversation. How would she react? Would she be scared? Disgusted? Elated? She wouldn't have run into the desert. She would take it all in stride. If she were here she'd say, *I always knew there was something extra-cool about us!*

I knew Saren would never consider going back. I was here in her stead. I would do what Saren would do. I slowed to a steady walk, then turned around to get my bearings. The Starlight Diner was a dark shape with flickering windows, doll-sized in the distance.

I couldn't run forever.

Resigned, I headed back to the diner at a slower pace, trying to think of the bigger picture. The universe seemed impossibly large. I'd never given much thought to aliens before. I didn't like space movies. I barely paid attention when we did a unit on astronomy last year. The only time I had ever given a second thought to things that happened beyond the Earth was when Saren became briefly obsessed with wishing on shooting stars and we spent a few weeks comet gazing. But according to Dr. Lowry, I was alive because of alien DNA. Did that make me less human?

Relax, little sister. Focus on your breathing and let everything else disappear.

I gasped aloud, stumbling as my smooth gait faltered, still not used to the sensation of Ren in my head. I did as he suggested, inhaling for four, exhaling for four. I thought only of those numbers, picturing them written in my head — one, two, three, four — and the sound of my own breath whistling in my nostrils.

That's better. You might think about coming back. Daisy will be worried.

The Starlight was closer now. I could make out shapes in the dusky twilight — the wings of the motel, the Dumpster and Ren, standing near the picnic tables.

I can't believe this is happening.

What, the fact that we're talking or the fact that we're part alien?

I don't feel part alien.

Of course not. You're you. You can't feel anything else. Knowing your origins doesn't change anything about you.

I came to a stop in front of Ren, holding on to the feeling of running and the chord in order to keep our connection.

What did you do when you found out?

I was fourteen. My nightmares were real bad. I was afraid to go to sleep. It's funny, once Bitsy told me what SuperGen was, what I was, the nightmares were easier to take.

Do you still have them?

Sometimes. Together, Bitsy and I worked out a way to deal with them without any sort of drug. Lately I've been dreaming about you.

"What?" I was so startled I spoke aloud.

"I didn't know it was you at first," Ren said. His hands were shoved in his pockets, his arms bent at the elbows like wire hangers. His speaking voice was gravelly. It sounded like it hurt. I wondered if that's why he preferred to communicate telepathically. "I dreamed of a girl running. Then I pulled up to the house, you came out and I thought, there she is. The runner. She's real."

"Do you dream about the fire a lot?"

Ren tilted his head back, looking at the moon. "I haven't for a long time. I think seeing you brings it back. You look like her," he said. "Your mother, I mean."

"Was it horrible?" Ren grew quiet again. I looked at the dirt, feeling bad for asking.

"It was. I tried to forget it for a long time. But in the middle of that horrible, horrible day were moments of good."

"What do you mean?"

"Well, Bitsy, for one. She found me and drove me to safety and raised me as her own. And second, your mother."

"What?"

"Bitsy rescued me, but your mother saved my life."

I didn't know what to say.

"I can show you, if you like. It won't be pleasant. But you would get to see her as I remember her. As a hero."

"How?"

"I can't be certain, but I think you might be able to

relive the memory along with me, the way you can read my thoughts or slip into my dreams." Ren shrugged. "It may not work, but it's worth a try. If you're up to it."

I thought of the photos pressed in Gumps's album, Mom always posed, always smiling. The memories he and Grandma tried to pass down by telling me stories. I could relive a memory of my mother, through Ren's eyes, see her as she was, not as a princess in Gumps's fairy-tale version of her life. Ren called her a hero. I needed a hero right now.

"Yes, I do want to see."

"I thought you might. You don't seem like a person who shies away from the hard stuff," Ren said. "I'm going to recall it. You'll need to slip into that place in your mind, the dream place. It's the same place you go when you're running like a cheetah out there."

"I think of it as the chord," I said.

"Whatever you want to call it. You slip in there and I can show you exactly what happened."

I looked around at the dusty ground and the sun-burned picnic tables. "Right here?"

Ren shrugged. "Why not?"

I perched on the edge of a picnic table, closed my eyes and thought of running. I willed my heart rate to increase, imagining how it felt to pump along, faster and faster. It worked. I listened for the humming, blotting out all other noises.

Easy, little sister, Ren coaxed me on.

Hearing his voice gave me something to focus on.

Keep talking, I asked.

If it helps. And remember, you're experiencing a memory and a memory can't hurt you.

Underneath the purr of his voice I felt the chord pulling at me like an undertow. I felt for it and held on.

My ears were ringing. I blinked, waiting for the sound to come rushing back to me, waiting for someone to come in and tell me what happened, but the world was still. Other than the ringing in my ears, the pain thudding at the back of my head and the burning of my skinned hands, there was nothing. Like I was the only person in the world.

Then a voice cut through the ringing and Ms. Stone — my mother — *was there. I was both me and Ren at the same time. It was a strange feeling, but things happened so quickly I didn't have time to reflect on it.*

"Ren!" She held a blue scarf with yellow flowers over her mouth and nose. She lowered it when she saw me cowering under the window.

"Ren! We're going to get out of here."

I watched, shaking, as Ms. Stone wrapped her scarf around her arm and smashed it through the glass of the window, which fell apart in large, jagged pieces. I flinched, backing away from the glass as it fell.

Next she crouched and patted her knee. "I'll boost you," Ms. Stone said. I hesitated, not liking the idea of going through the window. "We can't go back the way we came in," she said. I glanced over my shoulder and saw the rest of the bathroom had been swallowed in smoke.

"But I'll hurt you," I said, looking at Ms. Stone's bent leg.

"Oh, you sweet boy, you'll do no such thing. Come here." She reached toward me with both hands and hauled me up under the armpits. With the extra boost I could grab the ledge and pull myself through.

"Watch the glass!" she cried. The ringing in my ears had gotten quieter, but it was hard to hear over the roar of

the fire. I couldn't see it, but I heard it ravaging my school. I pulled my sleeves over my hands and knocked the bits of glass out of the window, then hauled myself through. I fell head over heels to the ground, landing flat on my back.

What little breath I had was knocked out of me, and I lay there, head throbbing, gasping at the air and waiting for Ms. Stone to come through the window. I could hear sirens in the distance. The smoke was pouring out of the bathroom window now. I shimmied backwards on the grass, trying to get as far away as I could.

The smoke and the heat and the panic faded, replaced by the grain of rough wood from the picnic table against my legs and the faraway clink of dishes in the kitchen. When I opened my eyes, they were wet with unspilled tears. I looked over at Ren and saw his eyes glinting silvery in the darkness and I knew his were wet too.

"I only know what my grandparents told me about her. They're full of funny stories about how she was so smart and interesting, but I didn't know she was so brave."

"Maybe bravery is the kind of thing that gets passed down," Ren said.

I shrugged. I certainly didn't feel brave. Things kept happening around me and all I could do was respond. Was that brave?

"A lot of things are about to change," Ren said softly.

"What do you mean?"

"You and Kamal coming here is the first major step Winfree has had in a long time. Feels like the wheels are in motion now, you know? Won't be long before everything's out there in the open for people to deal with."

"Am I still people?" I asked. "Now that I'm . . . part something else?"

Ren considered me for a moment. It was a bit unsettling, the way he took me in with his silvery eyes, the iris a pale shadow underneath the milky glow. Now that I knew he was unwinnowed, I looked for signs of alien DNA in him. He was tall and thin, but lots of people were tall and thin. His arms and face were smooth, with no sign of hair, but maybe he shaved or he had some condition. It was really only the eyes that gave it away.

"I hate to disappoint you," Ren said. "But you just look like a person to me."

I smiled. "Thanks."

"You ready to go back in? Daisy will be worried."

I slid off the picnic table, feeling a thousand years older than I did when I woke up. Why is it that knowing things makes you feel old?

Where's Daisy?

Probably in the diner. She doesn't like to miss the evening news. She eats her dinner at the bar so she can watch it every night.

Are you coming?

Nah, I've got some things to do. Good night, little sister.

'Night.

Inside, the kitchen was empty and spotless, the piles of dishes from before cleaned and stacked, the radio turned off and the sole light bulb above the stove left on. A rack of sticky buns was cooling on the island. My appetite returned at the sight of them, but I resisted in favour of real food. One can't exist on sticky buns alone.

In the fridge, I found a plate covered in plastic wrap with my name written across it in black marker. Daisy had left me dinner. I smiled in the pale light of the fridge, feeling less alone. I peeled back the plastic to find a generous slice of meat loaf and a mountain of mashed potatoes. I poured myself a glass of chocolate milk and headed for the diner. It was late and things were quiet. Surely it would be okay to sneak out for ten minutes, just enough time to eat and tell Daisy thanks.

I bumped the door open with my hip, and sure enough, the diner was empty save for Daisy, who was sitting on a bar stool, gazing up at the TV, her hands wrapped around a giant mug of coffee. Before I could call out, the chimes at the front door rang and a woman walked in. She was pretty, her hair loose and her jacket straight out of a magazine. But even out of her scrubs I recognized her in a second.

Roya.

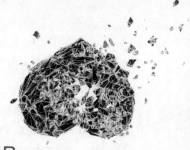

CHAPTER
TWENTY-ONE

Roya was angry. Her cheeks were flushed and her eyes narrowed, brow furrowed to a point. She's looking for me, I thought. Barton has sent her on a search and she's found me. All this time we were expecting police and sirens and teams of soldiers to swarm the diner, when in fact all they needed was one person.

I stepped away from the door, letting it come to a close as gently and quietly as possible, hoping Roya hadn't caught sight of me. For a moment I stood frozen in the kitchen, clutching the glass of chocolate milk in one hand and the plate in the other. The only thing to do was run. I could be out of there in an instant, far into the desert. But the desert was cold at night and there was nowhere to hide. I was fast but surely a car or a whole convoy of cars would catch me if they knew I was out there.

And then there was Kamal. I looked at the stairs. Was he in his room? Was he still with Dr. Lowry? What would they do if they caught us? Kamal and I would likely be winnowed, but Dr. Lowry was a fugitive. My conscience throbbed but I didn't have time to warn them. I had to get out of there. Now.

I placed my untouched dinner on the island and ran for the kitchen door, running smack into Abbot.

He was surprised, then happy to see me. "Marivic!" he said.

"Shhh!" I hissed, verging on hysteria. "She's here! We have to go. I have to go!"

Abbot got the message, lowering his voice to a whisper, but he still stood in the doorway, blocking my way. "Who?"

"Roya! She's here; they found us!"

The kitchen door burst open and the room blossomed with light. "Marivic!"

I was too paralyzed to turn around. All I saw was hot, red panic as Roya called my name. I was trapped. Desperate, I felt for Ren's presence, remembering what he said about panic leaving you wide open. If that was the case I couldn't possibly be more open than I was now.

Ren! Help! We've been discovered. I need you.

I didn't know how far he was or if he could hear me, but it was my only choice. I pushed against Abbot, who was surprisingly strong for someone so skinny.

"Marivic, what are you doing?" he asked.

Tears of frustration burned in my eyes. Maybe I wasn't a natural revolutionary but I wasn't ready for it to end like this, not even twenty-four hours after escaping. It was no use.

Roya rushed over, looking relieved. "When I found out what Abbot had done I was furious. Of all the dangerous, irresponsible things to do!"

She put her hands on my shoulders and smiled into my face. For a moment I thought she might hug me, but instead she frowned. "What's wrong?"

"She doesn't know," Abbot said. "I didn't tell her." To me, he said calmly, "Roya is one of us, Marivic. She's Winfree."

Realization dawned on Roya's face and this time she did hug me. She smelled like strawberries but there was a hint of that antiseptic Barton scent on her that set my heart galloping again. "Oh, you poor thing!" she said, speaking directly into my hair. "You thought I had come to take you back! No, no. You never have to go back to that place. You're safe now. You're with us."

Roya broke out of the hug and glared at Abbot. "We're not finished talking about this," she said.

"She's here, isn't she?" Abbot said, looking at me. "And Kamal? Is he here too?"

"Upstairs!" Daisy confirmed. She stood in the doorway. I hadn't seen her come in with Roya.

"So everything's fine," Abbot said, although he still looked a bit green.

"It is *not* fine!" Roya said. "You do not break Intakes out of Barton without consulting anyone, without a plan or a thought about the consequences."

"I had a plan!" Abbot insisted. "It worked perfectly well."

"You may have succeeded in getting them out, but now Barton is on high alert. Security has doubled. Staff inquisitions have begun. You've put me — and Winfree — in a very precarious situation."

I felt bad for Abbot but I was fascinated by this new, angry Roya. At Barton she had seemed like an extra-nice cheerleader, the kind of girl who gave valentines to every single person in the class and covered her textbooks with smiley faces. This Roya was powerful and crackled with energy. She would kick the other Roya's butt.

"Roya, dear, have you eaten?" Daisy asked. "Let's fix you something to eat. Abbot, you take that poor girl upstairs. The two of you just about gave her a heart attack."

Daisy started rummaging in the fridge, humming to herself. Roya hesitated, clearly not ready to let Abbot off the hook quite yet. But Daisy called for her to help and Roya turned, leaving Abbot and me to walk upstairs.

"You could have told me about Roya," I said, still shaking.

"I just didn't want Roya to find out I was there. She's the one who got me in the first time to do some searching in the records rooms, which are sealed, unless you're travelling by air vent."

"Is that how you got those videos?" I asked, remembering the ghostly images of Barton60 and the police officers flickering on the tiles of the pool.

Abbot nodded. "Exactly. They don't keep proof like that hanging around where anyone can find it. Roya has basic access, but that doesn't give her much security clearance. That's where I come in." Abbot looked extremely proud of himself. Even I had to admit that sneaking into secret rooms in Barton was an impressively dangerous thing to do.

"Then why is she so mad at you?"

"There were a few close calls with some of the Barton staff and Roya decided it was too dangerous for me to continue my missions, so I've been sneaking in unofficially. That's why I couldn't tell you that she was one of us. You might have mentioned me to her and then my cover would be blown." Abbot smiled ruefully. "Not that it matters now. They'll keep me so busy here I won't be able to get back in for a long time."

Abbot took a paper folded into thirds from his back pocket and gave it to me.

"What's this?"

"It's your dream map."

I unfolded the paper and stared at a series of graphs and strings of letters and numbers. Other than my name and basic medical information across the top, the rest of it made no sense to me, including the line I had read back in the lab at Barton: *Level 4 ATP, Recommended action unknown*.

"What does this last part mean?" I asked, pointing it out. "What's a Level 4 ATP?"

Abbot shrugged. "No idea. I don't understand all the medical stuff; I just steal things."

"Have you stolen dream maps before? Have you ever seen this line before?"

Abbot hesitated before answering, "Yes." He flushed. "Saren's dream map had the exact same conclusion."

The little balloon of pain I carried in my chest with Saren's name on it expanded, pressing against my lungs, my heart, my stomach, making my whole body ache.

Abbot rushed on. "It probably doesn't mean anything, but after I heard — I mean, after she died — I looked for Saren's winnowing report. I stole it too. Dr. Lowry has it. Maybe she can tell you more about what it means."

The silence stretched on between us. I could feel Abbot waiting for me to say something, but I felt like I had forgotten my lines in a play. What did it mean that Saren and I had both been designated a Level 4 ATP? Was that why she died? Was I at risk? Did running away from Barton mean that I had saved my life, or was I in even more danger? And, as always, why, why, why did Saren have to die? I had more questions than an entire year one class.

"Where's Kamal?" Abbot asked.

I shrugged. "I'm not sure. One of these rooms is probably his."

"I'm going to say hi," Abbot said. "You don't have to come."

"No, I want to." That wasn't exactly true, but I wasn't ready to be alone. I tried not to think about how much I wanted to talk to Saren. Whenever I had too much going on in my head, I would talk to her and she would make me laugh and see that nothing was as bad as it seemed. Only right now everything *was* exactly as bad as it seemed, made worse by the fact that she was gone.

It turned out Kamal's room was directly across from mine. He was sitting cross-legged on the floor with his eyes closed. Without opening them, he said, "Whoa, Stone. Your heart is beating extra fast. Does this mean you're excited to see me?"

"Are you meditating?" I asked. It was a relief to be annoyed at Kamal. It was an easy and familiar mode to slip into, so much better than the anger, grief and panic churning in my head and heart.

His eyes fluttered open and he grinned. "Sort of. Turns out the friendly giant also has bog ears. He taught me some cool tricks."

"Who's the friendly giant?" Abbot asked.

"Ren. You two are clearly unrelated, Termite. Even Stone here is taller than you."

"You can hear my heartbeat?" I asked.

Kamal grinned. "You wouldn't believe the crazy things I can hear."

"Did you hear our conversation?" Abbot asked, looking askance at me. He hadn't made eye contact since he told me about Saren's dream map. I think he was worried I would burst into tears.

"Nah, I don't need to listen in on you two lovebirds. I had more exciting things on my mind. Like the sound of earthworms tunnelling."

Now that was impressive. "Really?"

"Yes, really. You two are more boring than the most boring creature in the world."

Abbot sat on the edge of Kamal's bed. "Have you met Dr. Lowry?"

Kamal nodded. "Yeah. She told us about, you know, *us*."

We were all silent for a minute, each of us considering the sheer craziness of all we had learned. Kamal spoke first. "Ren said you could talk to each other telepathically."

"Yeah," I admitted. It hurt a little, knowing Ren had shared this information with Kamal. It felt intimate, like a secret. "It's weird."

"Can you read our minds right now?" Abbot asked.

"No, Ren said it only works with telepaths."

"I guess I'm a lower class of alien," Kamal joked. "Just bog ears for me."

"The Kesla," Abbot said. "That's what they called them, the ones they recovered from the ship. The Kesla."

"Kess-la," Kamal said, enunciating both syllables with care. "It doesn't sound very alien."

"It's not. It's the last name of the guy who recovered them."

Kamal snorted. "Figures. Just once I'd like to discover something cool and have it named after me."

"The Kesla," I said, trying the word on for size. I am part Kesla. In a weird way it was like hearing the name of a long-lost cousin you didn't know about until recently. Only that cousin was from another planet and might be the only reason you existed.

Exhaustion crashed over me like a tidal wave, sending my thoughts swirling in every direction. As full as my brain was, I wasn't going to figure anything else out that night. I needed sleep, or what little sleep I could get before the ACES took over.

"I'm going to bed," I said.

"Okay. I'm glad you're here," Abbot said meekly. He looked over at Kamal and added, somewhat reluctantly, "Both of you."

As I left, I heard Kamal say, "'I'm glad you're here'? We need to work on your game, Termite."

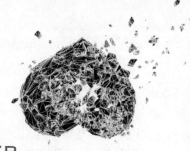

CHAPTER
TWENTY-TWO

My feet felt cold and my bare arms clammy. I was in some sort of dark, dank tunnel, but I couldn't see the walls or ceiling, just blackness. They felt close, as if I could spread my arms to the side and brush them. This wasn't like the other tunnel, a narrow plastic tube where the outside world was a blur of sound and movement.

Wherever I was felt older and less man-made, as if the tunnel had been here for years. The ground was uneven and I felt stones and possibly bits of tree roots through the thin soles of my shoes. Was I underground? I kept walking blindly ahead.

I was one of many; I couldn't see anyone, but I could sense other people in front and behind me. We were walking in single file. It was too narrow to do anything else. Once I got used to the darkness, I could make out the white flash of feet in front of me, but the rest of the body was swallowed in darkness. I tried to listen for footsteps, thinking maybe I would be able to tell how many people were in the line, but the tunnel muffled noises and it was eerily quiet.

Someone whimpered ahead of me. It was a soft sound but it startled me just as much as an explosion or a sudden scream. From somewhere near the back of the line a gruff voice said, "Keep moving!"

We walked in silence. Finally, in the distance, I saw what we were walking toward. There was a light. As we neared it, I realized the circle of light was cast from a hole high above. The light proved that we were indeed underground, the tunnels made of a mix of packed earth and concrete. The light also showed that we were approaching a dead end. A wall with metal rungs cemented into the earth led upward.

"One at a time now; up you go." The woman at the front of the line had a long white coat. I still couldn't make out her hands or her head, so she appeared as a ghost, a white, featureless, limbless shape floating in space.

The line paused and I saw that there were two people in front of me in identical grey T-shirts and shorts. One at a time, they tentatively climbed up the rungs.

I shuffled forward when it was my turn and grabbed hold of the rungs. The metal was cold and clammy against the skin of my palms. I counted the rungs as I climbed. Five. Six. Seven. Around fifteen, my shoulders burned and the muscles in my forearms started to shake. Twenty. Twenty-one.

Finally, my head popped above the ground. I blinked at the harsh light. Someone reached down and tugged me up by the armpits. He set me back on solid ground, only this time it was clean, swept concrete, no earth. I was in a vast empty building, the ceiling at least two storeys above me.

The space was sporadically lit, harsh spotlights illuminating various parts of the building so I couldn't be entirely sure how large it was. In the middle stood a pillar of darkness. I didn't know how else to describe it; it was like a shaft of pure darkness was cutting through the hazy light. I shuffled a bit closer and realized it wasn't a shaft, it was pyramid shaped and appeared to be solid. But what was it?

I sat up, tangled in sheets. At first all I could hear was my own ragged breathing. Where had I been? What had I just seen? It didn't feel like a regular dream, but surely it wasn't a typical ACE. Whatever it was left the hairs on my arms on end and my throat drier than paper. I stumbled out into the hallway intent on finding a bathroom and getting a glass of water, but voices coming from the kitchen stopped me. I picked out Daisy's lazy drawl and Roya's urgency, but I couldn't hear their words. I crept down the hall, closer to the kitchen. I sat on the top step and leaned forward. If only I had Kamal's bog ears, eavesdropping would be a cinch.

"They shouldn't be here."

"He apologized already. Go easy on the boy, Roya. He wanted to help."

"We're not equipped to break out Intakes. We have nowhere to house them, no plan to integrate them."

"We'll manage. It's just two more mouths to feed."

"And what happens the next time he goes rogue? Do you have any idea how paranoid they are at Barton now? It's going to be ten times harder to get anything in or out of that place now."

Abbot, I realized. They must be talking about Abbot. I lifted myself from the step and shimmied down a few more.

"I don't see why you're surprised. She's all you've talked about for months. Is it any wonder Abbot took it upon
himself to bring her to you?"

She? As in me?

"In any case, we have her now. What an incredible
stroke of luck."

Daisy's voice was full of reproach. "Mind you keep
your priorities straight, Roya. She's a living, breathing
human girl, not a rabbit's foot."

My heart picked up speed. They were they talking
about me. I was 'the girl'!

"She's the key," Roya insisted. "We can get to him
through her."

"Be careful with her. She's been through an awful lot.
You tell her about her grandfather and it might destroy
the poor thing."

Gumps again. Maybe Abbot didn't know much about
his Barton years, but Roya and Daisy seemed to know
something. Something bad.

"It's going to come out anyway. Isn't it better she hear
it from us?"

Hear what, I wondered. But the conversation became
inaudible again. Desperate to hear the rest of the conversation, I crept down a few more stairs and froze when the
bottom step let out a thunderous creak. Roya was there
in less than a second.

"Marivic? Is everything okay?" I could tell by the way
her eyes were boring into me that she was trying to assess
how much I had overheard. I bet she'd have given anything at that moment to have Ren's telepathic abilities. I
licked my dry lips and wrapped my arms around myself,
the perfect picture of a sad little orphan.

"The ACES," I said, my voice cracking. "They woke me up."

Roya's face softened. "You poor thing. Dr. Lowry will teach you how to deal with them soon. In the meantime, I have some Somnease if you think it will help you sleep. You've had such a hard day. Go up to your room, and I'll be there in a second."

I made my way back to my bed and busied myself by straightening my twisted sheets while I waited for Roya. I thought about what I had overheard. Roya said I was the key. That they could get to Gumps through me. But what did they want from him? What sort of secrets was Gumps keeping? Daisy had said that if I found out about him it would destroy me. Oh, Gumps, what did you do?

Roya appeared with a pile of clothes, a glass of water and a familiar purple pill.

"I thought you might need a change of clothes," she said, setting the pile on the chair opposite the bed. "It seems like you escaped in a hurry. Some of this might be too big, but it'll do for now."

"Thanks," I said.

"Now, I don't believe that drugs are the solution to every problem," Roya said. "But in this case, I think half a dose is necessary." She split the pill and handed me one half. It was so small I didn't need the water to swallow it, but I accepted the glass anyway. My throat was still parched.

I felt a surreal sense of déjà vu. There we were, acting out our usual roles — she handing me a pill, me in bed, accepting it — except the circumstances had completely changed. I felt like I was living in an alternate universe.

"How do you do it?" I asked. "Pretend to go along with the Barton agenda when you don't agree with it?"

"I won't lie, it's hard sometimes. But it's a necessary evil."

My insides cringed. "How can something evil be necessary?"

"Sometimes you have to do horrible things for the sake of the bigger picture. If the end result is right and just, then you have to do whatever it takes to get there."

There wasn't a hint of regret in Roya's voice. It must be nice to be so sure of something and not always be full of maybes and whys and what ifs.

"And you're absolutely sure that Winfree is in the right?"

Roya nodded once, an end to a sentence. "Absolutely. You'll see."

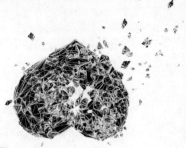

CHAPTER
TWENTY-THREE

Despite Roya's well wishes and the Somnease, I slept fitfully for the rest of the night, slipping in and out of dreams, some of them my own, some of them belonging to Ren. I saw my mother, scarf held over her mouth, in a cloud of smoke. I saw the cold, concrete walls of the maze, heard the snarling dogs coming closer. I also heard Roya's voice, repeating Gumps's name over and over again. When I awoke I felt relieved but not rested.

Downstairs, I found Abbot and Kamal, smushed into one side of a booth, glaring at Roya across a red Formica table flecked with silver and gold. Abbot had a stained trucker's hat pulled over his distinctive red hair and Kamal was wearing sunglasses. Roya had her jacket on over her scrubs and was drumming her fingers across the table. Her hair was still loose; she hadn't yet pulled it back into her efficient Barton ponytail. When I shuffled over, she got up and motioned for me to slide into the booth. She looked around to make sure nobody was watching.

"There's no one here, Roya," Abbot muttered.

"I have to go to work, but before I do, I want to make some things clear." Roya did not sound pleased. I had been considering asking her about Gumps, but now I wasn't so sure. Maybe the Roya who had come to my room with a glass of water and a sympathetic smile would be willing to tell me what she knew, but this Roya looked like she would just as soon bite my head off for eavesdropping as share information.

I was beginning to understand there were two Royas: the sweet, efficient Barton intake coordinator and the no-nonsense, do whatever it takes Winfree rebel. It was this second Roya we were sitting with now. She counted off her stipulations on her fingers with their delicate seashell-pink nails. The nails were at odds with the steely tone in her voice.

"You are not to be seen in the diner unless Daisy allows it. You do not go outside or do exploring of any kind. That includes the motel wings. You are not, under any circumstances, to bother Dr. Lowry."

Kamal looked up, unable to keep quiet a second longer. "We weren't bothering her. She asked us to stay!"

"After you broke into her office," Roya said icily.

"The door was open," Kamal muttered.

"I don't think you understand how dangerous it is that you're here — for Daisy, for Winfree and for yourselves." Roya sighed, dropping her drill sergeant shtick. "It's not forever, just until things calm down." She turned to me with hope in her eyes, looking for an ally. I wasn't sure I was ready to grant her that status yet. "Are we good?"

"So what *can* we do?" Kamal asked.

"You will learn to control your imps and the ACES.

Ren will help you. Once that's taken care of, we'll talk."

Roya stood, ending the conversation.

Kamal was incredulous. "That's it? Termite's been crawling through vents and stealing documents and you want us to just sit here?"

"Abbot is not technically Winfree. He has the same restrictions as you do."

A muscle in Abbot's jaw twitched but he didn't say anything.

"Are we clear?" Roya said.

One thing I knew for sure, Roya wasn't going anywhere until she had the answer she wanted. I spoke for the three of us.

"We're clear."

*

Roya left Kamal in a poisonous mood. Abbot offered me the leftover hash browns on his plate. I covered them in ketchup before digging in.

"What exactly does Roya do?" Kamal asked. "Is she leader of something?"

"I don't know how high up she is," Abbot admitted. "She's definitely our key contact person. She's the one who reports back from HQ but she could be just a messenger for all I know."

Kamal got up in Abbot's face. "You know what's funny? How you keep saying 'our.' And 'we.' As if you're a part of Winfree when Roya made it pretty clear that you're not."

"I am," Abbot insisted. "I'm like — a junior member."

"The thing is, Termite, Marivic and I risked everything to join Winfree because we were under the impression that you were part of Winfree. That you were someone who could speak on their behalf, not some junior member who's looking to collect brownie points."

Abbot swallowed. "They need you; they just don't know it yet. I know you can make a difference, both of you. But right now they underestimate you like they underestimate me."

It was exactly the right thing to say. I've known Kamal long enough to know that he did not like to be underestimated. If someone said why, he said why not. If someone said no, he said watch me.

Mollified, Kamal backed off. He helped himself to my hash browns and chewed thoughtfully. "Where does Dr. Lowry fit in?"

"Dr. Lowry used to be more involved but she's getting old and sad and spends a lot more time hidden away in her office," Abbot said.

"Doing what?" Kamal pushed.

"Looking back at her old files. She's obsessed with the ACES. She thinks Barton has it all wrong."

"Has what all wrong?" I asked.

Dr. Lowry appeared at our table, as silently and suddenly as a ghost. Before we could recover from the shock, she said, "I was wondering if you three could help me this morning."

Abbot blushed, probably because he had just been talking about Dr. Lowry behind her back. "Sure, Aunt Bitsy, with what?"

"My office is in a bit of a disarray."

Kamal and I immediately looked down at the table.

"I was wondering if you could help me put things in order again."

"Roya told us not to bother you," I said, still too ashamed of the mess we made of her private space to make eye contact.

"I'm not in the least bit bothered. Besides, I think even Roya would agree it would be rude to ignore an invitation."

"*Very* rude," Kamal added. He perked up considerably. I'm not sure what appealed to him more: the invitation to actually do something or the fact that he would be doing something Roya specifically told him not to do.

I looked up, and though Dr. Lowry's face was as expressionless as a mask, there was a twinkle in her eye that let me know she wasn't truly mad at us for destroying her filing system. Relief spread through me like a cool breeze.

"Finish your breakfast," she said. "Then come join me. I imagine you remember the way?"

Kamal laughed as she turned to leave. "Grandma Lowry's pretty cool," he said.

Abbot scoffed. "Show some respect, that's DOCTOR Lowry."

"I know who she is! Besides, you're the one who said she was getting old and sad."

"What did she do at Barton, exactly?" I asked.

"She was head neurologist," Abbot explained. "The first one. She's the one who invented dream mapping."

I thought of my strange dreams and how Tavi had also dreamt about escaping the lava. If anyone could explain what was going on in my sleep, it was Dr. Lowry.

*

Less than an hour later, plates cleaned, teeth brushed, we filed into Dr. Lowry's office, in the bright light of mid-morning. Inside, a desk and chair were pushed up under the window and an orange couch took up most of the opposite wall. Dr. Lowry was seated at the desk, her glasses perched at the edge of her nose.

"Ah, my young scientists!" she said as we entered. She pointed at the couch and we arranged ourselves on the lumpy orange monstrosity. It was misshapen and missing one foot, a pile of large red books propping up the one side. Dr. Lowry caught me looking at the books and said, "Good old Encyclopaedia Brittanica always comes in handy."

I sat between Abbot and Kamal, my hands pressed to the sides of my knees so I wouldn't have to brush either boy's sweaty legs. We were crammed in like crayons in a box.

"I'd like you to re-sort the ACES for me. It seems they got mixed up in yesterday's visit."

"Sort them how?" Kamal asked.

"The ACES fall under four broad categories: the Melting Road, the Abandoned City, the Net and the Crash. The dream maps will have these designations in the top right corner, in red. Your job is to put the dream maps in the corresponding files."

"So everyone who goes ACES has a version of those four dreams? But, that's not in the Barton Guide!" I protested.

"I think you'll find there is a lot they don't tell you in the Barton Guide," Dr. Lowry said gently.

Saren had said as much to me only days before. It hurt to have her words — some of the last words she ever said to me — thrown back in my face. All the studying and preparing for the winnowing and where had it gotten me?

Dr. Lowry passed each of us a folder before leaving the room, taking a moment to rest her hand on Abbot's shoulder. He turned away, refusing to acknowledge the gesture of kindness. His irritation rolled off him like waves. The second she was gone, he bounced up and took her chair. I moved to the other side of the couch, relieved that my knees were no longer pressed up against anyone else's sweaty leg.

"What did you get?" Kamal asked, as if I'd been handed a term paper with a grade on it and not a secret file full of nightmares.

"The Crash," I said. "You?"

"The Melting Road. Cool name for an album."

"Have you had that episode before?" I asked.

Kamal shook his head. "Not yet."

"I don't think you'd find it so cool if it was you running through lava," I muttered, remembering the smell of burning flesh and the feeling of sinking deeper and deeper into the molten road.

"I'd be cool," Kamal said. Then his eyes slid over to Abbot, who was silently fuming and hunched over his own file. "I don't know if Termite could handle it, though."

"Stop calling me Termite," Abbot said through clenched teeth.

"You would not be cool. You'd be the opposite of cool," I said. "You would literally be burning."

"I'm just saying, you and I are built for crazy stuff, superhero stuff. I can hear things that happen miles away. You can run like a cheetah. What can you do, Abbot? You've never told us what your imps are."

"I'm not sure bog ears qualify as a superpower," Abbot said dryly.

"Plus, some of the imps are really dangerous," I said.

"Didn't you hear what Dr. Lowry said? They're abilities, not impairments," said Kamal.

"Oh yeah? What about Simon?" I asked.

"Who's Simon?" Abbot asked.

Kamal waved the question away. "Just this kid we met at Barton. A little guy, like you."

I was infuriated with how casually Kamal brushed Simon off, as if he was nothing more than a fly. "He couldn't feel temperature," I explained. "Kamal thought it would be fun to do a little experiment and he burned his hand really badly."

Kamal shrugged. "He wanted to do it. It's not like I held his hand under the water."

"You might as well have! He only did it because you pressured him."

"So what's your point?"

"My point is, I don't think we're any stronger or smarter than anyone else."

"But we don't know that for sure, do we? Ren is the only unwinnowed adult we know, and he's not that much older than us. Who knows what we'll be able to do when we're fully grown."

"Ren looks pretty full-grown to me," I muttered.

"But he's just one guy. The more SuperGen kids who grow up unwinnowed, the more powerful we get."

I snorted. "So what, you're going to enslave everyone else with your alien mind control?"

Kamal flashed a wicked smile. "Maybe."

I was getting sick of this macho take-over-the-world

crap. "We're supposed to be helping Dr. Lowry," I reminded him.

Abbot and Kamal glared at each other for a moment longer before Abbot broke eye contact. Kamal continued to gloat like he had won something.

"If I read one more thing about lava I'm going to go mental!" he said. "Can we switch?"

We put the files back in order, then passed them around. I ended up with the Melting Road and then the Abandoned City. The more I read through the files, the less connected I felt to these other Barton kids and their nightmares. I had experienced the Melting Road, but why hadn't I also been lost in the Abandoned City or felt the panic of free fall in the Crash? I felt like a fraud.

When Daisy stuck her head in to tell us lunch would be ready in ten minutes, I was thankful for the interruption.

"Boys, it's your turn to help me out in the kitchen. That fried chicken's not going anywhere unless some nice young man puts it on a platter and carries it in."

Abbot got to his feet without a word, but Kamal mumbled under his breath.

"What, not used to helping out?" Abbot asked. "I guess at home your *mommy* does everything for you. Well not here. If you want to be part of Winfree you have to do your share, and that includes dishes."

"I know how to set a table," Kamal said, his voice dripping in acid. "And don't you dare talk about my mom."

I don't know what gave me a bigger headache, the two of them arguing, or trying to piece together the mystery behind the ACES. The silence that settled over the room once they had left felt like a sigh. I dallied, looking for things to do until Dr. Lowry returned. I wanted to talk to her about my ACES and my dream map. Maybe Level 4 ATP had something to do with why my ACES didn't match up with the ones in her files.

When she came in, she took in the files piled on her desk and the books on her shelves, which I had dusted and lined up neatly. "Thank you, Marivic. Why aren't you at lunch?"

"I have some questions."

Dr. Lowry sat at her desk and took her glasses off. She leaned forward slightly, focusing all of her attention on me like the narrow beam of a flashlight. I could imagine her sitting in an exam room at Barton, conducting my intake exam.

"You've collected four kinds of episodes. Are you sure there aren't others?"

"Why do you ask?"

"I had the Melting Road dream a few times but I've never had any of the others."

"Some children only ever experience the one dream, over and over. You can imagine how that contributed to the madness that has become associated with going ACES."

"But in the guide it says that once you start going ACES, they escalate until the winnowing. You don't have any other regular dreams. I've had other dreams, and they've felt real, just like the Melting Road. Only they don't fit with the ones in your files."

"And these dreams are markedly different from the dreams you would normally have?"

I struggled with how to explain what it felt like to be chased by dogs in that maze, or tied down in the tube. "They feel more physical, like if something bad happens to me in the dream, I'll wake up with injuries."

"That's not an unusual feeling to have during a common nightmare. That's what makes it frightening."

"This *is* different," I insisted. "Plus, I feel like I've been dropped into another world, one that makes sense to everyone but me. I can see and think and feel things, but my body doesn't respond. Almost like it's not mine."

"That is unusual. Can you tell me about one of these dreams?"

I told her about being trapped in the tube and being chased by the dogs in the maze, so scared I could barely think. "And then the other night I entered Ren's dream, about the Darby Fire. I wasn't watching it. I experienced it like he did."

"If that's the case, then perhaps these dreams actually belong to someone else and you've been tapping into them. It's clear your telepathic abilities are very strong."

Tapping into someone else's dreams was almost as crazy as having alien DNA. "Is that normal?" I asked.

"Normal isn't a word I like to use in my profession. It is unusual, although perhaps it's an ability that gets stronger with age and practice. Ren is quite skilled at it, but he wasn't at the beginning."

I was confused. "But I thought it was just Ren and I who were telepaths. How do you know how strong we are if there's only been two of us?"

"I mean among the Intakes. At Barton they test for telepathic ability during dream mapping. It has to do with how quickly you access the suspended cycle, and for how long. My guess is you would be an ATP, maybe level 4, if the dreams are that vivid. Instead of experiencing the episodes, your telepathic abilities have been allowing you to slip into someone else's dreams, perhaps because they are more pleasant." Dr. Lowry patted a file next to her. "Now that you've read about the range of episodes, I'm sure you understand it wouldn't take much for a dream to be more pleasant."

The room felt a few degrees cooler. Level 4 ATP. That diagnosis had been a death sentence for Saren. And maybe for me, if I hadn't escaped.

"A Level 4 ATP? Is that a bad thing?"

"No, it just means you'll have to work harder to control it so it's manageable. Why do you ask?"

"I've seen that phrase before. Abbot showed me my dream map. It had that exact wording on it. It was also on my friend Saren's dream map and she . . . died." I swallowed a few times to keep the tears from coming. Would there ever be a time when I would be able to say her name without crying?

"So you do have extraordinary abilities. ATP stands for Acute Telepath and level 4 is the highest designation. At least, it was when I was in charge. I don't think it's a fatal ability," Dr. Lowry said carefully. "I'm sorry about your friend. But I don't think her telepathic designation had anything to do with her death. It must have been a coincidence."

"If I am slipping into someone else's dreams, how do we figure out who they belong to?"

"You're going to have to be extra vigilant. I taught Ren how to step out of dreams and simply observe them. I can teach you too."

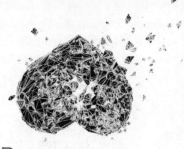

CHAPTER
TWENTY-FOUR

That afternoon I had my first official lesson in telepathy from Dr. Lowry and Ren. Unfortunately, Kamal insisted on coming.

"Can *you* talk to Ren in your head?" I said, knowing full well he couldn't.

Kamal hesitated. "No, but isn't that the point of a lesson? We're both unwinnowed, so why shouldn't we both learn about telepathy?"

I couldn't argue with that. Besides, Dr. Lowry had been delighted to have another student join us. I was jealous. Now I had to share her with Kamal, prize student, first-rate athlete and all-around champion. Just my luck he would end up being a natural telepath, the likes of which she had never seen before.

We met in her office. Dr. Lowry smiled when she caught me staring at the files on her desk, tabbed and colour-coded.

"Just brushing up on a few things," she explained. "Some of these I rewrote from memory. They're incomplete, of course, but better than nothing. Others Abbot has copied for me from Barton more recently." She opened a drawer in the desk to reveal stacks of spiral-bound journals. "These belonged to Ren."

"You kept a diary?" Kamal said with a snigger.

"Those are my dream journals," Ren said calmly. Unlike Abbot, who was becoming increasingly annoyed by Kamal's constant teasing, Ren was unaffected by Kamal's jeering. "I write down everything I see in my dreams. It helped me separate my ACES from other dreams."

"It might help for you to keep a dream journal too," Dr. Lowry suggested. Kamal balked and I bit the inside of my cheek to keep from laughing. So there, I thought.

"Please, sit." She gestured to the sad old couch.

I perched on the edge while Kamal plopped down in the middle only to get sucked between the cushions. "What is this thing made of, quicksand?" he complained.

"I'm sorry it's not very comfortable. We could do this in Marivic's room, if you prefer."

"No, it's fine," I said. I didn't want Kamal in my room. It was the only place at the Starlight that felt like mine and mine alone. Plus, I liked that I could hear the noise from the diner in Dr. Lowry's office. It was reassuring to know that there were people close by. Normal people with normal problems.

Dr. Lowry perched on her desk chair and opened a notepad to a fresh page. "Ren tells me that you hear a chord when you run, Marivic. Is that true?"

"Yes. I can feel it too. It hums."

"Try and think of the chord as an entrance to the suspended cycle. When you find it, it opens up other minds and therefore other dreams to you. You're still learning, so right now only one option presents itself. But eventually you can be like Ren. He can sense all of his dream options and choose which to slip into."

"I thought only telepaths could talk to each other in their minds," I said.

"Slipping into another person's dream is not the same as communicating directly with them," Ren explained. Somehow he had managed to pull his legs up under him and was sitting cross-legged on Dr. Lowry's desk. He was all dangling limbs, like a marionette. "Only true telepaths can converse with each other without speaking, but a person doesn't have to be telepathic for me to enter their dreams. When Naturals dream, their minds are open. I can slip in and dream with them, but I can't communicate with them."

"That's mega-creepy," Kamal said. "Do they know you're there?"

"I don't think so," Ren said. "And I don't do it often. I used to pick up on other people's dreams when I was younger, especially if they were intense, like nightmares."

"Like how I picked up on your dream about the fire?" I said.

Ren nodded. Like everything about him, it was a slow and careful movement. "Exactly."

"Telepathic ability first shows up in dreams," Dr. Lowry explained. "Even with Naturals, the mind is more open during sleep."

That was the second time they had used that term. "What do you mean by Naturals?" I asked.

"People born without the aid of SuperGen," Dr. Lowry said.

"Whoa, whoa, whoa. I thought it was impossible for

babies to be born without SuperGen," Kamal said.

"Not impossible, just very, very unlikely," Dr. Lowry explained.

If people born without SuperGen were Naturals, then that made me an Unnatural. Is that how Dr. Lowry and other people saw me? The term made me feel like an experiment gone wrong.

Dr. Lowry continued, "Remember that the suspended cycle is an extension of REM sleep. Once you can control your access to the dreams, and regulate your ability to slip in and out of them by using the chord, then you can start to access other minds while awake too."

"I can access it when I'm running."

Dr. Lowry smiled at me. "Fascinating. Running can induce a meditative state of mind or focus not unlike the suspended cycle. It seems your powers are strong enough that you have quite by accident stumbled upon the cycle in a waking state. That's the first step."

I smiled back at Dr. Lowry, feeling like a teacher's pet. That is, until Kamal spoke up.

"I'm a good runner. I won the hundred-metre dash in the bantam category at state last year," he said. "Maybe I can access the suspended whatever-you-call-it when I'm running too."

Dr. Lowry nodded patiently. "That's a distinct possibility, Kamal," she said, but I could tell she was more interested in me.

"Next step for you, Marivic, is to identify a neutral space. When you want to leave a dream, this is the place you return to. Falling out of someone else's dream and back into your own reality is shocking. In the early days, many of the Barton children had trouble distinguishing between the dream spaces and their own realities. Both felt equally real to them, not unlike people with acute schizophrenia." Dr. Lowry shook her head sadly. "It's no wonder so many were driven to a point of madness."

"What's your neutral space?" I asked Ren.

"It's a place that's special only to me. Try and pick something very specific, something few people know about. It helps to recognize it as your own and not part of the dream. It should be a place you feel calm or at peace."

Easy. My favourite place on earth was Saren's backyard in the summer. We spent hours there. I knew that place like the back of my own hand. Only now I would never see it again. Never again would I sink into an old lawn chair next to Saren, eating Popsicles until our lips turned purple and giggling until our sides hurt. My grief picked up, brewing inside me like a storm.

"Got one," Kamal said.

"Have you found one, Marivic?" Dr. Lowry asked.

I had to take a few shallow breaths before I could speak, imagining my breath was a strong wind blowing all stormy thoughts of Saren away. "Yes."

"Good. Now we're going to try to get you to open your minds without running or falling asleep. Since you're both such runners, we'll start there. I want you to imagine that you're running. Imagine all of the things that happen to you as you pick up speed, both in your body and in your mind. Try and find that calm, meditative space. Once you're in, grab on to a dream. Ren, maybe you can explain a little better."

"You said you hear a chord, right? Imagine each of the notes in that chord is a different dream. Hold on to one like the tail of a kite and let it pull you in."

"What if there's no chord?" Kamal asked. "I've never heard one while running before."

"It may take awhile for us to figure out how you individually access the cycle," Dr. Lowry said. "Let's try this way for now. Are you ready?"

Dr. Lowry and Ren were smiling so sweetly at me. I was nervous but also excited and I desperately wanted to please them.

"Ready," I said, hoping I sounded surer than I felt.

I closed my eyes and pictured myself running. I inhaled and counted to four, then exhaled for another count of four. I imagined my breath cycling through my body at an even, measured pace and my arms pumping along in time with my breathing. I imagined my feet pressing into the ground and the sweat gathering at my temples, the back of my neck and under my arms. I was sure I felt my heart rate increase, even though I was still sitting back in Dr. Lowry's quicksand couch.

"When you hear the chord, reach for it and ease on in," Ren was saying. He sounded far away. "Stay in the dream for a count of thirty, and then I want you to imagine your neutral space and return to us."

Kamal's voice broke my concentration.

"It's not working," he said. "I don't feel or hear anything."

"Keep trying," Dr. Lowry murmured.

The chord was shimmering close by. Exhilarated, I reached for it and slid in. I was swimming in sound. It was beautiful, rolling and swelling like the ocean, echoing in my bones. I wanted to float in it forever. I listened to the chord until I could pick out individual notes. I focused on one and held on to it and then—

I was sitting in a small, dark room, looking down at a maze. The air felt close, too close, as if I could brush it away from my face. The maze was complicated, built of unforgiving concrete, about the length of the entire Darby schoolyard. The walls were thick and at least one storey tall. Looking down at it gave me a feeling of dread, oily and toxic in the pit of my stomach.

I'd been in that maze before, and now I was looking down at it. I remembered the sound of dogs and the running until I thought my lungs or legs would collapse. I leaned forward, as close to the greasy double-paned glass as I could stand, and looked up, shutting my eyes instantly against the glare of very bright lights. They were too blinding to look at, obscuring the ceiling from the victim in the maze. Because that was what you were in the maze: a victim. But what did that make me, up in this box, watching?

There was a loud, ugly buzzing noise. A metal door at the far end of the maze opened and a boy stumbled through. He was too far away for me to see his face clearly, but he looked young and scared — shoulders rounded, skittish — and when the metal door clanged shut behind him he beat his fists on it uselessly. I couldn't hear him but I knew by the shaking of his shoulders that he was crying.

The buzzing noise sounded again and the boy started walking through the maze. He trailed his left hand along the wall, as if there were lots of people rushing by and he was trying to keep out of the way. Every once in a while he would glance behind him. He looked so small and lost, and I felt a surge of anger. I resisted the urge to tap on the glass, capture his attention and wave. It wasn't likely that he'd be able to see me with the lights obscuring everything, even if he could hear something as feeble as my knuckles on glass.

The noise sounded a third time, but this time the metal door rolled up, and even from my distant position I heard the snarling and barking of the dogs. Regardless of how loud I might be I started banging on the glass with both hands. "Run!" I yelled, as if he could hear me. As if anyone could hear me in this forgotten soundproof room.

The boy started to jog, still hugging one wall. I watched, frustrated, as he ran into a dead end. He turned three small circles, blinking, like a cat about to sit down. Only this cat was about to be torn apart by dogs.

Go, go, go! I thought. My host clenched her teeth, and I could feel it in my own temples. Three dogs had entered the maze. They were big and muscular, with giant jowls that flapped when they ran, exposing vicious-looking teeth — the kind of dog that people kept illegally on a chain in their backyards.

I felt my host compose herself. She stood with both hands on the glass and focused on the maze below.

GO LEFT.

The force of her thought almost shook me right out of the dream, out of her head. Because that's where I was, in her head. I was seeing the boy in the maze through her eyes. Realizing I was in a dream made me feel calmer. This isn't real, I told myself. I'm inside someone else's dream. But those dogs sure sounded real. And if they were, what chance did that boy have?

GO LEFT, she thought again. GO LEFT, GO LEFT, GO LEFT.

In the maze, the boy hesitated, cocking his head, before taking the left path at a run.

YES! NOW LEFT AGAIN.

The boy picked up speed and took the next left pathway.

NOW RIGHT, THEN RIGHT AGAIN.

As the boy did just as she instructed, I realized it wasn't a coincidence or wishful thinking. He could hear her. She was giving him directions telepathically. My host led him through the maze one turn at a time. When he reached the last stretch, he held his hands above him like a runner approaching the finish line. He ran at the wall, hitting a large red button with both hands. An alarm sounded and the dogs came to an abrupt stop in the middle of the maze, dropping to a seated position. The overhead lights dimmed to half and regular house lights flooded the maze. It looked less foreboding in kinder lighting.

This isn't real, I thought. This is a dream. Think of your neutral place. I tried to close my eyes but found that I couldn't. I was in someone else's brain; they controlled what happened. They were desperately worried about the boy, and now so was I. But I could leave, if only I could get back to my neutral space. Ren had told me to count to thirty, but I had been too caught up with the boy in the maze. How long had I been gone? Was time different in a dream?

I thought of our spot in Saren's backyard, the grass poking the small of my back where my T-shirt had ridden up, away from my shorts. I thought of how itchy the sun made my skin. I imagined the whine of an insect that flew too close to my ear. I imagined how the straw of my hat smelled, resting over my face. And suddenly I was there. I thought about the chord until I heard it shimmering around me, then I slipped in, let go of the kite tail and opened my eyes.

Ren and Dr. Lowry were beaming at me. "Excellent work, Marivic! Truly excellent!"

"It took me weeks to master that," Ren admitted.

I blinked slowly, letting the room come back to me. "It was just like you said. I imagined the notes as separate, and then as kite tails. I held on to one and . . . I was there."

Kamal was glowering beside me on the couch. "This is stupid," he muttered. "How do we know she actually went anywhere?"

"Kamal, I think perhaps we've stretched you to your limit today," Dr. Lowry said. "Let's pick this up just the two of us tomorrow. A private lesson."

Kamal looked stricken. It was probably the first time he had ever failed at something. He pushed himself off the couch and stalked away. "Fine," he said, slamming the door behind him as he left.

Once he was gone, Dr. Lowry clicked her pen open and leaned forward, giving me her full attention. "Can you tell me what happened?"

I felt more relaxed with Kamal gone. "It was the maze dream again, only this time I was watching it from above. There was a boy, and my host was giving him directions — telepathically."

"Did you recognize the boy?"

"Yes. I mean no, I didn't recognize him, but my host seemed to know who he was. I felt how worried she was about him."

"She?" Dr. Lowry prompted.

"Or he, I guess. I'm not sure."

Even in Dr. Lowry's bright, airy office, with the smell of sun-baked grass floating under the door and laughter bubbling up now and again from the diner, I was shaken. I remembered what it was like to have those dogs on your tail. The boy had looked so scared, and the host had been so hopeless. If this was what being a telepath was like, I wasn't sure I wanted to be one.

"Are your dreams always this bad?" I asked Ren.

"No," he admitted. "That one sounds like a doozy."

"How can you tell if the dream is happening in real life or if it's just another dream, made up by the host's brain?"

"That's fairly advanced, even for us," Dr. Lowry said with an apologetic smile. "The important thing is you found your neutral space with ease. Whenever you feel threatened, or the dream is too much for you, seek the neutral space."

"Okay," I said, taking a shaky breath. "Now what?"

"That's enough for one day," Dr. Lowry said. "Your brain will be tired. I wouldn't make you run a marathon every day, and I'm certainly not going to do the same to your brain."

I was relieved. I was proud of what I had accomplished, but I felt wiped, as if I had been running for real.

Dr. Lowry handed me a slim red journal. It was smooth and felt like leather. Inside, the pages were stiff and creamy, the edges tipped in gold paint. "As soon as you wake up, write down everything you remember. Ren and I will help you interpret your episodes and categorize your ACES."

"Thank you," I said. I was about to say more, but Ren tilted his head and held up a finger for silence.

"What's wrong?" Dr. Lowry asked.

"Listen," he said. "Can you hear that, or is it just . . ."

he tapped his ear, indicating his extra-strength hearing.

We fell quiet. I wasn't sure what I should be listening for until a car horn started blaring. My leg muscles tensed, ready to spring into action if the moment called for it.

"What is it? Barton? Did they find us?"

Ren shook his head but he still looked concerned. "No. Bitsy, you stay here, just in case."

"What about me?" I asked. I wasn't sure if I wanted to walk into the unknown with Ren or be left behind, safe with Dr. Lowry.

"You can come, but try not to stand out." Ren took the ball cap off his own head and pulled it down over my eyes. The sweatband was warm and smelled like grass and gasoline, with a whiff of something else. Essence of Ren. I tucked my hair under the collar of my shirt before following him out of the room.

"Don't worry, Dr. Lowry," I said, wishing I could heed my own advice.

Ren didn't appear to be hurrying but he covered an enormous amount of ground with his deep, smooth strides. I had to jog to keep up. I knew better than to ask him what was going on. We exited the back of the motel and ran around the side, staying close to the wall.

When we reached the front Ren paused, peering around the corner at the parking lot. The horn was still blaring insistently. A small crowd of people were standing in an empty parking spot just in front of the diner. One man, his face shiny with excitement, raised his fist and chanted, "Fight, fight, fight!" He looked the type to have been in a couple of fights of his own.

I had a bad feeling about the fight. I elbowed through two truckers to get a better look and was not surprised to see Kamal and Abbot tangled in a knot of arms and legs. So much for keeping a low profile.

Daisy was standing at the edge of the circle with her head in her hands, crying, "Boys! BOYS!" over and over. It made my heart lurch to see her so distressed.

"You — liar!" Kamal said between heavy panting breaths.

"Let go! You're crazy!"

Kamal had Abbot in a headlock but Abbot bit down hard on his arm, causing him to shout and loosen his grip. Abbot took the opportunity to roll away. He scrambled to his hands and knees. His nose was bloody and his elbows were scraped bare.

"What happened?" I said, to no one in particular.

"Just a little scrape. Nothing to worry about," said the man who seconds ago had been urging them on.

But I knew it was more than that. Kamal was a bully and a pain, but as far as I knew he never got into actual fights. And Abbot seemed like the kind of kid who preferred reading to fighting.

Ren stepped in, looking more like a stork than ever, and put one hand on each of the boys' shoulders. The effect was instantaneous. They both paused in their cursing and sniffling and squinted up at him, momentarily calm. I wondered if maybe this was another one of Ren's abilities, a lesser-known imp he had honed over the years.

"All right, nothing to see here," he said. "Show's over, fellas."

The truckers grumbled and filed back into the diner, taking their seats at the bar, picking up their abandoned forks and digging back into their meals.

Daisy hauled Abbot to his feet, brushing grit from his cheeks and shaking her head. "What got into you?" she scolded. "Fighting in the parking lot like that. That boy is our guest!"

"Show them your arm!" Kamal shouted, a vein throbbing at his left temple and a trickle of blood staining his lip. "Go on, Termite! Show them your arm!"

"What is he talking about?" I asked Abbot.

I saw Daisy and Ren exchange a glance, the kind of look adults give each other when they don't think children are paying attention. It made me wonder about Abbot and what he was hiding.

"What's wrong with your arm?" I asked.

Abbot's face was red with rage but instead of screaming he fell into Daisy's arms, defeated. "Show them," he mumbled into her flowered apron. "I don't care anymore."

"Oh, baby, it's nothing to be ashamed of," she said, mostly to him, but we all heard it.

Abbot wrenched himself free of her grasp and thrust his left arm under my face. He shoved his left sleeve up with his other hand. "There. See? Are you satisfied?"

Abbot's arm was pale, freckled and flushed pink from fighting.

"I don't understand what I'm looking at," I said, feeling dumb as a sheep.

"Nothing!" Kamal shouted. "You're looking at nothing. There's no scar there or on his other arm. I checked."

Abbot pushed up the sleeve on his right arm, proving Kamal right. I looked at my own left arm, at the small star-shaped pucker, a scar left from the SuperGen inoculation I had, along with everyone else, way back in year one.

"You don't have the scar," I said. "How is that possible? Everyone scars. Do they give you a pill or something in the city?"

"I never got the inoculation," Abbot said, his face twisted in rage. I shrank back from his anger. "Not everyone is born to a nice family in a nice town like you."

Daisy came forward again, wrapping Abbot in her cinnamon-scented arms. "I'm your family. I wanted you."

"But if you don't have an inoculation, then how are you—"

"Abbot is a Natural," Daisy interrupted, looking at me through watery eyes over Abbot's red hair. "Born without SuperGen."

I looked from her to Kamal to Ren. Everyone looked exhausted.

"Let's all go inside," Daisy said. "I think we've drawn enough attention to ourselves for one day."

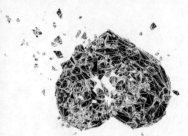

CHAPTER
TWENTY-FIVE

Daisy took Abbot upstairs. He followed her like a puppy, allowing her to smother him in kisses and rest her arm around him. He didn't seem to care that we were watching. Ren went to the kitchen to grab Kamal some ice. We waited for him in a booth in the back, away from the other diners.

"What happened?" I asked.

"We were arguing. It was no big deal. I just wanted to know what the little guy could do. He knows all about us. Didn't you think it was weird how he never talked about his own imps?"

Now that Kamal mentioned it, it was a little strange, but I had been so consumed by everything else that it had barely registered. "I guess."

"And then he was in my face, shouting, and I pushed him. He took a swing at me and I grabbed his arm, and there was no scar."

"So you just beat him up?"

"You make it sound like I'm this big jerk."

"You were acting like a big jerk."

Ren ambled up and passed a chunk of ice wrapped in a tea towel to Kamal, who pressed the bulky package against his swelling lip.

"You need to know a few things," Ren said. "First, you're right about that scar. It makes you special. Seems it's only in Darby that kids are given a SuperGen booster shot."

I ran my finger over the raised scar. "Why?"

Ren shrugged. "No one knows. Not yet, anyway. The rest of the fertility test centres only administer SuperGen to women who are trying to get pregnant. But at Darby, the Barton folks roll up at school each year in their big white van and make sure every child gets a good, healthy dose of SuperGen."

That didn't make any sense. Why would one test centre mandate booster shots and not the others?

Ren continued, "Now this next thing I'm telling you only so you get a sense of where Abbot is coming from. I'm not in the business of telling other people's stories, but maybe this will help y'all understand. Daisy came across Abbot when she was doing social work in St. Louis. She heard him crying in the alley behind the drop-in shelter where she worked and went out expecting to find a kitten. She certainly didn't expect to find a baby. No one had seen a baby outside of the clinics in thirty years."

"But SuperGen was introduced in 1955," I said.

"Only in Darby," Ren explained. "And only under strict monitoring. It wasn't until 1965 that the process was used elsewhere. Even then, it was closely regulated. The city of St. Louis wasn't approved as a fertility test centre. Back then St. Louis was a poor city, full of crime. Still is for all I know. The powers that be seemed content to let chaos run rampant. They were probably waiting for the people to run it into the ground on their own. It would save them having to swoop in and clean up the streets."

"But then someone had a baby."

Ren nodded.

"How can you be sure he's a Natural if he just turned up?" Kamal said. "Maybe his mother had the shot, ran away and left him for somebody else to take care of."

"We weren't sure until he hit puberty. Abbot is fourteen now. His voice has deepened, he's had a growth spurt — for all intents and purposes, he has entered puberty. But he's never shown any abilities like the two of you have and he's never experienced an episode like those of the Barton children." Ren looked at Kamal. "As you have so frequently pointed out, Abbot is a few inches shorter and much slighter than the average boy his age."

Kamal looked sheepish. Good. He should feel bad about how he constantly picked on Abbot, who had never been anything but kind to him.

"At Barton, they keep medical charts of children born before the Infertility Crisis, without SuperGen. Bitsy discovered that on average they were slightly smaller than SuperGen children. So while you may find his size odd, it is in fact perfectly average for children born before the SuperGen age."

"So he's human," I said.

Ren frowned. "So are you."

"No, I'm not. Part of me is Kesla. Abbot is a hundred percent human."

"Dr. Lowry prefers the term Natural," Ren said.

"Why didn't Daisy tell anyone about him?" Kamal asked.

"There would have been too many questions. Where did he come from, how was it possible that after all this time, a baby was born without SuperGen, and in St. Louis of all places? They would have locked him in a lab and made his life one big test. Daisy decided they couldn't stay there. It would have been too hard to hide him as he grew older. So she and her husband moved out here shortly after discovering him. It was close enough to Darby that no one would look twice at a baby. They were used to seeing children in this neck of the woods. What is it Roddenberry called the town? The Nursery of America?"

"The Cradle of America," I said.

"Exactly. You'd expect to find a baby in the Cradle of America. In other places, people would be spooked. Or worse, hungry for a child of their own."

Kamal was full of questions. "But if he is truly a Natural, shouldn't he at least do basic testing? Maybe there's another solution to the Infertility Crisis, something other than SuperGen. I can't believe Dr. Lowry of all people would just sit back and let her own sister ignore the scientific possibilities."

"Daisy loves that boy more than anything. She thought she had a chance to give an abandoned child a loving life. If she turned him over to medical science he would be no better off than a laboratory rat with no life to speak of."

We lapsed into silence. I thought of how passionately Abbot disliked Barton, how obsessed he was with experiments and how the Intakes were treated like rats instead of people. His passion was starting to make a lot of sense.

"How many other people are there like Abbot? How many Naturals?" I asked.

"I don't know. I'm not sure that anyone knows that number. There are always exceptions. Even in a widespread infertility crisis, some women may conceive. But the chances are extremely low, and those children conceived naturally often died before reaching their second birthday."

"Why didn't he tell us?" I asked.

Kamal snorted. "Because he's afraid of us. He's just a human; we're something more."

"I don't think that's true," I said.

"Which part?" he said with a sneer.

"Both! Abbot's not afraid of us. He broke us out of Barton, didn't he? Plus, he stole all those files, even though it was dangerous. And we're not something more. We're something . . ." I thought wildly about how to describe what we were, ". . . different."

Kamal rolled his eyes. "Okay, so he's not afraid, but he's definitely jealous. It's obvious. I mean, wouldn't you be?"

Ren cleared his throat. "Abbot is a good kid, and his heart is in the right place. I think he's finding it harder than he realized to be faced with children like you, children with abilities, children of the future."

"That thing I said about enslaving people, I didn't mean it," Kamal said. "I was kidding around."

"If Winfree succeeds and the next generation of children grow up unwinnowed, a sort of class war between the winnowed and the unwinnowed is possible. It's one of the things we have to be prepared for. Where there is difference there is prejudice. History has shown us this over and over again. And if we can't accept each other within the movement itself, what hope is there for the rest of society?" Ren touched Kamal's shoulder lightly.

"Give Abbot some time. Be his friend. That's what he needs right now."

Ren left, ambling off to wherever it was he spent his time. It occurred to me I didn't know when or where he slept. Just one more question in the mystery that was Ren.

"Does this mean we have to get our own dinner?" Kamal asked.

I scoffed. After all that, the only thing Kamal was worried about was where his dinner was coming from. "Do you even feel a little bit bad?"

"I said I was sorry."

"Not to Abbot."

"You heard Ren, he said to give him some time. I wasn't going to do anything. I just wanted him to come clean."

"Did you have to beat him up?"

Kamal pointed to the bite marks on his arm and to his lip, which had swollen to almost twice its size. "It's not like he didn't fight back. Stop looking at me like I'm the bad guy. I thought we were on the same side."

"Abbot is also on our side."

Kamal stood angrily. "I'm going to my room. I'm sick of being treated like a criminal."

I watched him go, feeling only the slightest bit sorry.

*

Abbot didn't come down for dinner, so I took a plate up to him instead. I knocked on the door and called his name a few times. When he didn't answer, I let myself in anyway. He was sitting on his bed, looking out the window as the hot pink sun melted into the desert. He didn't even turn to look at me when I walked in. If it was Saren who was upset I knew just the right things to say to make her smile, when to tease her a little, when to be silent. Abbot I knew so little about.

I set the plate on the bed beside him. "I brought you dinner."

"Thanks."

"You know Kamal is an idiot, right?"

"Yeah, but that doesn't mean he's wrong."

"About what?"

"If Winfree succeeds, everyone will know the truth about the Kesla and SuperGen."

I shrugged "So? Isn't that the point of Winfree? Isn't that what you want?"

"Yes, but where does that leave me?"

"You're lucky."

Abbot turned to face me with a look on his face that clearly said, you are crazy. At least he was acknowledging me. Anything was better than the cold shoulder.

"You're a Natural," I told him. "You're what everybody wants, a healthy, normal human kid."

"I'm not normal, I'm *natural*," Abbot said, his voice full of acid.

"What's the difference?"

"The difference is, I'm a scientific aberration, the exception to the rule. I might have been conceived naturally, but the fact is I'm the last of my kind. The future of civilization is not people like me, it's you and Kamal and the SuperGen children."

"They could still solve the Infertility Crisis. People could start having babies again. Without SuperGen, I mean."

238

Abbot shook his head. "They're not even trying other solutions anymore. In Darby, they teach you that the crisis is over; meanwhile lots of places all over the world are still in crisis."

"I get it, I'm an ignorant hick who grew up in a bubble where everybody lied to me. You don't have to rub it in."

"That's not what I meant. We are at the dawn of a new era, a new stage of human development. People like me are old news."

"For someone who hates Kamal so much you sure sound like him right now."

"He's right! Once Winfree succeeds, kids will grow up with all of these amazing abilities. You can enter people's dreams, Marivic. Do you have any idea of how crazy cool that is?"

I frowned, remembering the smoke in Ren's eyes and the dogs at the heels of the boy in the maze. "It's pretty scary, actually."

Abbot went on. "And what about your running? And Kamal can hear things that no one knew even made sounds before."

"That's a pretty lame superpower."

"My point is that if superhuman is the new normal, then where does that leave me?"

"Kamal was just joking. No one is going to enslave you."

Abbot looked hurt. "You're making fun of me."

I lost my temper. My empathy only stretched so far before it snapped. "Well don't be so ridiculous, then! Maybe we have superhuman abilities but that's because someone injected us with alien DNA. You're the miracle — you were conceived naturally in the middle of an infertility crisis. You're a, a — beacon of hope!"

Abbot smiled. "Now who's being dramatic?"

With some effort I was able to calm myself down. "You're not less of a person, if that's what you're worried about. You figured out how to break in and out of Barton, didn't you? You found all those secret files, the Barton60 recordings . . . that's not nothing. And you did it without the help of any imps. You have the makings of an international spy, even without the superpowers."

A smile tugged at the corner of Abbot's mouth.

"I wouldn't be here if it wasn't for you. Neither would Kamal."

Abbot touched the gash in his cheek from Kamal's fingernails. It still looked tender. "Sometimes I wish I had left him in that bathroom."

"Me too. But we're all part of this now."

"Maybe you should get Bitsy to add pep talks to your list of imps."

"They're not imps, they're abilities," I reminded him.

"Super-abilities," he corrected me.

"You're being super-annoying."

"I guess I have a superpower after all."

I laughed and eventually Abbot did too. I nudged the plate toward him. "Now are you going to eat those fries? Because if not, I could use a second helping. Pep talks require a lot of energy."

*

That night, when sleep came, I was ready. I recalled the exercises Ren had taught me, visualizing the notes as kites in the sky, ready for me when I needed them. I thought of my neutral space and imagined I was lazing around on my back in the grass behind Saren's house. When the chord came, I listened for the strongest note and grabbed hold.

I was on my knees, breathing hard, someone holding my left hand. My right hand was pressed against my chest, as if I could slow my heart just by pressing on it.

"Again!" a man demanded, cold and controlled.

I let go only for a moment to brace myself on all fours. I stood and the girl grabbed my hand again.

I held out my right hand and someone else took it. There was a group of us, holding hands around an inky black statue. I swayed slightly, feeling faint with hunger. If it wasn't for the people on either side, squeezing my hands, I thought I might fall over.

"Surely you can manage this together," the man jeered. "This should be nothing for your combined power!"

I looked back at the statue. It was inky black, and without a single mark. I wasn't sure what we were expected to do. No one seemed to know.

"On three," a voice said, only it was in my head — my host's head — not aloud. I realized they could all communicate with each other telepathically. I stepped closer to the statue and suddenly the surface of it started to move. It rippled like water, or silk, and my reflection appeared, murky at first, as if in muddy water, and then clear as glass.

I recognized the face staring back at me as if it was my own. High forehead, almond eyes, freckles. But it wasn't my face I was looking at in the mirror — it was Saren's.

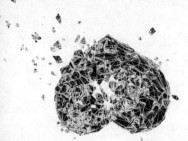

CHAPTER TWENTY-SIX

None of Ren's exercises had prepared me for the jolt of shock that came with seeing Saren's face. I wanted to get closer, to push my nose against the reflective surface of the statue so I could examine every detail of her face, but of course I couldn't do anything Saren didn't do. I had no physical power; I was only there inside her head. Dr. Lowry said that my dreams weren't like the other ACES because my telepathic abilities were so strong that they were overriding the ACES. Instead of dreaming about the Melting Road or the Abandoned City, I was tapping into someone else's dreams.

That someone was Saren.

I had seen the reflection of her face. I could still see it. That meant she was alive; she had to be. How could I tap into the dreams of a dead person? She was the girl in my dreams, my host. I forgot all about the neutral space and tumbled out of the dream, back to the bedroom.

I tried to wrench my arms free but they were pinned down. I expected to see the hands of the kids in my dream, but instead it was Kamal and Abbot, each holding me by an arm. I could tell by their strained faces and cords of muscle popping in their necks and furrowed brows that they were shouting. But caught between Saren's world and my own, I couldn't hear them.

It was Ren's voice, silky smooth, that got through to me. *Calm down, little sister. Let go of her and come back to us.*

But I didn't want to be with them, I wanted to be with Saren. She was alive! With a blink of an eye I was back there, in Saren's head — had I been in her head all along? In the tube, in the maze, shuffling along the dark tunnel? — and as I watched the shock play across her face in the strange obsidian statue, I knew she felt me too. She let go of the hands on either side of her and backed away, confused and horrified.

Marivic? Is that you?

"It's me!" I screamed.

Marivic?

Ren's cool voice echoed in my head. *You're caught between places, Marivic. She can't hear you. Find your neutral space.*

I blinked and suddenly saw Kamal's face, horribly contorted with the effort of screaming. "Saren can't hear you!" he shouted. "You're speaking out loud!"

And then Ren, smooth and calm as milk: *Think of your neutral space.*

I gulped for air and lay back. I listened for the birds and the wind chimes Saren's mother hung at the back door, old spoons pounded flat and strung up on fishing line. I imagined the sun on my face, my feet bare and resting in the baby pool, slipping against the blue plastic painted with yellow fish.

The physical reality of the room started to come together. The flowered sheet of my bed at the Starlight was twisted around my knees. My arms hurt where Kamal and Abbot were gripping them.

"Finally," Kamal muttered. He let go and I melted against the pillow, panting hard.

"It was Saren. It's her head I've been inside at night. She's alive."

"We got that," Kamal insisted, gingerly touching an angry-looking scratch on his cheek.

"Did I do that?" I asked. "I'm sorry."

Kamal laughed. "Yeah, right — you've been wanting to get me good for ages. If you and Termite keep attacking me, I'm going to look like a real rebel. We shouldn't have tried to wake you anyway; you're not supposed to wake someone when they're going ACES." He touched his cheek gingerly. "Now I know why."

"But you're not going ACES, are you, Marivic?" Dr. Lowry was in the doorway.

I shook my head. "No, they aren't ACES and they aren't someone else's dreams. What's happening to Saren is happening now, in real time. I'm in her head, like with Ren, except it's like I'm actually there. I see what she sees, I do what she does."

"You were right, Aunt Bitsy," Abbot said. "The Barton children are connected."

"Some more than others," Dr. Lowry said, shaking her head slowly. "Extraordinary."

"What do you mean connected?" Kamal asked.

"Connected in that you share a consciousness. I don't think it's easy to access; in fact I'm not sure if all Barton children can. But it's a theory I had when I discovered

244

the similarities in the accounts of the ACES. It is not uncommon for people to have similar dreams. But for dozens of children to experience similar dreams, children who are completely unrelated and have no common traumatic experience . . . I would call that unusual."

"But they have SuperGen in common," Kamal said.

"Exactly. They have SuperGen in common. In addition to the imps, something about SuperGen has connected these children on a deeper, subconscious level, a sort of hive mind they may not be aware of unless, like Marivic and Ren, they are acute telepaths. But it wasn't until Roddenberry's murder that this became clear."

"What does Roddenberry's murder have to do with anything?" Kamal asked.

"Because of what happened with Barton60," I said.

Dr. Lowry smiled encouragingly. "Very good, Marivic. Why do you say that?"

"Nine people confessed to the murder," I said. "But there was no way nine people actually went to the hotel, broke into Roddenberry's room and drugged his juice. Only one person did those things, but they were connected . . . telepathically. It was like they were all there, even though only one went in and crushed up the pills."

Dr. Lowry was beaming at me like I was something miraculous. "Yes, that was the conclusion we came to, only not so quickly as you."

"So the underground tunnel, the maze, these are all real-time experiments, things that have been happening to Saren, and not some muddled-up dream," I said.

"It would seem so," Dr. Lowry said gravely.

"But who is running these experiments?" Ren asked. "And where?"

"She's at Barton," I said, knowing the moment it came out of my mouth that it was true. "And not just her," I said, remembering the others walking in the dark tunnel and the people holding hands around the statue. "There are others."

"Can you find out who they are?" Kamal asked. "Maybe Saren can tell you."

"I don't know. I've only just realized it was her. She heard me, I know she did — but actually talking to her is another story."

"But you and Ren can communicate," Kamal said.

"It likely has something to do with proximity," Dr. Lowry said. "Ren and Marivic can talk to each other telepathically because they're never more than a few feet away from each other. In order for her to reach Saren, Marivic has to be deep in the suspended cycle. Even then, she's only been an observer."

"But this time she heard me," I insisted, remembering the shock — not totally unpleasant — when Saren realized it was me in her head.

"So go back in," Kamal suggested. "Talk to her there."

I wanted nothing more than to close my eyes and be with Saren again. She was alive!

"No," Dr. Lowry said. "Marivic has been through a great mental strain." She patted my shoulder. "Tonight you rest. When you hear the chord, you need to ignore it, Marivic," Dr. Lowry said. "Picture your neutral space, do whatever you need to do to keep from entering the suspended cycle. You need a regular night's sleep. It might not feel like it now, but entering the suspended cycle for long periods of time can wear a person out."

Dr. Lowry refused to leave until I agreed to heed her

advice. The others filed out of my room reluctantly. I could tell Abbot was worried about me, and Kamal looked like he was ready to run over to Barton and stage an uprising that very minute. Ren steered them out, a long-fingered hand on each of their shoulders.

I went about the business of going back to bed, knowing that as tired as I was, I would ignore Dr. Lowry's advice. Saren was alive and only I could help her. Once the others returned to their rooms I stayed up late scribbling feverishly in my dream journal. I wrote until my pen ran dry and my fingers cramped, recalling in as much detail as possible all the dreams, nightmares and ACES I could remember from just over a week.

*

In the morning, feeling sluggish but determined, I showed my journal to Dr. Lowry. Together we studied it and pieced together what was going on inside my head and somewhere in the bowels of Barton.

"I can't believe I've been with her all this time."

"Not every time." Dr. Lowry pointed out that the first time I had been in the maze, Saren was still at Barton. She tapped on the first maze entry in my journal. "Here you slipped into someone else's consciousness. It seems to me that the first time you shared Saren's experiences was during dream mapping, when you dreamed of the plastic tube. That must have been what they wheeled her out of the operating room in."

I thought of Saren, scared and alone in that narrow plastic coffin. "Do you think she was reaching out to me on purpose?"

"I doubt it. That would require very advanced control of her abilities. My guess is that you picked up on her panic while you were in the suspended cycle and after that her note, as you so charmingly describe it, was familiar to you."

I thought about how well I knew Saren, how many times we had blurted out the same thing at the same time. Sometimes I would be thinking about phoning her and she would show up at the front door as if I had summoned her there. Was it possible our friend-sense was because of SuperGen?

"Do you think she ever enters my consciousness? Could she be here right now, listening to us talk?"

"It's possible. Based on your journal entries, they are keeping Saren very busy with specific tasks that require her utmost concentration. Almost like they are training her for something. It seems she was unaware of your presence until your last episode."

"But now that she knows it's me, she can help us. She can tell me exactly where she is and we can rescue her."

"From what you've said about Saren, she sounds like the kind of person who doesn't shy away from a challenge."

"She's not afraid of anything."

Dr. Lowry smiled. "You two must be quite the pair. Be very careful she doesn't put herself in danger. We don't want anyone to grow suspicious."

"She'll find a way. She's smart."

Saren was alive and I was going to rescue her. After that she could join me at the Starlight and become a member of Winfree like she had intended. I was giddy at the thought of being together again, saving the world, side by side. Suddenly it didn't seem so impossible.

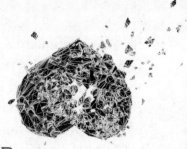

CHAPTER
TWENTY-SEVEN

I played Bloody Mary at a birthday party once. Five kids crammed into a bathroom, no lights, a single candle, staring into the mirror and chanting "Bloody Mary, Bloody Mary, Bloody Mary" over and over again. It was supposed to call up the spirit of a dead Scottish queen. Nothing happened, but I had felt properly spooked. Safe in my neutral space, I thought Saren's name over and over again, only this time I desperately wanted the chant to work. *Saren. Saren. Saren.*

My eyelids fluttered open. I was seated at a table with a group of kids ranging from my age to their late teens. We faced another row of kids with their backs to a metal wall. Behind them, on the wall, was what looked like eye charts, the kind with letters arranged in increasingly smaller font sizes.

My heart lurched as I recognized Cal Stark sitting directly in front of me. He was five years older than me and had died due to complications during the winnowing. Yet here he was, with shaggier hair and stubble on his chin, definitely alive. The girl next to him looked familiar too. And at the end of the table — I'd recognize that skinny neck and those round glasses anywhere. Lex Silver. Saren's dead brother, sitting at a table with a bunch of other kids who were supposed to be dead. Every one wore the same Barton T-shirt I had been issued on my arrival and an expression of sheer exhaustion.

Saren? Is that you?

Nothing. How would I know if I was in her head? What would that feel like? My host reached down to scratch an itch on her knee. I tensed, waiting for a glimpse of a familiar scar, a souvenir from a nasty bike accident last summer. Saren called the scar the caterpillar because of the way it wiggled over her knee. My spirits dipped as an unfamiliar hand scratched at a smooth, scar-less knee. No caterpillar, no Saren. But maybe she was somewhere in the room. Maybe I could see if she was okay.

"Children."

Everyone straightened up, including my host, as an imposing man in a lab coat entered the room.

Abrams.

I could feel my host's mood change like a shift in temperature. My ears buzzed and my vision got spotty. Dr. Abrams was part of this. Of course. How could the head of Barton, the man who had perfected the winnowing, allow children to die on his watch unless he was part of the conspiracy?

As the faces started to swim in front of my eyes, I remembered what Ren said about focusing. I was having trouble concentrating on the chord. I needed to calm down, otherwise I was going to start flickering between my host's consciousness and my own. I imagined breathing all my air out through my nose and that seemed to help. My vision cleared and I was back in the room. Dr. Abrams was talking.

"On paper, you are the best of the best. Your ATP scores are off the charts. Together you should be able to move mountains and yet you can't even open a door."

So Dr. Abrams was collecting telepaths. But for what? What were they trying to open?

"I did not introduce a SuperGen booster and pluck you from your lives to satisfy my own curiosity. You are here to serve a grand purpose. You are here to protect the lives of every person on this planet."

Even though he couldn't see me or possibly know I was there, I felt exposed, like at any moment Dr. Abrams would point at my host — at us — and call my name.

"Project Hive is not a game. It is our last hope. You and only you stand between us and the next invasion. It is your connection to the Kesla hive mind that will provide us the insight into their next step, and yet you sit here, playing games."

Dr. Abrams unstuck one of the charts from the wall, removed the tape and rolled it into a smooth cylinder. Somehow his controlled actions were more alarming than if he had ripped it down in a rage. He thoughtfully tapped his open palm with the edge of the tube.

"Your training is not working. I've been too soft. If I expect great results, I shall have to raise the stakes."

Someone whimpered. My heart — or perhaps it was my host's heart — was beating so quickly it made me uncomfortable. The sound filled my left ear completely and the glare of the overheard lights on the metal table intensified, blotting out my vision. *Focus, focus*, I told myself. Breathe! In two three four, out two three four. In two three four, out two three four.

But it was no use. Panic — springing from me or my host, I couldn't tell anymore — had set in. I wanted to close my eyes to the blinding light but I couldn't feel them or anything else. The pounding heartbeat in my head turned to hoofbeats and then a stampede and I was swept away by sound and light.

I imagined the light was the blazing August sun and the sound was a distant train travelling through Darby. I was in Saren's backyard and not stuck in someone's head in a nightmare, held captive by a crazy scientist. The intensity faded, and I could hear the chord humming softly, like the purr of a contented cat. When I opened my eyes, Dr. Lowry was there, a cool, dry hand on my forehead.

"Come back to us, Marivic."

"The telepaths!" I gasped. "He's collecting the telepaths."

Dr. Lowry's grip was firm but gentle. "Who?"

"Dr. Abrams. They're part of a project. He called it Project Hive. He thinks they can read the Kesla's mind. He thinks they're going to attack."

"Who's going to attack?"

"The Kesla!"

"Did Saren tell you this?"

"No, I was there. I heard him. But I wasn't in her head. I didn't see her. I need to go back."

"No, you need to rest. Stay in our present for a while, build up your strength. Your pulse is weak and erratic, and you could be doing more damage than good."

"I can't! Saren is still there."

I let go of Dr. Lowry's hand, closed my eyes and imagined I was in a boat, casting her voice off like a rope and floating back across the tide of the chord. I let it pull me farther along a crest of sound, listening for a sweet note among the sour. I coasted until I found a strong one and held on tight.

*

The next thing I knew, I was walking briskly along a dimly lit hallway, my steps clanging with each heavy footfall. The floor, the walls, the ceiling — everything was made of metal, and everything felt close. Too close. The ceiling was less than a foot from the top of my head. I had to swallow the feeling of claustrophobia that clawed its way up my throat. It was like being in a submarine. With a jolt, I realized the man I was walking with was Dr. Abrams.

"When did he arrive?" he asked.

"1700 hours." My host's voice was deep, not the voice of a child. Somehow I had jumped into the mind of a grown man. I didn't have time to marvel at the how or why of the situation. Dr. Abrams was still talking.

"Alone?"

"Alone. He requested you specifically. When I asked if he had an appointment, he said you'd make the time."

A slow smile spread across Dr. Abrams's face. "Yes. Very good. Thank you, Sawyer."

We came to a stop outside a door. A man was seated inside, his back to us. He was hunched over, hair sprouting straight up from his head and his ears in wiry tufts. I knew him before he turned around. But when he did, the defeat in his face wrung my heart like a dishrag. Gumps.

If he was surprised, Dr. Abrams didn't show it. "Ah. Humphrey."

Gumps stood, nodded his head in recognition. "Cain."

"It's been a while since you've been to visit."

"I hardly recognize the place."

Dr. Abrams cocked his head slightly, the hint of a smile playing on his lips. "Is that a compliment?"

But Gumps wasn't smiling. "We both know I'm not here for a tour, Cain."

Dr. Abrams paused. "The last time you were here, I believe you stole something from me."

Dr. Abrams towered over Gumps, but I could tell by the determined set of his jaw that Gumps was not intimidated. "It's been a long time; perhaps you can jog my memory."

"Yes, it has been a long time. Eleven years in fact. Perhaps this will help your memory."

Dr. Abrams took a folded sheet of paper from the pocket of his lab coat and handed it to Gumps, who read it, then handed it back, his expression as blank and inscrutable as his Scrabble face.

"Well?" Dr. Abrams said.

"What do you want?"

"I want what you took from me."

"I don't have what you're looking for."

The men stared each other down, and I couldn't help but feel like a whole conversation was unfolding silently between them. What happened the last time Gumps was here? Why? What was on that paper? So many questions screamed inside my head, but I was trapped in the body of Sawyer. Dr. Abrams turned and smiled curtly at me — no, at Sawyer.

"Thank you, Sawyer. I can take it from here."

My host clicked his heels together and saluted. "Sir."

No! I screamed. *No, no, no!* But Sawyer was obviously

military-trained to obey. He shut the door and marched down the hallway, but not before I caught a final glimpse of Gumps with his head in his hands, and Dr. Abrams smiling like a cat with a canary.

*

I don't know how long I slept. Hours, days, years seemed to pass. I saw glimpses of the metal prison where members of Project Hive were being held captive, felt the barking of hungry dogs in my bones, saw Dr. Lowry's face swim in and out of my waking nightmares. Twice I remembered leaning over the side of my bed and dry heaving into an empty bucket.

Someone swept my damp bangs from my burning forehead. Someone was singing.

And then, finally, nothing.

*

When I awoke, I was alone. I lay in bed, trying to put the pieces of what I knew together into something that made sense. Saren and Lex were alive. They were being held by Dr. Abrams somewhere in Barton as part of a project to stop the next Kesla invasion. They were connected somehow, because of their telepathic ability. An ability I also shared. I shivered despite the oppressive heat. There was only one piece that didn't fit. One thing I couldn't make sense of.

But I knew someone who could.

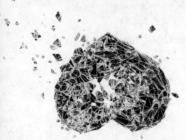

CHAPTER
TWENTY-EIGHT

Somehow I mustered all the energy I had to make it down the hall and stairs and into the kitchen. I felt like I had aged seventy years, as if my bones were made of rock-solid granite. Everyone was huddled around the island, so wrapped up in their thoughts they didn't hear me thumping down the stairs.

"You all look like somebody died," I said.

They all jumped, as if someone had dumped cold water down their backs.

"Marivic!"

I would have laughed at the shock on their faces, but I was afraid I might faint. They all spoke at once, flocking to my side like anxious birds. Ren helped me to a chair. Roya gave me a glass of water. Abbot patted my arm.

"You've been asleep for a day."

"More than a day."

"And you haven't had a bite to eat!"

Daisy hopped to it, throwing leftovers on a plate, hollering at Abbot to put the kettle on.

Dr. Lowry held my hand, and I knew she was the one who had been by my side all day and into the night. "You're a foolish child," she said, though not unkindly. "And now you're paying the price."

"Did you learn something at least?" Kamal asked.

Daisy gave him a light swat. "Shush! Give the poor lamb some room. Here you are, cupcake. You eat as much as you want."

I dipped a spoon into Daisy's fluffy mashed potatoes, shocked by the weight of the silverware. I had to rest between bites.

"Why am I so tired?" I asked.

"It takes a lot of mental effort to slip into someone's mind, let alone multiple minds. And for a novice like you . . ." Dr. Lowry trailed off. "It's best you eat up. And maybe take some Somnease tonight."

I told them about Lex, Dr. Abrams and Project Hive between bites of mashed potato and meat loaf. Dr. Lowry looked concerned. "It's not the first time I've heard of that theory. A few radicals floated the idea of a Kesla hive mind back in the mid-sixties, but they couldn't prove it."

"Is there any way it could be true?" Roya asked.

"I can't say for sure . . ." Dr. Lowry admitted. The potatoes turned to dust in my mouth. She patted my hand gently. " . . . but it seems unlikely to me."

"Roya?"

She flinched at her name, as if she knew what I was about to ask. "What did you mean when you said I was the key?"

"What?" Roya blinked, but the truth was in the blush that spread from her neck up to her ears.

"I heard you and Daisy in the kitchen one night. I was on the stairs. You were talking about Gumps, about how I was the key. What did you mean?"

Daisy flushed. "You weren't meant to hear that, cupcake."

"But I did. And I saw something, at Barton. Gumps was there, with Dr. Abrams. He accused my grandfather of stealing, and then he gave him something. A piece of paper, like a letter or something. Do you have any idea what it could have been?"

Dr. Lowry and Roya shared a look over my head. I was too tired and too hungry to protest.

"It was probably proof," Roya said.

"Of what?"

"Of his involvement in the Purge."

Roya grabbed my hand and squeezed. I was too numb to squeeze it back. She brought her face close to mine, forcing me to look her in the eyes. "Marivic, I know this is a blow, but it's better that you know the truth. I wanted to tell you from the beginning. I know you're strong. I know you can handle this."

Was I? I certainly didn't feel strong.

Dr. Lowry spoke in her calm, reasonable scientist's voice. "When I ran away, I expected them to pin the Purge on me. At Barton I was a very vocal critic of Dr. Abrams. After Roddenberry died, Abrams proposed that the winnowing become a mandatory procedure. He was convinced the Kesla had access to the minds of SuperGen children and had orchestrated the murder. The winnowing would be a way to sever that psychic connection. It was a farfetched idea, totally without evidence, but people were scared. I had my reservations about the procedure, but it wasn't until he recommended the Purge that I knew I had to leave."

Dr. Lowry continued, "I kept waiting for the news to brand me a fugitive, for the police to show up in New York City. After all, I was the perfect scapegoat, last seen at the scene of the crime, then never heard of again. To the outside world, I was acting like a guilty person. But they deemed it an accident. Years went by and nobody came knocking on my door to take me away. I found that odd. And then a few months ago, Abbot found the confession in a file at Barton."

I stared at Abbot, who had sworn that he had no idea what my grandfather had done at Barton. "*You* found it? You mean you knew all this time?"

The confession they were talking about must have been the paper Dr. Abrams had given Gumps to read. He was using it to blackmail him. And Abbot knew all along.

Abbot looked miserable. "I'm sorry," he said.

"Did you convince me to leave Barton and join Winfree just so you could get to Gumps?"

Their silence told me everything I needed to know. All this time I thought I was part of the team, valued for what I had to contribute, when really I was the bait they were using to get to Gumps. I was nothing more than a lowly worm, torn from the muck and stuck on a hook, hoping to catch something bigger and better.

"You're using me."

"No," Dr. Lowry said. "That's not it at all."

"It's not just about Gumps," Abbot said.

"Don't call him that!" I snapped.

Abbot apologized. "It's not just about your grandfather. Your telepathic abilities led us to discover Project

Hive. A whole bunch of kids are going to be rescued because of you. The fact that you're Humphrey Stone's granddaughter is just . . . a bonus."

Roya clasped my hands between her own. "Winfree needs you. Who better to convince Humphrey Stone to go public with the truth about Barton and the Purge than you? Imagine how powerful it will be: the man responsible for the Purge coming clean for the sake of his granddaughter, a member of Winfree. You'll be the most powerful symbol of the revolution."

"And if I refuse to ask him? Am I still a part of Winfree?"

Daisy tried to put her arms around me but I backed away. "Of course, cupcake."

Roya wasn't letting go that easily. The fire was back in her eyes and she was butt-kicking Roya, any hint of the sweet cheerleader nurse gone. "Marivic, we need Humphrey to speak out. Without a public confession we have nothing to pin the Purge on Barton. You're the only one he'll listen to."

"What makes you so sure? According to you, he set a whole school full of kids and teachers, including his own daughter, on fire!" My voice broke and I struggled to remain calm. "What makes you think he cares about me any more than he did about all of them?"

Kamal spoke. I had almost forgotten he was there. "Why do you think he asked my mom to give you a ride to Barton?"

That I couldn't answer. My heart still stung remembering it, even with all the other bigger, more horrible things I now knew about Gumps.

Kamal continued. "It's because he couldn't bear to

take you himself. He didn't want to leave you there, knowing what he did, what Barton still does. He felt guilty." Kamal's eyes were warm and brown and kinder than I had ever seen them. "If he feels guilty then he can't be all bad."

Dr. Lowry agreed. "Truly evil people don't feel any remorse."

Roya opened her mouth to argue but Daisy cut her off. "I think that's enough. We'll leave Marivic to her thoughts. Not one of us can understand how she's feeling."

*

It took two full days and two nights before I felt anything close to normal. I had had food poisoning once but this was worse. Dr. Lowry urged me to take the Somnease offered by Roya, but I hid them away in my pocket in case I had greater need for them later. I was getting better at avoiding the suspended cycle. When I heard its siren song calling to me, I ignored it, imagining the whine of backyard insects, the gentle lapping of waves against a boat, anything soothing and disconnected to the winnowing, Barton or Project Hive.

During the day, it was harder not to think about these things. Every second I spent in recovery was a second Dr. Abrams was testing Project Hive, potentially putting Saren and Lex and maybe Gumps in danger. Kamal, Roya and Abbot came to visit me. Kamal complained about being stuck at the diner all day.

"But the training is cool."

Ren was teaching him how to hone his hearing and turn his bog ears into something useful. "I'm getting really good at this echolocating thing," he boasted. "Maybe we won't even need Abbot's maps."

"What maps?" I asked.

Abbot grinned. "These ones." He unrolled blueprints for a building, fine blue lines on white paper.

"Is this—?"

"Barton," Abbot confirmed. "At first I thought they were earlier plans that had been abandoned. But then I thought about what you saw and I realized they're the original plans from when Barton was a military base. And these ones include five whole levels below sublevel three."

"Where Barton supposedly ends today."

"Exactly."

"But what are you doing with these maps?" I asked.

Abbot shrugged. "Maybe they'll come in handy. You know, if we decide to make a break for it."

But Roya was adamant that we stick to her plan. "First, we get a message to your grandfather that you're being held hostage."

"Held? Like a prisoner?"

"Obviously you're not a prisoner, but in order to convince him to do anything drastic, we'd have to hint that you were in danger, or at the very least being held against your will. Once we've got him, we can explain everything and he'll understand why we had to go to such great lengths." Roya said all this casually, as if she was explaining how to make sticky buns.

I kept thinking about what she told me about the necessary evils in life. She may have been on the good side, but she was just as merciless as Dr. Abrams when it came to getting what she wanted — all in the name of Winfree.

"But he's at Barton," Kamal pointed out. He snuck

a glance at me before adding, "And it sounds like he's working with Abrams. Now what?"

The solution was as plain to me as bread and butter. "We break into the bunker underneath Barton. That's where I saw Gumps last and it's also where Project Hive is being held. We could rescue them all in one go and bring an end to the project."

Kamal and Abbot were nodding but Roya was unconvinced. "We don't know for sure that Gumps is at Barton. Even if we did, it's extremely risky. Winfree isn't prepared for a rescue operation. We're not a military group. We don't have the resources or the numbers to invade Barton."

"We don't need a lot of people," Abbot pointed out. "Maybe it's better if a smaller group goes in. We'll be less likely to be detected."

Roya shook her head. "No. I can pass on the new information, let the group decide what to do with it. Our best bet is to send that message to your grandfather."

"But if Gumps goes public, Dr. Abrams might take it out on Project Hive. He might get rid of them altogether and tell people that the project never existed! We need to get them out of there before Gumps does anything. If he does anything at all."

Roya started to pace. "Marivic, I'm not trying to say that Project Hive doesn't deserve to be rescued. Of course I think they do! I'm simply suggesting we need a plan first. If we waltz in now, a hundred things can go wrong. I could blow my cover, and even more importantly, people could get really hurt."

"So we're just going to sit here and wait?" Kamal said, his voice incredulous.

Roya was determined. "Until we can formulate a plan, yes."

"I'm sick of waiting; I want to *do* something!" Kamal cried.

"What if we don't like the plan?" Abbot asked.

"Then that's too bad!" Roya's voice rose. "The three of you are still kids. There are people out there who are putting their lives — their families — on the line for Winfree. They've spent years gathering information for the cause. I'm not saying you aren't valuable, but when it comes to major decisions, I'm sorry, but you haven't earned a vote. You will stay here, inside the diner, until I tell you what our next move is."

Abbot rubbed his hair until it stood straight up. Kamal looked like he was ready to explode. I sighed.

"Fine. I'll do it."

Everyone looked at me.

Only Roya looked excited. "Do what?"

"I'll pretend to be your prisoner. You take my picture and send it to Gumps. You're right, if he thinks I'm in danger he'll be here in an hour."

Roya knelt in front of me. The hope in her eyes was unbearable. "Marivic, are you sure?"

"Yes. On one condition."

"What's that?"

"I get to write the letter."

Roya let out her breath in a noisy sigh. "That's fair. And it makes sense. Good thinking."

For the first time in ages I felt like we were on the same page. "Now, what did you have in mind?" I asked.

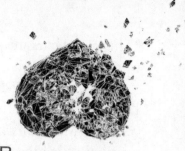

CHAPTER
TWENTY-NINE

We decided to use the cellar. Daisy led us out back and down a short flight of dusty stairs under the kitchen. "We used to keep wine down here. Not for the diner, mind you, we're not licensed for that sort of thing. Just for my husband and me. Special occasions, you know."

Despite the punishing sun, once we were underground, the temperature dropped considerably. A single window cast a bluish square of light on the packed-earth floor. An empty wine rack and a stack of wooden crates were collecting dust in a dark corner. They looked like the skeleton of something that had crawled into the cellar by mistake and died hundreds of years ago.

I nudged a crate with my toe, sending clouds of cobwebs into the dank air. I gagged as they brushed my lips.

"Pull one of those crates over into the light," Roya said, surveying the setting with a director's eye.

Daisy muttered under her breath and tried to rub away the goosebumps that had popped up along her arms.

"This place gives me the willies," she said. "I'm sure you won't mind if I wait outside."

Roya barely looked up from her camera. "Not at all, Daisy. We'll be five minutes."

"Now, Marivic, sit on the crate. Good. Try holding your hands behind you like you're tied up. Now slump your shoulders a bit."

Roya gazed at me through the viewfinder of a Polaroid camera. Saren had wanted one just like it. She wanted to sneak up and get pictures of people when they least expected it, catching them as they were, not as they wanted to be. I wondered what she would think of me now, playing the part of a prisoner to lure my own grandfather.

"Okay. Good. Now look up at me. I want to be sure we get a clear shot of your face . . ."

I blinked as Roya took the first picture. The camera whirred and then spit out a photo. Roya pulled it out gently without touching the surface, shook it lightly and then set it on the bottom stair to dry. "Let's do a few more, just in case."

I shifted slightly for each one, letting my hair fall forward and my face show exactly how miserable I felt. It didn't feel like acting at all.

"That should be enough; there has to be one good one in that bunch."

I stood, leaving the crate where it was. A memorial to our treachery. "Can I go now?"

"Yes. And Marivic — thank you. I know this is hard for you. I wouldn't have asked you to do this if I didn't think it was the only way."

"I know." I brushed by her, anxious to get back to the surface and the light. "I better go work on that letter."

"Of course. If you need any help—"

"No, I can do it myself."

"Remember, don't mention the diner itself. Tell him to wait by the pay phone at the gas station on Dundas Street at 4 p.m. Thursday. Someone will call with instructions, got it?"

"Got it: the pay phone on Dundas Street. Thursday at 4 p.m."

*

I thought a lot about the letter. I stopped and started eight different times, chewing the end of my pen until it was so mangled it looked like a wild dog had been gnawing on it. How do you find the words when you know no matter what you say, you're going to break somebody's heart?

When I finished I stretched, listening to the bones in my neck pop like corn on a hot skillet. A whiff of roast beef floated up from the kitchen and I decided I had earned a change of pace.

"Daisy, can I help with dinner tonight?"

"Of course, cupcake. If you're feeling up to it."

I nodded and pulled an apron out of the drawer. She smiled. "It's so nice to see you back to your normal self."

"What would you like me to do?"

Daisy pointed me in the direction of the stove. "You can start by stirring that gravy."

I smiled. "Perfect."

Fifteen minutes later, Abbot bounded down the stairs, sniffing dramatically. "Roast beef?" he said.

"My little bloodhound," Daisy said, bopping him on

the nose with a carrot. "Make sure you wash your hands and tell the others it's just about ready. I set the table in the corner for us."

I cleared my throat. "Hey, Abbot. Can you give me a hand?"

"What is it?"

"There's a letter in my back pocket. Can you grab it? My hands are all greasy."

Abbot blushed. "Sure."

I turned around, allowing him easier access. He slipped it out of my pocket and leaned in conspiratorially.

"Is this *the* letter?"

"Yes," I said. "Can you put it on Roya's desk?"

His eyes widened. "Sure."

"But before you do, can you give it a read? Make sure I didn't get anything wrong?"

"Okay."

"Thanks. And when you're done, get Kamal to look at it too." Abbot looked hurt. "I just want to be doubly sure. Plus, he's good at spelling and grammar stuff."

"Whatever you say."

✻

The Starlight Diner was deserted, a sudden heavy downpour keeping people from pulling off the highway for dinner. Nobody had much to say at what I had come to think of as "our table" in the back. Our minds were too busy and our hands were preoccupied with stuffing as much of Daisy's tender roast beef into our mouths as possible.

"Is Dr. Lowry joining us?" I asked.

"No, I'm afraid the strain of looking after you these past few days has taken its toll," Daisy said. "Now, don't look so worried, she wouldn't have it any other way. I'm sure she'll be right as rain by tomorrow morning. She just needs a good night's sleep."

"And Ren?"

Daisy waved her hand in the air, as if shooing an invisible fly. "Goodness knows where he got off to. I can't keep track of him. He'll come home when he's good and hungry. Gravy, dear?" With two hands, Daisy offered the yellow ceramic gravy boat that looked an awful lot like Aladdin's lamp to Abbot.

He smiled politely. "No thanks," he said.

"Kamal?"

Kamal grinned and patted his stomach. "No can do. I'm in training," he said.

"Ah, well. More for us ladies, then."

"None for me, Daisy," I said. "This beef is good enough on its own."

I watched as Daisy poured a steady stream of thick, piping hot gravy over Roya's potatoes. She groaned, "Daisy, no more," but I noticed she mopped every bit up with her bread. I finished quickly and offered to get a start on the dishes.

"Now wait just a hot second, cupcake! You helped make this dinner. Perhaps the boys should wash up."

Abbot and Kamal looked at each other and shrugged. It might have been the first time they agreed on something without an argument. I wasn't the only one who noticed.

"It sure is nice to see you boys getting along," Daisy said. "You know, I'm feeling a bit peaky. I may close up early and head to bed with a nice cup of tea."

Roya stood, stifling a yawn. "Me too. I have an early shift tomorrow."

I followed the boys to the kitchen, where they ran the water and started the dishes in silence. We worked for a good half hour before speaking.

"How much Somnease did you put in that gravy, Marivic?" Kamal asked.

"Four tablets. Do you think it'll be enough?"

"I don't know. We should probably act soon."

Abbot shook his head. "I can't believe I drugged my own mother."

Kamal clapped him on the back. "It's the revolution, dude. Desperate times. Besides, if it makes you feel any better, it was Marivic who did the deed. You're just a willing accomplice."

Abbot groaned.

"And you! Stone! That 'can you check my spelling' act was genius! Up top!" Kamal held his open palm up and I smacked it against my own in a high-five.

"I just hope Roya thinks so when she wakes up and finds it on her desk."

"Not a chance," Kamal said, laughing. "But by then we will have sprung those kids outta Barton, saved your grandfather and pretty much saved the world."

"I'm glad one of us is sure."

Kamal grinned. "I was *born* sure. Termite, you go check on Dr. Lowry. I'll go make sure Sleeping Beauty is in fact sleeping. Stone, you use your brain mind-meld thing to call Ren. We're going to need a ride."

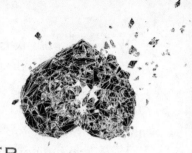

CHAPTER
THIRTY

The drive back to the Barton Flats was quiet. Ren offered to turn the radio on to distract us from the enormity of what we were about to do, but Kamal wanted to practise echolocating and I wanted to try and contact Saren and let her know we were on the way.

Kamal was skeptical. "But you've never been able to talk to each other, not like you and Ren."

"Dr. Lowry thinks it's because we're too far away. But we're closer now, and getting closer every minute. I have to try." I reached for the chord but I was too jittery to concentrate.

I cleared my mind and tried again. I heard a cascade of notes but I couldn't catch a single one. Dr. Lowry had cautioned that I had done too much too soon and it would take time before I was able to access the chord and sort through all the notes. Frustrated, I gave up and instead thought over and over to myself — and anyone else who might be listening — *Saren, I'm coming.*

You need to calm those nerves, little sister.

I'm trying, but what we're about to do seems so huge.

It is huge. It's change-the-world huge.

That's not helping.

I felt Ren's laughter ripple in my brain like a breeze on a warm day.

What's so funny?

It wasn't so long ago that you and I were in this very car and you almost jumped clear out of your skin when I popped into your head. And look at you now. The student surpasses the master.

I laughed too, only I did so out loud.

Kamal's face popped up in the rear-view mirror, frowning. "Hey, no super-secret telepathic conversations. It's rude."

"Don't worry, we weren't talking about you."

"Whatever you say, Stone. I know you love me." Kamal leaned over the headrest, making kissy noises near my neck. I jerked out of his way and he laughed like nothing funnier had ever happened.

"Are you picking up on anything yet?" I asked, pointedly ignoring his previous comment.

"No, let me concentrate."

Kamal tilted his chin upward and I watched as the whites of his eyes swirled, blotting out the irises, the pupils, any bit of colour. I wondered if that's what my eyes looked like when I ran. Did the Kesla have pure white eyes? Did they have eyes at all? Ren and I fell silent as Kamal clicked, then waited. Clicked, then waited. After a few minutes of echolocating, his eyes opened and he frowned.

"What's wrong?" I asked.

The Flats were closer now, dark shadows morphing

into houses and shrubs. From this distance Barton was a few tiny lights, like fireflies. Something manageable you could catch in a jar. Everything in my body felt wound up; I was a girl made of springs, ready to pop. "Kamal, what's wrong?"

Kamal shook his head and the last of the white film disappeared, leaving his eyes brown, like cream melting into coffee. "I'm not sure yet."

Ren pulled the car to a stop. "This is where I leave you."

"What will you do?" I asked.

"I'm going to stay in this neck of the woods with my mind open. You know how to reach me if you run into trouble."

My stomach tightened at the word *trouble*. I wanted to rescue Saren more than anything, but it didn't mean I wasn't scared.

*

The Flats felt eerie and still. Too still, as if the houses were sucking the energy out of the world. I watched Ren drive away until the car was out of sight. I kept reminding myself that he would be close by, that Kamal was there and that Abbot was also on the way to Barton with one of Ren's Winfree contacts to create the biggest diversion in the history of Winfree. Clouds floated across the sky, fracturing the moonlight like pieces of a shattered mirror. Kamal clicked his tongue a few times, then tilted his head to listen. I watched, fascinated. His bog ears were totally foreign to me. My telepathic abilities may have been strong, but there was nothing special about my hearing. Kamal turned to the left and took off briskly down the road.

"This way," he whispered.

Kamal jogged down the driveway and along the side of the closest house. We picked our way through the gardens, keeping low. If we needed to hide, we could duck among the shrubbery and shadows. I understood that it was safer than walking down the middle of the street where anyone could spot us without much trouble, but it didn't make me feel less nervous.

"Okay, here. Stay low." Kamal stopped at an unremarkable house, indistinguishable from the others. We crouched under a bay window, dry, raspy weeds tickling our knees. "According to my incredible bog ears, there's an underground tunnel leading from this house to Barton."

"How will we know what the entrance looks like?"

"It'll probably be a door."

"I *know* that."

"No, I mean a door hiding in plain sight. Termite said these houses all have the same plan. What doors do you remember from the pickup house?"

I leaned back against the nubby wall of the house, surprised at its warmth. Aloud, I retraced my steps in number four. "There was a closet in each bedroom, a linen closet outside the bathroom and a pantry."

"Is that it?"

"I think so. Which do you—"

"Shhh. We're not alone." Kamal tugged on his earlobe and said with a grin, "They can't hide from me, remember?"

"You mean there's somebody here?"

"Some*bodies*. I'm picking up four heartbeats. But three are crazy-fast."

I frowned. "What does that mean?"

Kamal shook his head. "I'm not sure."

"But you're sure the entrance — the only entrance — is in this house here?"

"I'm sure."

"And there's someone inside?"

Kamal sighed. "Yeah."

"So do we wait?"

"No. Diversionary tactics 101. I'll draw them out, and you do what you do best—"

"I don't—"

"Run."

Despite my nerves, I found a reason to smile. "Are you saying that I'm a better runner than you?"

"All I'm saying is, run. They'll never catch you, Stone. Get to the kitchen door and run."

Before I could protest, Kamal ran into the middle of the road and started singing the national anthem at the top of his lungs. I was torn between wanting to laugh and wanting to pull him back into the bushes. Instead, I remained crouched against the house, my muscles zinging, poised for action. Light flooded the front yard and I skittered back even farther, like a spider, scratching my shins on the hardscrabble earth. A screen door slammed, and out of the corner of my eye, I saw a man walk out onto the front stoop. He stopped less than four feet from where I was hidden. I didn't dare look up, but I could see his pants, and his hand reaching back for a holstered gun.

Be careful, Kamal.

Kamal turned. "Good evening, sir! I think I'm a little lost! I was looking for the fireworks, but I can't seem to find them."

The man took two steps forward. "What fireworks?"

"What do you mean, what fireworks? It's the fourth of July!"

The man moved a little closer. I shifted, trying not to make a sound. "It's only May, son."

Kamal stopped careening around and pretended to be genuinely confused. "It is? How can that be, it was just June."

"Where did you come from?"

"Barton, I think? I mean I was there, and then I was being prepped for surgery . . . it's all mixed up in here." Kamal twirled his finger near his head and then laughed. As diversionary tactics go, it was a good one. Kamal was pretending to be an escapee from the readjustment centre. It made him less threatening. The man seemed to think so, as he let go of his gun and approached Kamal slowly, with his hands open and held out in front of him, like you would a strange dog.

Five feet, six feet, seven — the man got farther from the door and yet I couldn't bring myself to make a move. In this moment, I was safely hidden. The second I made for the door, I was exposing myself. There was no going back. *C'mon, Marivic, move!* I chided myself. *Saren is waiting!* Maybe I wasn't a revolutionary, maybe Roya was right. I was just a kid, how could I possibly—

"Ooooh say can you seeeee!"

Kamal started singing at the top of his lungs again. The man was nearly at his side. He was saying something but

I couldn't hear him over Kamal's truly awful singing. As covers go, it was the only one I was going to get. I slipped out of the bushes, up the stairs and into the house, barely straightening from my crouch.

I made my way to the kitchen, hoping Kamal's guess was right. I didn't have time to be wrong. A single bulb lit the kitchen table, where a half-eaten sandwich and a pickle sat waiting on a plate. *Hurry, Marivic.* The pantry door was unremarkable. I wondered how many people had come to visit, had tea or smoked a pipe at the table, not knowing that the entrance to a secret underground tunnel was so close by.

I turned the knob and the door opened easily. Instead of a pantry with shelves of cans, I was looking at a set of cement stairs leading down to another door. This was it. I'd made it. But the sudden sound of whimpering behind me scared me out of my wits.

I whirled around, flattening myself against the door and searching the kitchen with my eyes. It was still empty, but two pairs of yellow eyes were watching me from behind a screen door.

Dogs. Big ones. I hadn't seen them before; the door was hidden in shadow, beyond the pool of light cast by the single fixture. One of the dogs whined and pawed at the door. Its toenails clicked against the mesh of the screen, making my skin crawl. Kamal said he heard four heartbeats, but three were faster. One of those must have been the man outside. The other three belonged to dogs. Which meant there was a third dog somewhere.

I didn't wait to find out where.

I ran down the steps, slamming into the second door with all my weight. I ignored the pain in my shoulder as the door gave way, opening to another yawning, dark abyss. Cold, dank air settled around me. I tried to breathe through my mouth but discovered it's better to smell foul air than to taste it.

I stumbled, adjusting to the smell and the darkness and listening for the chord. It was faint, but I heard it. I started to jog, following the sound as it got stronger. I reached my hands out to feel the tunnel. It was maybe six feet high and four feet across, roughly hewn of packed earth and supported by metal beams. It would be a close fit for someone of any significant height. It wasn't very high-tech, not at all like the rest of Barton, but I supposed a secret tunnel didn't need much in the way of bells and whistles.

I pumped my arms harder, holding on to the feeling of total freedom. Abbot estimated that the subdivision was less than ten miles from Barton. With any luck I would be there in half an hour. Maybe less. Every once in a while I felt for Saren, sending messages out to her or anyone in Project Hive who might be paying attention.

My name is Marivic Stone and I'm coming to rescue you.

I had to tell myself to keep breathing, keep running, as I waited for a response. There were a hundred possible reasons why no one was responding. Unfortunately, many of them had to do with Dr. Abrams and what tests he might be putting them through.

My name is Marivic Stone and I'm coming to rescue you. Project Hive, are you there? Saren? Lex?

I sifted through the notes of the chord, trying to find one that felt strong enough to hold on to, but Dr. Lowry's warnings gave me pause. If I slipped into someone else's consciousness now I could get caught or leave myself vulnerable to capture. I had to do this the natural way — no telepathy. In the back of my mind, a faint sound grew more insistent. It didn't belong to the chord. In fact, it wasn't in my mind. It was out there in the real world, getting louder and closer.

Barking.

*

I ran faster than I ever had before. The dogs were on my trail, but I was almost at Barton. I would not give up now. I could feel the air change as I approached a bunker door. The tang of metal filled my nostrils but it was still incredibly dark and hard to see. When I reached the bunker it came up so quickly and I was running so fast that I didn't have time to come to a proper stop. Instead I gritted my teeth and braced for impact. Something crunched as I collided with solid metal and then bounced backwards, landing hard on the ground. I heard nothing but ringing in my ears, not even the dogs. But that didn't mean they weren't closing in on me.

I got to my feet, my lungs and heart burning and the left side of my face throbbing from the impact. I grasped the wheel and cranked. I heard the levers falling out of place and the door popped open. I slipped inside, not daring to look behind me.

I tried to pull the door closed but it was heavy and I couldn't afford to waste time. Instead I moved forward, stepping through a low-ceilinged entryway, and found myself staring up at the maze from my dreams. No, not my dreams. It was real and the proof was in front of me.

If only I had a photographic memory, something to lead me through. After all, I had been in the maze, taken its sharp turns, felt its cold walls beneath my fingers. And I had looked down on it from above, guiding another to safety. But staring up at its imposing high walls now, I was at a loss. I moaned as I heard the dogs rushing through the tunnel, wishing I had locked the door behind me. It couldn't end here. I was too close.

Marivic. Get a move on!

Saren?

Look up.

I lifted my head and saw Saren looking down at me from the isolation box. Her hands were pressed against the glass and she looked determined.

You have to move, now!

Somewhere I found the strength to start jogging again, ignoring the shooting pains in my legs and the fire in my chest.

That's it. Now go left, and then take a quick right.

Behind me the dogs were barking. It sounded like an entire pack of them, but I couldn't think about that now.

I followed my best friend's instructions without pause, barely seeing the walls as I twisted and turned through the maze.

Left. Now Right.

I might as well have been blind. Saren was my eyes.

Right.

The dogs closed in on me. I could feel their hot breath on the back of my calves. Suddenly I was back in my dreams, deep in the ACES, with lava grabbing at my ankles and a stampede behind me. What were we running from? Would we ever outrun the lava that threatened to swallow us whole?

Left. You're almost there, Marivic, LEFT!

Hot jaws clamped down on my shin. I felt the skin tear and I screamed as teeth closed around my ankle, warm blood gushing forth. I pitched forward, tears in my eyes.

KICK HIM!

I twisted in the dirt and with my other foot kicked the dog squarely in the nose. He yelped and let go, and I clawed at the ground, forcing myself to stand, to go on. I hobbled on my good leg, swinging the injured one beside me.

I wasn't going to make it. I could barely outrun the dogs before I was injured. I wondered if they would eat me alive, or if they just wanted a taste of my blood. Suddenly an air horn blasted, clearing all thoughts out of my head. The dogs fell back on their haunches, and I fell too, my good leg giving out below me. The overhead lights turned on, and I blinked in the sudden light.

Did I make it? Am I safe?

No response came. I looked up at Saren. Her hands hung limply at her sides, and even from two storeys below, through my own hot tears, I could see she was crying.

I'm sorry, Marivic.

A pair of impeccably shined shoes stepped into my vision. I sat back, only half-surprised to find Dr. Abrams smiling down at me.

"Ah, Marivic Stone. I see you've experienced our little maze. How did you find it?"

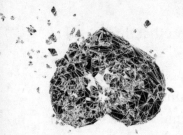

CHAPTER THIRTY-ONE

I sat on an examination table, my swollen, mangled ankle in Dr. Abrams's hands. I hissed through my teeth as he dabbed the tooth marks with antiseptic. The cotton came back dark with blood.

He smiled sympathetically. "Stings, doesn't it?"

"What are you going to do with me?"

"First I'm going to clean this up."

I swallowed. "And then?"

Dr. Abrams patted my knee. "Then we're going on a little trip. Don't worry, we'll take a car. You won't be running for a while."

"What kind of trip?"

"Not far. I have a little project I need your assistance with." Dr. Abrams held my ankle still and started wrapping it in feather-light gauze.

"You mean Project Hive. I know all about that. You're collecting telepaths. You fake their deaths and then you kidnap them and train them. You think you can use them to find out the Kesla's plan. But you're crazy! You can't prove that there's any connection to the hive mind at all!"

"You're right, I can't prove it. But the project is in early stages. And despite your remarkable telepathic abilities, it's not Project Hive I need your help with." Dr. Abrams tore a strip of medical tape from a roll and secured the bandage.

"Then what is it?"

"Many years ago your grandfather worked on a top-secret project called Humpty Dumpty, tasked with unlocking the secrets of the downed Kesla ship. The project seemed to be going well, until Humphrey left. Your grandfather was a brilliant engineer, and it took years for us to figure out that there was a piece missing. I believe your grandfather stole a part of the ship — a sort of key — knowing that without it we wouldn't be able to enter and the project would be abandoned."

"My grandfather is not a thief."

Dr. Abrams's mouth quirked. "I think we've established that there is much about Humphrey Stone that you don't know."

"But why would he steal from you?"

"Insurance. It was his way of letting me know that even though we had a deal, he wasn't happy about it."

My head was spinning. It was a lot of information to take in and the pain was making my brain fuzzy. "What kind of deal?"

"After the murder of Roddenberry, the four remaining members of the Barton Five, myself included, found ourselves in a quandary. The actions of Barton60 pointed to something sinister and beyond our control. A connection to the Kesla hive mind that the aliens could use to orchestrate revenge. As a group, we were divided on what measures to take. In the end we voted three in favour, with only one — Dr. Lowry — opposed."

I shivered, thinking of the memorial wall at Darby Public School, a hallway of golden name plaques stretching floor to ceiling, bearing the names of the dead. All because three people didn't know what else to do.

"Of course, we made the fire at Darby Public School look like an accident. But Humphrey Stone figured out the truth. He knew it wasn't a faulty boiler and cheap building materials that were at fault. He guessed, correctly, that Barton was behind the fire. And he threatened to go public."

Hope stirred in my heart. If Gumps threatened to go public, then he couldn't be behind the Purge. Roya was wrong. "So why didn't he go public?"

Dr. Abrams held my injured leg out straight. "Flex, please."

I did as he asked, grimacing as the bruised muscles and tendons stretched.

"Very good. That should heal nicely."

I took my leg back, tucking it gingerly under the examination table, away from Dr. Abrams. More than anything I wanted to get down from that table and run as far away as I could. But I wasn't going anywhere. My foot was as good as useless. I was stuck in that small examination room, Dr. Abrams positioned in front of the door. The only other possible escape route was a window with a heavy curtain tightly drawn.

Dr. Abrams leaned back in his chair. "Now this is where the deal comes in. Despite what you might think, I am not a heartless man. Your grandfather and others at

Barton seemed to think that because I ordered the Purge I *wanted* to do it." Dr. Abrams looked genuinely hurt. "I work at Barton in order to *preserve* life. I take no pleasure in destroying it. If I believed I could have avoided all of those deaths, I would have.

"When I ordered the Purge I had forgotten one crucial detail. Humphrey's daughter, Victoria — your mother — taught at the school. When she died you were orphaned. So when Humphrey Stone burst into a private Barton meeting the next day, ranting about his daughter and his poor motherless granddaughter, I saw a chance to save two lives: his and yours."

Dr. Abrams stood, putting his supplies neatly back in a box that resembled an oversized first-aid kit. "We agreed that your grandfather would never speak of the Purge or the experiments at Barton to anyone. In return, he got to live a quiet, simple life with his granddaughter. If I suspected even a hint of rebellion, I would produce documents that blamed him for the so-called accident at Darby Public School. He would spend the rest of his life in jail, and goodness knows what would become of you."

"So the confession?"

Dr. Abrams gave a tight little smile. "Fake, naturally."

A wave of conflicting emotions flooded my heart and threatened to sweep me away. Relief that Gumps was innocent. Love for my loyal, heartbroken Gumps. And rage at the impossible situation Dr. Abrams had put him in.

"You're a murderer and a liar!" I said.

Dr. Abrams considered my accusation. "Yes, I suppose I am. But there was too much at stake. After what happened with Barton60, I had to protect the world from a generation of children who were potentially dangerous.

I had to protect the program so Barton could go on with the important business of fertility, ensuring future generations. And your grandfather got to be with you."

Dr. Abrams spread his hands. "So you see, I couldn't draft you for Project Hive. To do so, I would have had to fake your death. Humphrey would have been furious and there was a risk he would consider the deal null and void. Without you to protect, there was nothing to stop Humphrey from going public and stirring up trouble." Dr. Abrams narrowed his eyes. "But then you disappeared anyway."

I squirmed, scrunching the paper below me. How much did Dr. Abrams know about Winfree?

"I didn't believe for a second that Humphrey was responsible for your disappearance. Like I said, we had a deal. He would never put you in jeopardy. But it gave me an excuse to contact him after all these years. To recover what he took.

"As a friend, and head of Barton, I took it upon myself to deliver the news of your disappearance personally. Humphrey was devastated and returned to Barton to assist in finding you. I asked him about the key and he swore he didn't have it. We went many rounds on the topic and eventually I realized he wasn't lying. He did have it, but it was no longer in his possession. It wasn't Humphrey who had what I needed, it was you."

I stared blankly at him, resisting the urge to laugh. It was stupid to laugh at someone who was so obviously crazy, not to mention dangerous. He thought I knew something about a missing piece of an alien spaceship? I had never seen anything resembling a key to a spaceship in my life. Dr. Abrams seemed calm, but there was an undercurrent in the room that felt electric — dangerous. I didn't want to risk upsetting him, but I couldn't lie. "I don't have anything."

Dr. Abrams reached into the pocket of his lab coat. My body tensed, preparing to run at the first sign of a weapon or syringe. I rotated my injured ankle, testing its strength, and winced as pain rippled up my leg. Dr. Abrams noticed and showed me his hands, weaponless and empty, save for a small wallet-sized photo. "It's all right, I'm not going to hurt you."

He held the photo out to me and I took it. It was soft around the edges and as familiar as my own face. In it my grandparents were squished together in an old-fashioned carnival bumper car, Gumps grinning with his arm around Grandma, his eyebrows practically shooting off his face. Grandma held on to her hat with one hand, her mouth open, laughing in delight. Gumps had kept the photo in his wallet. I used to sneak it out of his jacket and stare at it when I was missing Grandma.

"This belongs to Gumps! Where did you get it?" I said.

Dr. Abrams took the photo back. "Your grandfather is not in need of a wallet at the present time."

Cold began to trickle down my spine.

Dr. Abrams continued. "It's a very nice photograph. I can see why he would carry it with him. But one thing in particular caught my attention. That's a very unusual stone your grandmother is wearing. At first I thought it was onyx or perhaps a black opal, but we enlarged the photo and my team and I agreed that it wasn't either of those. And then I realized I had seen that necklace before."

Without thinking, my hand flew to my chest where

Grandma's charm was resting against my jackrabbiting heart.

Dr. Abrams smiled. "So you *do* know what I'm talking about."

"But . . . it's just an old *necklace!*" I protested. There was nothing key-like or even special about it. Grandma had worn it every day, not like the pearl earrings she saved for special occasions. "How can it be part of a spaceship?"

"The Kesla ship was built out of a material unlike any substance we have on Earth. It changes state from solid to liquid in milliseconds. It resists water and extreme heat. No one knew more about that substance than your grandfather. Somehow he managed to disguise the key as a trinket and then gave it to his wife. She probably had no idea she was wearing a piece of stolen government property around her neck for all those years."

"It's not government property; it belonged to my grandmother." It was true that the charm never seemed to get wet. But was it possible? Was I wearing a piece of alien technology around my neck?

Dr. Abrams's nostrils flared and his temper began to show. "It belongs to the project. We're going to return what was stolen and then we're going to discover what I've been searching for all these years."

I stepped back, putting distance between us. My legs were already urging me to get out of there. "No. Gumps didn't want you to have this and neither do I."

"Oh, I think you will."

Dr. Abrams pulled back the curtain, revealing a window that looked into another examination room. Except in this one a figure was lying in a hospital bed with an

IV drip and a monitor beeping above it. Gumps.

I forgot all about my ankle and lunged toward the window, ignoring the pain that shot up my leg. I pressed my hands to the glass and shouted.

"Gumps? Gumps! Wake up!"

"I'm afraid he couldn't hear you, even if he was conscious." Dr. Abrams rapped the glass with a knuckle. "Soundproof."

"What have you done to him?"

"Nothing. Yet. Right now your grandfather is safe. Like most pharmaceuticals, Somnease isn't dangerous unless one takes too much for the body to handle, or mixes it with other drugs. Something Roddenberry found out the hard way." I stiffened at the mention of Roddenberry, remembering his death at the hands of Barton60.

"I have given instructions for your grandfather to receive a double dose every half hour. Combined with the Paxocet I crushed into his dinner, in one hour he will go into a coma. In two hours, he'll be dead." Dr. Abrams patted the pager on his hip. "With one message I can call off the dosage, or increase it, if need be."

I opened my mouth to protest, but no sound came out. Not even a squeak.

Dr. Abrams checked his watch. "If we leave now we can get to the ship in fifteen minutes. I'll make the call, and your beloved Gumps will wake up feeling rested. If not, well, I can promise you that his death will be painless. The choice is yours."

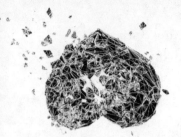

CHAPTER THIRTY-TWO

In the end, I had no choice and Dr. Abrams knew it. I would never leave Gumps to die. I hobbled after Dr. Abrams as we made our way through the bunker to an underground parking lot, row upon row of spotless military vehicles glittering like beetles.

Dr. Abrams helped me up into the passenger seat of an open Jeep. I reached wildly for the chord, sending out distress calls to Ren, Saren or anyone who could hear me, but the notes slipped away. It was like trying to catch a hat toyed with by the wind. Whenever I imagined my neutral space, faces would swim before me. Between Gumps and Saren, my mind was so full of worries I couldn't make any room for anything else.

Two armed guards cleared us for exit and a metal door cranked open. Dr. Abrams put the Jeep into drive and we took off into the darkness. The ceiling and floor of the tunnel were marked with strip lighting, narrow green ropes of light that stretched as far as I could see.

"Where's Saren?" I asked, raising my voice over the crunch of the tires.

"She has served her purpose."

The air froze in my lungs, making it hurt to breathe. "What does that mean?"

"It means she performed admirably and I'm pleased."

"What do you mean 'performed'?"

"We had to get you through that maze alive somehow."

"You knew about our telepathic connection?"

Dr. Abrams was amused. "Of course. I am head of the project. I know everything about my subjects. I heard her talking to you by the ship. She called your name more than once. I know enough about the suspended cycle and her advanced telepathic abilities to be sure it wasn't the incoherent mutterings of a dream or a mad woman. She was connecting with you telepathically. You owe your life to her, you know. Although you will have a nasty scar. Animal bites rarely heal nicely."

All this time I thought we had been so clever, so careful, when really I had done exactly what Dr. Abrams wanted. I felt sick with worry. "Where is she?"

"Safe."

"I don't believe you."

Dr. Abrams's voice sharpened. "You don't have a choice."

It was clear Dr. Abrams wasn't going to say anything more on the subject. But silence did nothing but feed my panic. I had to get him talking. Anything to keep me from worrying.

"Why do you want to get inside the ship so badly?"

"There are many reasons. By exploring the Kesla technology, we could learn more about them as a

291

species. Perhaps there are innovations and technology we can apply here on Earth . . ." Dr. Abrams trailed off and I knew there was more to it than that.

"And?"

Dr. Abrams sighed. "And Project Hive is stalled. None of the members have successfully been able to connect with the Kesla. I believe there is a communication device inside that ship. If we can access it, learn its secrets, perhaps we can use it to communicate with the Kesla hive mind and accelerate the project."

"I don't understand. If you think the Kesla want to destroy us, why bother communicating at all? Why not abandon Project Hive and winnow everyone so the Kesla can't poke around in our minds at all? Wouldn't that solve the problem?"

"Until we find out for sure what the Kesla want, we'll always be waiting for the next attack. Why did they come here in 1947? What did they want? What would have happened if they hadn't crashed? Project Hive is an isolated military operation to go deep into the mind of our enemy so we can destroy them when they return. By introducing a mandatory SuperGen booster shot, I increased the amount of hormone in the system, strengthening the imps and ACES. They became easier to test, to quantify. I could keep a secret group of powerful telepaths to study, and winnow everyone else. It was a perfect plan."

Dr. Abrams's theories were just as crazy as the ones in Kamal's issues of *The Canary*, but in that dark tunnel full of dead air, I couldn't shake the feeling of dread. If powerful people believed in a theory, it became real. It didn't matter if it was crazy. Dr. Abrams believed it, the military believed it, and people had died because of those beliefs. The headlights glinted off the chrome rungs cemented into the wall of the tunnel ahead of us, and déjà vu spread through my belly like nausea.

Dr. Abrams cut the engine and came around to the passenger side to help me down. "Up we go," he said.

*

As far as spaceships are concerned, the Kesla ship wasn't what I expected. When I had first seen the ship through Saren's eyes, I didn't even know what I was looking at. I thought UFOs were silver and shaped like massive Frisbees.

The ship in front of me was more like a bullet and was so dark it appeared to be sucking all the light from the room. It wasn't as big as I thought it would be — about the shape of a large motorboat if you stood it on the stern end, with the prow pointing up at the ceiling. It was propped up with thick metal braces painted in caution stripes of yellow and black. Up close, it seemed impenetrable. Whatever it was made out of had no imperfections or anything at all to suggest a way inside, as if it had been made of a single sheet of black silk.

Dr. Abrams sighed, like he was gazing at a work of art in a museum and not a downed alien ship. "You can touch it if you like."

I moved closer, still trailing my injured leg behind me, and hovered my hand over the ship. The surface rippled gently, like dark water. I gasped and pulled my hand away as if burned.

"It only reacts that way for unwinnowed children," Dr. Abrams said. He sounded regretful, as if he too wished he could have such an effect on the ship. "Go on, touch it. It won't hurt you."

I lowered my hand and stroked the smooth surface of the ship like it was a cat. It felt cool and solid under my fingertips, but it rippled under my hand, leaving an iridescent trail, like rainbows in a pool of oil. The rainbows quivered and disappeared moments later. I stared at my hand and wiggled my fingers, noting a pleasant tingling sensation.

I hobbled all the way around the ship, trailing my hand on the surface as if it were a cool stream and my fingers were troubling the water. The patterns I made were mesmerizing. I looked for bolts, screws, a keyhole, the outline of a door or window, anything to suggest a way in, but I saw nothing.

"How do you get in?"

"The ship didn't always look like this. It had a door, panels, the sort of features you would expect on a spacecraft. What you see now is a sort of cloak or protective shield, almost as if the ship itself is hibernating."

Hibernating, like something alive. Under my T-shirt, the charm felt warm. Maybe it had been warmed by my body heat, but somehow I didn't think so. It was reacting to the ship. Maybe it too had been hibernating, pretending to be a rock. Until now.

"Give me the key," Dr. Abrams said, as if he could read my mind.

Secret key to alien ship or not, the charm had still belonged to Grandma, something given to her by Gumps out of their big, goofy love, and I couldn't hand it over to someone as cold and calculating as Dr. Abrams. "No."

Dr. Abrams was patient. "Marivic, I thought you

understood. You give me the key and your grandfather lives."

"No, I want to do it. I'm the one with Kesla DNA. It should be me."

I retrieved the chain from under my T-shirt. To my surprise, the familiar black stone was now molten and swirling with red, like the lava that swallowed my feet in the ACES. Before, I thought it was an oddly shaped stone, polished to a high, fine gloss. Now I realized it wasn't a stone at all. Maybe it had been liquid all along, moving so slowly I hadn't noticed.

It was definitely getting warmer.

"What do I do with it?"

Dr. Abrams looked at it greedily. "Give it to me. I need a better look at it."

"No."

No way would I give him anything. I would have to figure it out myself. I approached the ship, holding the necklace in front of me like an offering. The charm began to spin, first one way, then the other, like a thing possessed. When I held it close to the ship, the blackness evaporated, roiling away like boiling smoke to reveal a dull pewter panel and bolts underneath.

"Yes, that's it!" Dr. Abrams said.

But when I stepped back, taking the charm with me, the blackness rolled over everything again, filling in the space. I walked around the ship, using the charm as a sort of flashlight, revealing the ship in bits and pieces, looking for anything to suggest an entrance.

I knew it was close, because I could feel the chord starting in my bones. It seemed to be vibrating in time with the spinning of the charm. Out of curiosity I pressed the charm against the ship itself. Those three seconds of contact seared the palm of my hand and I pulled back, trying to shake the pain off. The charm remained attached to the ship like a barnacle. An explosion of greenish light burst from the connection point as Grandma's chain fell to the ground.

I watched as the oily black substance, freed from the charm I once thought was a solid stone, changed again — this time flattening out into a patch the size and thickness of a playing card. The card seemed to melt into the ship and disappear in another burst of greenish light. I threw my arm over my eyes to protect them from the glare.

"Magnificent," Dr. Abrams said.

When I looked again, the ship was no longer black; it glowed as if it were made of light. Panels, windows, shapes resembling letters etched in the surface could be seen. A low tone, something you could feel in your belly, emanated from the ship.

"Finally," Dr. Abrams breathed. The green light danced across his face and I thought I saw tears in his eyes.

I lowered my arm and gazed at the ship. *I* had done that. For years it had been dormant, no more exciting than an old, dead log, and now it was lit up and pulsing and full of possibility. Pride made me feel twice as tall, like I could do anything.

What I needed to do first was save Gumps. "I did what you asked. Call off the next dose of Somnease."

Dr. Abrams blinked at me as if I had spoken another language. I repeated myself, pleased with how strong and sure I sounded.

"Call off the next dose of Somnease. I opened the ship for you and I'll go inside, but you have to hold up your end of the deal first."

Dr. Abrams unhooked the small pager — the kind they used in hospitals — from his waistband and tapped a message. "There," he said. "It's done."

"Do you swear?"

Dr. Abrams nodded once. "I swear."

"Then let's go in."

In a second, Dr. Abrams was behind me. He gripped my elbow with his hand, but it didn't feel possessive. He wasn't trying to direct me anymore. When I glanced at him over my shoulder, he looked less like an evil scientist and more like a little kid who was living his wildest dream. We were about to step foot on an alien spacecraft. I no longer felt like his captive. When I revealed the ship's true form, I stopped being his prisoner and became a partner. For better or worse.

Various colours rippled across the surface of the patch — once Grandma's charm — like a holograph. I still couldn't quite believe it had been around my neck moments ago. It wasn't a key exactly, but more like a security pass. Gumps must have removed it knowing the ship would go into hibernation mode, covered in that impenetrable black alien silk. I held my hand over the patch and a panel slid open, revealing an entrance.

We went in.

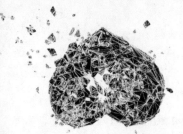

CHAPTER
THIRTY-THREE

The moment we stepped across the threshold, the ship sealed behind us. There was no click of a lock, but a bell-like note rang through the air. The sound put me immediately at ease. Everything about the Kesla was so musical. Dr. Abrams was obsessed with telepathy and analyzing the ACES for signs of danger, but no one seemed to notice how beautiful the chord was or how musical the Kesla were, and what that said about them as a species.

No other human — hybrid or not — had been inside the spacecraft in years, yet I wasn't nervous. Instead I felt a sense of calm settle over me, from the inside out.

There wasn't much room for us to move around. The front part of the ship had caved in and that area was still strewn with pieces of cracked consoles and twisted metal. That must have been where the ship took the greatest impact when it crashed back in 1947.

"It's not very big."

"Humphrey thought the ship was part of a bigger

structure or mother ship. This vessel was for short exploratory missions, or used when the Kesla needed to disembark very suddenly."

"Like a lifeboat."

The section we could explore consisted mostly of three chambers built into the curved walls, with a complicated set of straps, almost like a harness, in each one.

"This must be where they slept," I said.

I rubbed the straps of the harness between my fingers. They were rubbery but soft and very flexible, like seatbelts made out of chewed gum.

An insistent buzzing, like a mosquito whining, started to make itself known. I tilted my head and concentrated, trying to figure out the source of the noise that seemed to come from all around. I used my hands as a guide, trailing them over the walls and the rubbery straps, hoping to feel a telltale vibration.

"What are you looking for?" Dr. Abrams asked.

"That sound, do you hear it?"

"No," Dr. Abrams's voice was full of regret.

Finally, in the nose of the ship, I saw it. Stashed below a cracked console something was pulsing with colour. Red. Green. Blue. Violet. I climbed over the charred rubble, careful not to put too much weight on my bandaged ankle or get caught in a set of straps that may have belonged to a pilot's chair.

I was close enough to see it was a globe, a little smaller than a basketball. I reached for it, my fingers barely brushing the surface, but it was enough to give it a little nudge.

The buzzing got louder and the chord quivered in my bones as the globe moved on its own, rolling along the floor and then floating on an invisible breeze out from under the console.

"That's it," Dr. Abrams said, his pupils dilating two whole sizes as he watched the globe hover in mid-air. "The communication device, that has to be it."

The globe hovered in front of my face, still humming. It felt like an invitation, so I reached out and cupped my hands around its shimmering surface. The chord rang through my body. It was more deafening than ever before.

I felt the melody melt into my skin and bones until I *was* the song. There were so many notes, as if every tone and semi-tone in the world had come together to make the most complex and beautiful sound ever known.

Images flashed through my mind. They were starkly different from the song running through my veins. I saw fire burn and felt my skin bubble. I saw piles of blackened bones and the remains of an empty city, smouldering. I looked to the sky and saw the darkness speckled with colours I couldn't even name. My stomach lurched as I tumbled over and over, my ears popping as I was jerked about, straps biting into my neck.

Breathless, I pulled my hands from the globe. Instantly, the song disappeared, leaving ringing silence between my ears. I recognized the images from Dr. Lowry's dream files. The Melting Road. The Abandoned City. The Crash. The Net. These were the nightmares described by generations of Barton children.

"What is it?" Dr. Abrams asked.

"I'm not sure. I think I saw the ACES."

Dr. Abrams ran a finger along the dome.

"Can you hear the chord?" I asked. "All those notes?"

Dr. Abrams shook his head, frustrated. "Can you feel the Kesla hive mind?"

I shook my head. "No. I don't think it's a communication device. I think it's a message."

I put both hands back on the globe. This time when the chord started up I opened my mouth and the song poured out of me.

We are the last of our kind. After the planet opened up, flooding our lands in fire, pulling our sisters and brothers deep into its merciless molten core, those of us who were left set off to seek a new home in other parts of the galaxy. We take with us the gifts of our kind. May we always hear the song of life. May we always see the truth in stars. May we always heed the Great Spirit that directs us all. Remember our lives, our lost, and we will live forever.

I took my hands from the globe. I felt the Kesla's pain as if it were my own. In a way, it was. The ACES were real: the melting road, the ruined city, the terrifying free-fall, the net; those horrible dreams were real. The SuperGen children had inherited the memories of the Kesla just as we had inherited their amazing speed and hearing and sight capabilities. This ship was a lifeboat, a last ditch effort for the Kesla to find another place to live following the disasters that had befallen their planet. But they had failed. Dr. Abrams was wrong. We weren't part of the Kesla hive mind. We couldn't share a consciousness, because they were extinct. But we did share a collective memory.

"You were wrong. The Kesla are not coming back. They can never come back — they're all dead."

"I heard it, the message—" Dr. Abrams pointed at the globe, which still turned lazily in the air, but the swirling

301

colours had disappeared, leaving the insides dark, like a burned-out light bulb. "You spoke aloud, in English. I heard their message."

Dr. Abrams looked pained, but what he was feeling was tame in comparison to my own pain. I felt like I had lost my grandmother and Saren all over again. I wanted Dr. Abrams to feel as bad as I did. I wanted him to understand who the Kesla had been, what they had lost.

"The ACES aren't signs of a violent nature or secret messages to be decoded by a dream book. The ACES are the story — the *history* — of the Kesla. We were dreaming about their last days, living those awful moments as if we were there. No wonder they drove people crazy." My voice rose as I got angrier and angrier. "All this time you believed they were a violent species, looking to invade Earth, when they were just looking for a place to live."

"Refugees, not conquerors," Dr. Abrams said, his voice hushed. "It never occurred to us."

Dr. Abrams stopped. I'm not sure if he was overcome with guilt or grief or the knowledge that the last thirty years of his life — all the sacrifices, the murders and the experiments — had been misguided. His cheeks sagged and he put one hand against the wall of the ship for support. A part of me pitied him, but I wasn't ready to forget what he had done quite yet.

"Barton60 didn't murder Roddenberry because the Kesla told them to. They did it because they had been driven mad by his experiments. *He* turned them into murderers, not the Kesla. You wanted the Kesla to be the enemy and so you made up theories that supported you."

"Please, no more."

"Project Hive ends here. The winnowing ends here.

Winfree is onto you. It's just a matter of time before the world finds out the truth."

I scrambled out of the broken cockpit and exited the ship to find the members of Project Hive, along with Kamal and Ren, looking up at us. I could tell by their solemn faces that they had heard the message too. When the last words of the Kesla filled my head, they had filled all of our heads. I knew now that the melody that coursed through me was made up of all our notes — plus the notes of who knows how many other SuperGen children across the country — blending together. We were connected, and together we would honour the memory of our ancestors. It lessened the pain a little to know that it was shared among us, and that the memory of those we lost would never be forgotten, as the Kesla had asked.

I looked to Kamal. "Abbot?" I asked.

"He's at Barton. He set off fireworks in the old pool. The fire department and a news crew are on the way. And probably the military." He managed a smile, then added, "That Termite sure has style."

"Gumps?"

Behind me, Dr. Abrams spoke softly, defeated. I hadn't heard him exit the ship. "I gave you my word. I called off the Somnease. He's exactly where we left him. He'll wake up as if from a long nap, no damage done."

I searched Dr. Abrams's face for any sign of deception, but all I saw was an exhausted old man. I breathed a bit easier. Gumps was safe. There was only one more person I needed to find.

I searched the sea of faces, but I didn't see hers. I caught Kamal's eye.

Kamal shook his head.

I looked at Dr. Abrams. "Is she still in the bunker?"

"It's too late," Dr. Abrams said softly. "You'll never make it on time."

"Then I'll take the Jeep. Ren, you drive!"

I hobbled toward the Jeep, cursing the dog that bit me, crippling my ability to run and get to Saren in her hour of need.

Ren pressed a cool hand into my shoulder. "Marivic," he said. I felt his voice in my head and heard it with my ears.

I turned to look at Dr. Abrams, small and shrunken beside the darkened ship.

He shook his head. "It's too late."

*

One month later

Saren closed the red leather journal Dr. Lowry had given me that day in her office. It had only been a month, but it felt like another lifetime. The very same journal that had once held my scribbles about my dreams and ACES now told our story, as best as I could remember it.

"And it's true?"

"Every word."

We were in her room, me in a chair with my bad ankle resting on the bed, Saren stretched out next to it, staring at the journal in wonder. It was a familiar scene, a place we had been a million times, only everything was different.

"I wish I could remember it."

I swallowed. "Me too."

It turned out Saren's fate was to be winnowed after all. Not only had her imps been taken care of, but Dr. Abrams had ordered a very thorough scrubbing of her brain, destroying years and years of cherished memories.

"I seem kind of mean," Saren said.

"You're not!" I insisted.

"I said some nasty things."

"We both did. Sometimes friends fight. Even best friends."

"And that's what we are?"

My heart flip-flopped but I managed a smile. "Yes."

"Even when we go back to that — place?" Saren screwed up her face, scrunching the skin on her nose, and a wrinkle appeared above her right eyebrow. I was getting used to that expression. It was the face she made when something — a word, a face — was just out of reach.

Every day we discovered new things she had forgotten. Some could be re-taught, like her times tables or how to use the toaster. But others — conversations, birthday parties, sometimes whole people — were gone forever.

"What place?" I prompted. "Describe it."

"I can't remember the word. It's made of brick, like a house but for students—"

"School?"

Saren's face relaxed. "Yeah. That sounds right. School."

"Yes. We'll be friends when we go back to school. We'll always be friends." I wanted to hug her so badly my arms tingled, but I resisted the urge. Saren was different after the winnowing. Without her memories, we were practically strangers. It made her tentative, and so I was tentative too.

There was a knock at Saren's door.

"Come in," she called.

Gumps poked his head in. "Time's up, ladies. Marivic, we need to get home before curfew."

"I'll be there in a sec."

After the truth about Barton became public, the world was thrown into an uproar. Some people thought Super-Gen was an abomination, that all SuperGen children should be exterminated and Darby wiped right off the map. Others thought we were the next evolutionary step, that the Kesla's arrival and their restorative genes were a gift from the heavens, fate, science — you name it, there was a theory.

The military was dispatched to Darby to protect the town and everyone in it. Soldiers patrolled the town in pairs, their eyes hidden behind mirrored sunglasses. The *patta-patta-patta* of helicopters could be heard at all hours of the day. And a curfew was in effect, with all citizens expected to be home by seven o'clock.

"You're coming back tomorrow, right?" Saren asked.

"Of course!"

"Will you leave this with me?" Saren hugged the red leather journal to her chest.

"Of course. I wrote it down for you."

"It's a great story."

"It's our story."

Just outside the door, Gumps cleared his throat.

"I'd better go," I said, though I really wanted to stay.

Saren looked at the door, then down at the journal in her lap. "Gumps, right?" she said, still trying to connect names with faces.

I smiled broadly. "Yes, Gumps!" I said, then, to clarify, "My grandfather."

Saren looked pleased with herself.

We walked home slowly, Gumps mindful of my healing ankle. Dr. Abrams was right; I was going to have a scar. Not that I needed a reminder of that night. I relived it over and over again, rewriting the ending in my head. Me, bursting through the doors just as they were putting Saren under; me, telling Roya we were going to march into Barton a day early, no matter what.

Gumps sniffed dramatically at the air. "What's that I smell, burning? What are you thinking about so hard?"

"If only I had taken the time to shut the door behind me, I never would have been bitten by that dog and Saren—"

"Don't do that, kiddo. Don't play the 'If Only' game," Gumps said softly. "There are a thousand ways to play but you'll never, ever win. If only I'd never become an engineer. If only I'd never met your grandmother. If only I hadn't taken a job at Barton . . ." He smiled feebly. "See? I can't win. And neither can you."

"But I was there that night. I could have tried harder to reach Ren—"

Gumps cut me off firmly but gently. "If you're looking for someone to blame, blame Abrams. You'll be in good company."

Dr. Abrams was in Washington awaiting trial at a special international tribunal. Eventually Gumps would have to give his testimony about his work on the Kesla ship. It was going to be hard to let him go. Ever since he woke up in that bunker — groggy but otherwise fine — I had barely let him out of my sight. I clung to him like cat hair on a pair of black pants. The only time we spent apart was when I visited Saren.

I heard footsteps behind us and turned to find Saren running down the street toward us. I almost didn't recognize her without her cloud of hair springing up from her head. It had been cut and shaved close to the skull for the procedure. Just one more thing the winnowing had taken from her.

"Marivic!"

"Saren? Are you okay?"

Saren leaned forward, breathing heavily. "Did we make a cake once? Like a really bad one?"

I grinned. "Yes! We used baking soda instead of baking powder."

"I remember that cake," Gumps said, grimacing.

"So do I," Saren said, and for the first time in weeks I caught a glimpse of the old Saren, like sunlight cracking through heavy clouds. "I remember that cake too."

I laughed, throwing my arms around my best and oldest friend in the world, squeezing tight until she complained about bruised ribs. It was true that she didn't remember everything, and truer still that she might never recall what we had lost. But she was still here and we had the rest of our lives to make new memories. Together.

Acknowledgements

Writing a book begins as a solo journey and then evolves into a team effort. I am fortunate to be surrounded by brilliant, supportive, magical human beings who make my work stronger and my life richer.

In no particular order, special thanks to: Jenn Hubbs, for giving me a room of my own to hammer out the first draft and for being Head Cheerleader when it comes to Canadian authors. Marivic de la Cruz, who told me the origin of her name and allowed me to use it. You'll always sound like a superhero to me. Kallie George, Rachelle Delaney, Grace O'Connell, Suzanne Sutherland and Laura Hughes, for listening to me ramble on about plot and offering insightful commentary even when the draft included notes like "insert escape scene here." The mighty Scholastic Canada team, including Diane Kerner, Anne Shone, Erin Haggett, Denise Anderson, Nikole Kritikos and Aldo Fierro, who didn't balk at my detour into new territory. Or if they did, they never let on. Sally Harding, Ron Eckel, Rachel Letofsky and The Cooke Agency, for being Grade A champions of all my writerly endeavours. My PRH family, Shannon Ozirny and Miranda Mulholland, for all-around, everyday greatness. And, as always, my family, who believes I can do anything, and therefore so do I.

Vikki VanSickle is a Canadian writer and an active member of the children's book industry. Frequently referred to as "Canada's Judy Blume," she is the author of the acclaimed Clarissa books, including *Words That Start with B* (CBA Libris Awards Young Readers' Book of the Year finalist), *Love Is a Four-Letter Word* (an Indigo Kids Best Book of 2011) and *Days That End in Y* (a *Best Books for Kids & Teens* selection). Vikki's novel *Summer Days, Starry Nights* has been called "summer reading at its best" and was a finalist for the 2015 Red Maple Award. Vikki began her career as a children's bookseller and is now a popular children's lit blogger who is frequently called upon to speak about kids' books for radio panels and conferences.